Embers in the Dark

STEFANIE CASTRO

To those who feel like you have no fight left. You stand tall. You're not done. You've got this.

Content Warning

Thank you for reading Malloy and Baylee's story. Before continuing, I want you to know that the content you're about to read about is emotional and heavy. Baylee will be dealing with issues pertaining to domestic violence.

If you or someone you know has experienced domestic abuse, please know there are resources available at RAINN and National Domestic Violence Hotline.

For further content warnings, please check out my website using the link here or using the QR code provided.

Please use the QR Code below to find the Spotify Playlist or click the link here. Listen and enjoy!

Baylee

LAST FALL

I THINK *I love you and I want to have your babies.*

"Baylee?" Tucker pulls me from my thoughts.

"Yeah?" I look up at his forest-green eyes, and I have to stop myself from staring for too long or I'll give myself away.

I honestly love him so much, and I'm too chickenshit to admit it to his face. I came home yesterday with every intention of telling him I wanted something more than friendship. But, when I found him on the other side of my parents' front door I lost my nerve and now I'm just sitting here in my childhood home watching him move around my kitchen.

"I asked how school is going this semester." He looks at me as he makes us sandwiches.

"Oh, it's going really well," I say, grabbing the plate he hands me.

"Good. Your brother said you're liking your classes." He smiles at me as he takes a bite of his sandwich. Man, he's got the most gorgeous mouth. I can't help staring at him as he chews.

I bite my lower lip, once again lost in thought about how I want to devour him instead of the food in front of me.

"You okay?" he asks between bites.

"Yep." I try to look completely unfazed.

I have no clue how this guy has me tied up in knots. I'm not like this with anyone else—just Tucker Malloy. He's my kryptonite and I go gaga over him. I'm tongue-tied when he's around, or I stutter, or turn into Jello. Fuck. I'm Baylee-*fucking*-Rios. I'm confident. I'm strong. I'm empowered. Yet, here I am looking like the biggest fool because I'm head over heels in love with my childhood neighbor.

This summer I was home from college, and he was around a lot visiting his mom and seeing my brother. Tucker lives in Dover, which is roughly thirty miles outside of Boston. He visits often, but now that I'm in Connecticut, I don't see him frequently.

I can't say it was my imagination that I caught his gaze lingering on me a few extra seconds whenever we crossed paths. I know my feelings for him have been one-sided for years. But, based on his reaction to me this summer, I know he has something brewing for me too.

With any other guy, I'm direct. I'd come right out and make my move. But with Tucker, there's so much more on the line. He's pretty much part of my family. He's embedded in the fabric of my fucking life.

I tried to let this crush go as the summer passed. Honestly, I've been trying to move on for years. The problem is each moment that passes I feel like my feelings for Tucker are multiplying and it's getting out of control. I can't even go on dates anymore without thinking about him. I compare every guy to him. The last time I went on a date, I even watched the guy chew his food and decided I couldn't continue the date because he chewed differently than Tucker. Get a grip, Baylee!

I internally roll my eyes at how ridiculous I'm being. I've got to get this shit together and come out with it already. That's what this weekend was about. I promised myself that if I saw Tucker, I'd come clean and tell him how I'm feeling because I'm better than this.

The kitchen is silent as we eat our sandwiches. I look up from my plate to find him looking right at me. I can feel the heat of his gaze as he watches me, like my skin is on fire. God, he's attractive. My original thought stands—I want to have this man's babies.

I put the sandwich down and Tucker smiles at me. I can't help the smile I return.

"You've got mustard on the side of your mouth," he tells me.

I stick my tongue out and swipe at the side, hoping I got it. "Did I get it?"

"Not even close." He chuckles. He moves his thumb to drag at the corner of my mouth. The gesture is simple, yet incredibly intimate. The moment he does it I can't help but lean into his touch. I automatically close my eyes and feel my cheeks flame.

I flutter my eyes open, thinking Tucker will pull his hand away, but he keeps it on my cheek, cupping the side of my face. The gesture is so affectionate, I want to stay here for as long as possible.

Our eyes are locked and I bring my hand to cover his. It would be so easy to move my face in to kiss the inside of his palm. I could cross this line and see what happens. I could ignite whatever it is I feel is happening between us. Oh, how I want to push us a little further.

"Baylee, what are we—"

"Hey, Malloy, are you here?" my brother's voice echoes through the house and Tucker's hand moves so quickly away from my face, I almost think I was in a dream.

He straightens as my brother walks into the kitchen. I feel like a bucket of ice water was thrown across my body. I'm still trying to adjust to the change between Tucker and I, so I'm quiet as my brother looks between his best friend and me.

"Um, hi. Am I interrupting?" Danny says.

"Of course not," Tucker says. I can tell he's uncomfortable by his tone.

I can't look over at my brother. I'm looking down at my sandwich, still trying to figure out what just happened. What was Tucker going to say? Was he just being affectionate like the kind friend he's always been? Or was there something more to that gesture?

I finally compose myself and look toward my brother.

"Hey, Danny. How's my favorite brother?" I give him the best smile I can muster.

He comes over and gives me a hug, although it's awkward as I stay seated while he reaches over to squeeze me.

"I didn't expect to see you this weekend." Danny's gaze keeps bouncing between me and his best friend. "Everything okay?"

"Yeah, of course. Just wanted to get my laundry done here this weekend."

"I get that. Plus, Ma's cooking is hard to beat," he says. "Well, you ready to go?" He looks over at Tucker.

"Yeah, sure. Let me just finish this." He points at the sandwich.

"No problem." My brother leans a hip against the counter and crosses his arms over his chest.

They start talking about work at their respective firehouses and I zone out. I catch my brother looking over at me, his concern evident, but I keep a smile plastered on my face between bites of my sandwich, hoping my brother doesn't get suspicious. I honestly don't need him putting together that I have a massive crush on his best friend. That will only complicate things, especially if it's not reciprocated by Tucker.

———

I had to grab something from my old room and as I'm making my way back out, I hear hushed voices. I can't make out what's being said, but as I get closer the words get clearer. Before I reveal myself from the hallway, I hear Tucker's voice.

"Fine, I'll take Abby on a date."

I struggle to keep the sandwich I just ate from coming back up as I slowly retrace my steps back down the hall. My heart is pounding so hard, I fear my brother and his best friend will hear it from the living room.

The moment I'm safely behind the door of my childhood bedroom, I sink down and compose my breathing. I bring the heels of my hands to my eyes, the beginnings of a headache creeping up to the surface.

How could I have been this stupid? This crush I've let myself have on Tucker Malloy has consumed my thoughts since I understood what it meant to care about someone romantically. This infatuation has been one-sided, and I let myself believe it was growing into something more between us these last few months.

I left school yesterday, a smile plastered on my face, music blaring like a fucking idiot, thinking I would finally get some-where with Tucker after years of pining after him. Then I walked out of my room just now and discover him agreeing to a date with another woman? I should've known better. I've been a fool, and I fell for his charms.

That's the thing though. I'll always be Daniel Rios's little sister to Tucker Malloy. I'll forever be the annoying neighbor who chased him around years ago, because I was bored and wanted his attention. But to me Tucker has been the boy next door who hung the moon. He's a safe space; the person I run to, a shoulder to lean on when I feel scared.

But Tucker Malloy is no longer a boy. Oh no, he's built like a fucking ox if I'm being honest. One I'd like to climb like a tree now that I'm older. He just looks at me with those deep-green eyes and ginger hair, and my heart flutters in a way it never has for any other guy.

As I sit in my room, all those little wistful feelings are out the window now, because my blood is boiling. Fuck melting at his feet. He's seen the last of me falling for his charms, even if he doesn't know I'm head over heels in love with him—*was* head over heels in love with him. Not anymore. I'm done being this girl who pines after the guy. I'm not meant for this role.

I'm not this person for anyone. My sisters always taught me to be the woman men go after. Yet here I am, rearranging my life, waiting for the guy like a lovesick fool. I've been waiting for Tucker to see me.

I'm acting like this is some fairytale where he'll finally notice I'm perfect for him and we'll ride off into the sunset together. But that's never going to happen. I'm going to take life by the reins, find myself someone else and forget Tucker Malloy ever existed.

Fuck. This. Shit.

I'm no longer that gangly little girl running around trying to get Tucker's and Danny's attention in the yard. I'm a grown, confident woman. I can hold my own.

I'm the youngest of five children. The oldest Rios children are my sisters, who served as extra maternal figures in my life. My brother, who everyone aside from me refers to as "Rios," has always been incredibly protective of me. I clung to him the most as he was the one that helped me through all the major milestones; showing me how to ride a bike, walking me to school, teaching me to drive, and all the things my dad didn't have time to do. Both my parents were busy working two jobs.

I'm the "happy accident," as my parents like to call me. I was very much not expected, coming much later than the rest of my siblings. The thing with the dynamic between Daniel and I is that while we were close when I was little, the ten-year age gap between us eventually started to wear on me. As I got older I felt more smothered than protected by him, which caused epic fights between us.

Tucker served as our Switzerland throughout the years. He kept the peace between my brother and I when tensions got high. He became my hero, and the person I ran to when I needed someone to lean on without judgment. I learned pretty quickly that I could get away with a lot as the baby of the family. Though Tucker was never one to coddle me, he would lend a hand whenever I needed it.

Luckily, I was a tough kid, learning to stick up for myself when necessary. Being timid isn't really a personality trait I understand. My teachers always told my parents I wasn't shy. I was quick to speak up for myself if I felt like I wasn't heard, which I've carried through into my adult life. But right now, my voice is feeling numb as I process the fact that the one man I want is going on a date with someone other than me.

Tucker has grown into a brawny-looking man at six-foot-six, while I'm a petite woman at five-one. His laid-back personality has women falling at his feet, while I've been told I remind people of a black cat with my bold personality. I have an edge with my fashion sense, preferring to pair my dresses with a leather jacket and my favorite combat boots instead, of fancy heels.

I snap myself out of my thoughts and realize I can't be here right now. I start to move through the room and grab my belongings. I'm not finding the usual comfort my childhood home blankets me in. I need to get back to my apartment in Connecticut. My roommates will probably pepper me with questions. But after that, they'll shower me with chocolate and a chick flick, while they help me drown my sorrows in a tub of ice cream.

They're the only ones that know about my true feelings for Tucker. They knew the moment he arrived to help us move into our place that I had something for him. My eyes wouldn't stop tracking his every move through the small space. The second my brother and Tucker headed back home, they started questioning me.

I continue to grab items and throw them in my weekender, making sure I leave nothing behind. I wasn't planning to stay long, but my bag was already unpacked last night. I hate having to sift through it, even for a few days, so I immediately pulled everything out when I arrived yesterday.

I refuse to wallow in this little pity party any longer though. This ends now. The minute I leave this room, I'm leaving Tucker behind me in the process, along with everything I felt for him. I can't keep living in the past. I'm done waiting for him to notice me when I'm not even a blip on his radar. I'm nothing to him and the reality of that is fucking depressing.

Had I walked out there and not heard about the date, I would've told him how I felt. What a fool I would've made of myself. Thank goodness I saved myself from that humiliation. I deserve better.

If I know anything about Tucker, it's the fact he puts his friendship with Danny above everything. Nowhere near as important as my brother in his eyes. I know he won't do anything with me in fear of losing a friendship with Danny. Even if he did like me, I don't know what I was thinking believing he would ever consider dating me. Maybe he thought I was attractive this summer, but it was probably nothing more than that. I've matured and he probably just noticed that little fact. I made it out to be more than it was.

I'm better than this. Fuck this shit. I can go find my happily ever after somewhere else. I can conquer the world on my own, thank you very much. And Tucker can watch me from the sidelines.

I hear the front door close while I'm putting the last of my toiletries in my bag. I don't let that distract me. I shoot a quick text to my roommates, asking if they have plans for tonight because I need them. This causes a slew of text responses asking what happened, and I let them know I'll need a girls' night tonight to fill them in. They send me a few heart emojis and "love u" texts.

I zip my bag and sit on my bed to put my shoes on when a faint knock raps on my door.

"Come in," I say as I tie my sneakers.

"Where are you going?" Danny says as he pokes his head in, surprise etched on his features.

"I'm headed back. I have an assignment due that I forgot about," I lie.

"Can't you get it done here?" I know he can tell I'm full of shit.

"Nope. I need to get back because all the coursework for the class is back in my room. Sorry." Danny has no idea my feelings for Tucker have been growing throughout the years. If he did, he'd lose his shit.

I move past my brother.

"Hey," Danny grabs my free hand, "you good?"

"Of course, why wouldn't I be?" I continue forward. "I'm just needing to get back. This paper is really stressing me out and I lost precious time I don't have." I shrug. My brother doesn't deserve my attitude. I'm annoyed and I just want to get back to my place and forget about all this stupidity.

I finally look over at Danny and see him inspecting me a little longer, knowing he wants to push me, but decides against it. We're ten years apart, but something about him right now makes him look younger.

"You know you're the most important person to me, right Bay?" Danny pulls me into a hug. "I just want you to be happy."

Something about his tone gives me pause. Where is this coming from?

He kisses the top of my head.

I hug him back tightly. Right now, I think my brother is the only person that might have my back. Maybe the next guy I meet will be *the one,* and a better pick than Tucker Malloy.

CHAPTER 1

Tucker

PRESENT DAY—SUMMER

"YOU KNOW we could just run off together and be happy forever," I tell Abby as I hold her daughter Gabriella, who we usually call Ella, in my arms. We had to stop calling her Gabby after Abby kept thinking we were talking to her instead of the baby. She's tucked in her blanket and looks even smaller because of my size compared to her tiny body.

"Right because we're so in love?" Abby responds sarcastically from the kitchen as she speeds through grabbing her lunch. Apparently, she doesn't get much time to herself to eat an uninterrupted meal so she's taking advantage of this time while I hold her precious daughter.

"I love you as a friend though. Isn't that enough?" I throw back with a wink that usually has most girls melting into my arms. With Abby, though, it just conjures a laugh. She's one of my closest friends, that just so happens to be my fellow fire-fighter's ex-wife.

She just gave birth to their daughter at the beginning of summer, and they rekindled their love recently. However, they haven't made it official and remarried, although I do know that will soon change. He confided in me that he has a little plan up his sleeve.

"I love you too, Tucker. Am I in love with you, though? Nope."

"Harsh!" I exclaim.

She laughs and continues, "Also, I think Clay might be a little pissed to see me pick you over him, seeing as you just got on his good side." She sits beside me, tucking her feet under herself as she takes a bite of her salad.

"Is that a Caesar salad?" I look at her horrified. She got food poisoning from a restaurant Caesar salad during her pregnancy a few months back and I'd be surprised to see her eating it this soon.

She points the fork in my direction and mumbles, "Don't fucking utter those words in this house, Malloy. This is an iceberg lettuce salad with ranch dressing. Don't get it confused with that devil salad!"

I put my free hand up in hopes of taking her anger down a notch. Touchy subject, apparently. *Sheesh.*

"So, how's Baylee?" Abby asks, returning her attention to her salad as she preps another bite on her fork.

I sort of regret ever telling her about Baylee because she doesn't let up. She's been a hopeless romantic ever since she started back up with Clay. Probably long before that judging by her taste in reality TV love dramas.

I shrug my shoulders. "I have no clue. I know she still has that boyfriend of hers according to Rios, but that's it. I haven't seen her."

It's the truth. I haven't spoken to her since that day I accepted my fake date with Abby back in the fall. The fake date that I only took to appease Rios and confirm that I had no feelings for his sister. Seems it worked in Clay and Abby's favor and resulted in little Ella here.

The same day I accepted the date Baylee ran off back to school to Connecticut. Probably for the best though. She texted me a few times here and there, but I kept my distance because I didn't need to complicate my life further. Once I found out about my mom's cancer diagnosis, I focused on her care or picking up shifts at the firehouse.

I transferred from Dover to a closer firehouse in Boston to help Mom, which coincidentally ended up being the same firehouse as Rios, and Abby's boyfriend, Clay. Clay's identical twin brother River is also at the same station.

The mess from the date with Abby caused a huge disagreement between Rios and Clay, in turn the tension doubled between both brothers and Rios. I'm trying to keep the peace, but it's been hard, as Rios is still having a hard time believing I had nothing going on with his sister months ago. I miss my fucking friend. It's slowly starting to improve, but it still feels strained.

Luckily, I have Abby and in turn I've gained Kennedy, River's fiancée, as a friend. They've been a huge support system as I've navigated my mom's illness. My brother Eric lives in Ohio, practicing law with his fiancée and I want to see him get his law practice up and running.

We were raised by a single mom, and it was always hard for her figuring out life with two rambunctious boys. As my older brother, he did so much to help me get my life moving forward. It's the least I can do to take the lead helping our mom with her illness while he follows his dream. We speak constantly and he'd drop everything to be here if I were to ask him to come back to Boston.

"Earth to Malloy." She snaps her fingers. Ella flinches, then settles.

"Don't bother my girl, Abby!" I look over at the baby and shush her so she doesn't fully wake up.

"*My* girl will sleep through a train passing through. Don't worry. Plus, I know she loves sleeping in your arms." Abby takes another bite of food. "Malloy, don't avoid my question. Why haven't you spoken to Baylee? I told you to respond to her texts months ago!" Abby whisper-yells.

"Just because you told me to do something doesn't mean I listened." I roll my eyes.

"Did you just roll your eyes at me?!" she exclaims.

"Abby, she has a boyfriend. Plus, I've been busy." I bring my focus back to Ella, hoping I can end this conversation before it goes any further.

"*Oh please*, Malloy. Don't act like you've been too busy to think about Baylee. You're going on these lame dates with random women while you're thinking about *her*. It's written all over your face." She stabs her lettuce and stuffs it in her mouth as if Baylee is her best friend and I'm betraying something between them.

"Can you stop talking about Baylee? It's not like we had something going on between us. I didn't break her heart or anything," I say while repositioning Ella onto my shoulder, rubbing her back as she squirms and settles into the crook of my neck.

The silence is unsettling, until I look over to see Abby's fork mid-air and her mouth agape, while her eyes look murderous.

"What?" I can't help but ask.

"You're lucky you're pretty, because your brain really doesn't work sometimes. If you weren't holding my daughter, I would seriously stab you in the eye with this fork."

"I think we need to talk to Clay about your anger issues."

She brings her forefinger and thumb to that space between her eyes and inhales a breath, closing her eyes. "I swear Malloy, I need you to listen to me and listen well. She likes you. Just because she's dating someone else means nothing."

"I think it means something," I retort.

"Stop being an ass and pay attention!" Her frustration is quite fun to pull from her so I hold in the laugh, but a smile still frees itself, which causes Abby to pinch my bicep.

"Abby, I swear the last time you did that, I had a bruise.

Stop doing that!" I try to swat at her, but don't want to move too much because of the baby.

"Malloy, you're almost as bad as River, pretending he didn't like Kennedy all those years! I don't know why I even try." She tosses her fork into her bowl.

"I'm not asking you to do anything."

"You're miserable. Don't you see that?"

"I am not miserable. What are you talking about? I'm fine." I chuckle. I'm one of the happiest people; Abby's delusional.

"That's what you think. You're just showing up for everyone, playing a part, but you're not living life to the fullest. I should know, because that's what I was doing. I did exactly what you're doing now. Then I finally had someone pull me out of the hole I was living in, and guess what? I saw the life I could live. So, I'm going to be the person to push you to your limits. I'll be your Marissa!" She beams at me.

"You're no Marissa, sweetheart." I laugh.

"Hey, that's not nice." She fake pouts.

Marissa is Abby's best friend who lives in Southern California. She's one of the reasons I went on that crazy fake date with Abby months ago. Marissa's outgoing, speaks her mind, and has no problem grabbing life by the nuts. She takes what she wants from whatever situation is in front of her. Abby might be trying to give me the kick in the ass that Marissa gave her last year, but it's not hitting like she wants it to. She's one of my closest friends, but she's not Marissa.

"I appreciate you wanting to be my cheerleader in life. I think I'm fine and I'm not in some depressive state. I'm doing okay with you. Plus, Kennedy hooked me up with a gym to workout at near my house, so there's that."

Since my mom's diagnosis, I've needed an outlet. Rios and Clay used to be running buddies, but with their relationship still strained after the whole fake-date debacle, I've tried to hang out more at the gym with Clay. I'm not much of a runner though, so Clay has been finding a new crew to run with at the station, while I've been trying to find some new people to lift weights with. River spots with me at the gym sometimes, but it doesn't always work with our schedules.

Kennedy has hookups with her baseball franchise, so she was able to get me a great deal with a gym near my place with all the bells and whistles for me to lift weights. There's no way I would've been able to afford such a spot, but she gets an amazing discount, and she had an in for me, so I took her up on it. It will come in handy when the weather is dicey here in Boston come winter. Until then, I'll alternate between enjoying being outside and some indoor workouts at the new place.

"Speaking of workouts, have you seen the jump rope guy on social media? Oh my gosh, I think he recently moved to Boston. I watch his stuff when I'm breastfeeding Ella in the middle of the night," Abby says as she grabs her phone and starts scrolling.

"Does Clay know you're watching guys on the internet while feeding his daughter?" I make a face.

"Clay satisfies me just fine. Don't you worry," she says with a Cheshire cat grin across her face.

"Gross, I don't need that visual." I gag.

A blush paints her cheeks as she continues to scroll, and I honestly don't need to know what she's thinking. She can't find this person's account fast enough. The moment she stops scrolling, she turns the screen over to me.

"This guy. Have you seen him before?" she asks.

The image of a guy takes up the screen. Of course he's not wearing a shirt and he's got tattoos on his chest. He's got the quintessential defined physique, and he's jumping rope, doing some crazy maneuvers that look pretty impressive. With my body type, I'd be on my ass in no time.

"Nope, never seen him before. Let me see his handle." I take her phone and notice his account name is @huntsamillion. "Nope, never heard of him." I hand her phone back to her.

"I love his reels. He's always doing crazy stunts. He was in the military. Now he's back to civilian life. Some of his stuff has weight workouts, some has this jump rope stuff, and then he does runs in different cities he's in. It's pretty cool. But I've noticed he posts in Boston a lot lately. Makes me think he's here permanently now." She keeps looking down at her phone, completely lost in his page.

"Yeah, I bet you follow him for the workouts, Abs," I say, laughing to myself.

"Fuck you." She laughs, still not looking up.

"Why are you mentioning this guy, exactly?" I ask, lost to why she brought him up.

"Maybe he could be your friend." She finally looks up at me.

"Yes, this random guy in a city of over six hundred thousand people, I'll find him and we'll become friends. Maybe we can braid each other's hair and stuff. Maybe he could join us to watch *Love is Blind*, or come to smutty book club."

"Oh my gosh, imagine." She looks at me, hope evident in her eyes.

"I was fucking kidding," I say. "Oh wait, maybe you can stare at him when I bring him around even though you're with my buddy Clay. I bet it'll work out well for you." I roll my eyes again. "You can introduce your daughter to him while you're at it." I point to Ella, who's starting to squirm and she moves her little fist to her mouth, likely hungry.

"Okay, point taken," she answers sarcastically. "Now hand me my daughter. It's close to her feeding." She makes grabby hands for me to hand the baby over.

"Okay, okay." I kiss Ella's cheek and give her to her mother.

Abby takes her daughter and sniffs before bringing her onto her shoulder. Is that a thing?

"Malloy, back to Baylee," she starts and I moan, dropping my head to the back of the couch. I run my hands down my face.

"I thought we were done with the Baylee talk," I complain.

"You have to listen to me. I'm your favorite," she says.

"Not true. Ella is my favorite," I say as I reach out and grab the baby's little toes.

"Fine, second favorite. Baylee might be with this guy now, but you know she wanted to be with you. You ruined that by accepting that date with me. And you only accepted that because you were trying to save your friendship with Rios, which she doesn't know. And that didn't really salvage anything. Rios is still a dick. That friendship is holding on by a thread. And do you really think being miserable is worth it? Do you really think she's happier without you?"

I go back to looking up at the ceiling as she talks. I think avoiding her gaze is best, the moment she looks into my eyes, she'll know what I'm thinking. My reprieve is short-lived, because as soon as she looks into my eyes, she grasps my chin to ensure we are eye level.

"That's what I thought. You can't just leave things with her unfinished. Aren't you just a bit curious? Don't you want to see if this thing with her could lead to something real?" Abby's standing over me with Ella snuggled into her neck, although the baby's starting to get restless.

"When did you become this hopeless romantic? Weren't you the one pushing Clay away for so long?"

"Yeah, and you were the one making me open my eyes to the fact that I was wrong to do that to him. Don't let her go, because you'll regret it. She won't have a Malloy by her side taking her on fake dates. She'll have someone taking her on real dates, swooping her off her feet and then life will pass you by."

I can't let my mind wander to thoughts of Baylee falling in

love with someone that lights her world the way Clay does for Abby. Right now, when I see her current boyfriend, all I see is misery reflected in her photos on social media. She doesn't seem happy. There's no light in her eyes. The Baylee I've grown to love is nowhere to be found.

That's the thing Rios doesn't seem to recognize about his sister. Maybe his vision is clouded because he's too focused on keeping me away from her. He wants me away from his youngest sister so badly that he doesn't see what's right in front of him.

She doesn't seem happy; she's not even dressing like herself anymore. She's slowly peeling away the layers of who she was to conform into this new version of herself. She's trying to fit into a mold for someone else.

Baylee had this style about her that I loved. She wore clothes that radiated confidence, it was even palpable through the screen. Now all I see is someone closing herself off in the pictures staring back at me.

Her images were full of life before; they showed someone young, confident and charismatic. Her smile felt alive, now it looks forced and cold. Her clothes are uptight and feel as though she's hiding her skin from the world. She used to wear dresses and leather jackets with her combat boots, a style that felt uniquely hers. Now she wears modest outfits reminiscent of a fifties homemaker. It's uncharacteristic to the Baylee I know.

Even thinking about it now causes my blood to boil. I push myself off the couch to stand. I think a trip to the gym will fix the anxiety that's creeping up my spine.

"Listen, I appreciate you wanting what's best for me, but right now, what I need is to focus on my mom. These lunch dates and book club are all I can take on. It's fine, really. I'm happy with my life the way it is. And what I have with Baylee is what it is. We're in completely different stages of life. She's just starting her life and focused on school; while I'm already in my career. She still has a ways to go to become a physical therapist. I don't need to get in the middle of all that. I would only be a distraction to her," I say as I grab my keys from the coffee table.

"That sounds like an excuse, Malloy. And it sounds like something Rios would say to keep you away from his sister."

She isn't wrong, it's exactly what he said that day when he asked me to take Abby on a date.

"Yeah, well, it doesn't matter because nothing is going on. I appreciate you, Abby. You know I love you and this little girl." I kiss Ella on the head. "I'll see you later?" I ask.

"Yeah, I'll try to swing by the station one of these days. I know Clay loves when I swing by with her."

"Yeah, right. River's the one that goes crazy for her." I chuckle as I make my way to the front door. Uncle River will do anything to get Ella to call him "Dada" first, even if she's barely two months old.

"I know, right? It's actually pretty cute to see the two of them compete for her love. I don't mind it." Abby smiles at her daughter, playing with her dark hair.

I hug my friend one last time, kissing her cheek, then head through the door to the elevator. As I make my way home, I pull my phone out and scroll through social media. I still follow Baylee, and a few recent photos pop up on my feed. The ones with her friends are a little more carefree, but they're few and far between these days. I can tell something is wrong, but I can't pinpoint what the actual problem is.

I close my phone and realize she was never mine, so why am I preoccupying my time worrying about her now?

CHAPTER 2

Baylee

"HOW MANY CUBES of sugar do you want in your tea?"

"Two should be fine. Thanks, sweetie," Carolyn says from the other room.

I mix in the sugar and make my way back to the living room.

Carolyn Malloy is the sweetest woman and the fact she's sick breaks my heart. For as long as I can remember, she was a school nurse and had all the cool stickers in her office. Her warm smile always comforted me when I'd go see her at school when I didn't feel well. But next door, she welcomed me with fresh cookies and snacks whenever I swung by to say hello.

Being here while she's struggling through her own illness feels like the least I can do after all the times she's been there for me. From the outside, no one would be able to see she's dealing with cancer. When my mom called to tell me, I spent the rest of the day in bed crying. She feels like a piece of my inner circle, just as much a part of my family as a blood relative.

I cringe at the thought of my boyfriend, Myles, and his heartless comments when I first found out about her illness.

He was incredibly dismissive of my feelings when I told him, making me feel "less than" in ways I never expected. He made me feel like I was making it bigger than it was, not understanding this woman was not just a neighbor, but more like a second mother. Looking back, I don't know why I didn't break things off with him then, but I gave Myles the benefit of the doubt. I've given him shot after shot to be the man he was when we first met. But as the months have gone on it feels like he's gotten more heartless than kind.

"I assume my son has no idea you're here," she says as she brings her tea to her lips.

"No, he doesn't know I've been visiting, and I'd like to keep it that way," I say, my gaze out the window. I watch the kids playing outside, soaking in the last bits of summer as they kick a ball to one another, laughing much like I did with Danny and Tucker years ago.

"Hmm, you're still upset at my Tucker, I see."

"I'm not upset," I lie. I refuse to look her way because I've never been good at lying to her.

"Sure. You were never good at fibbing around me, Baylee Rios. Why don't you try that again." I hear her sip her tea and I keep my eyes trained on the kids outside the window. I will not look at her green eyes that match her son's.

I shake my head. "There's nothing to fib about," I continue my lie because there's no way I'm going to tell her my deepest feelings about her son. Those are packed away for good.

They have to be.

If I search in my chest, I'll crack open those feelings about Tucker that I hid away last fall and have all of them come seeping out. It doesn't matter how much time has passed, I still miss him. But maybe if I keep telling myself I don't want to see Tucker Malloy anymore, one day I'll crave him less. Even though I'm with someone else now, I still long to be around him just as much.

"It seems you've been avoiding my boy quite a bit since last year, if I'm not mistaken," she comments.

"Have I?" I play dumb.

"Gosh, you're just as stubborn as all the other Rios kids, aren't you?" Carolyn chuckles.

"Ah, maybe so. But I'm the most fun." This time I swing my gaze her way and I wink at her.

There's something about being around Carolyn that makes me feel like myself. I shed all my worries at the door, and I can simply *be* when I'm around her. It's a comfort sitting here with her.

"How's Daniel doing? Any new girlfriends?" she asks.

"Not that I know of. Still annoying the hell out of me. But he likes this boyfriend of mine, so that's nice. Gets him off my case for once," I tell her, rolling my eyes.

This is my first boyfriend Danny seems to like and that's probably why I've kept Myles around for so long. I like that Danny accepts him. I sort of hate that having Danny's approval matters to me, but it's nice to have it anyway. *Why is that comforting?*

"Yeah, Daniel always had this need to protect you. He was never like that with your sisters, but with you it was different. Like you were this delicate doll, even though you were born a spitfire." She chuckles. "I remember the moment your mama came home with you. Your brother looked at you with such adoration—such protection."

"Yeah, well, I can protect myself just fine," I say, although I feel less power behind those words than I did before.

"Oh, I know. But sometimes those we love still want to provide it. Daniel has always been hardheaded. Just because you say you can do something doesn't mean he'll listen."

I hum my acknowledgement.

"Tell me more about the internship you've been doing this summer. You seem to be liking it," she says, a small smile spreading across her face.

"It's been a lot of fun. I've learned a lot," I say, my smile genuine.

I attend a small university in Connecticut that has a kinesiology program I've fallen in love with. I could've stayed in Boston after graduating high school, where I was also accepted into the program at a university nearby. But I simply wanted to try something different and have some independence so I could spread my wings. I've never shied away from trying new things. If there's one thing about me, it's that I have no fear taking a leap off that ledge to see where the wind takes me.

With my degree, my goal is to one day become a physical therapist. This summer internship is my first step to attain that dream. This internship has opened my eyes that sports medicine is where I would like to specialize.

Unfortunately, at my current school, sports medicine isn't an offered major. If I hope to eventually work with athletes, it would be beneficial to add that to my studies. At one point this summer, without telling anyone—including my roommates or my family—I submitted applications to transfer to different programs that offer the double major.

It would mean possibly extending my graduation date, even though I'm supposed to be graduating in June of this coming year, but it would benefit me in the long run. I would also need to go to grad school after to further my specialty, but it's what I really want. Unfortunately, I haven't received an acceptance from any of the schools I applied to.

It's a shot in the dark at this point, but I did hear from two schools that put me on a waitlist. I had nothing to lose. I'll revisit sports medicine once I finish out my time at my current university and see what my options are once I have my diploma.

I spend the rest of the afternoon telling Carolyn about how much I've learned in the weeks since I started the internship. She asks me about everything involving the training and the physical therapists that work around me. It's hard to contain the smile that forms on my face when I talk about this career path I've fallen in love with.

My time with her flies by, and soon I have to run next door to say goodbye to my parents and start my drive back to my apartment. Luckily my parents have kept my visits to themselves, knowing I don't want them sharing my impromptu drop-ins with Carolyn with anyone else in our family. Carolyn and I share a special bond, and I honestly just want this to be our unique uninterrupted time together.

Halfway through my drive home to Connecticut I get a call from a number with a Boston area code. My finger hovers over the decline button, almost clicking the red icon when I decide to tap the accept button in case it's an emergency with Carolyn or a family member.

"Hello?" I'm always weary when answering these unknown calls.

"Hi. I'm calling for Ms. Rios, please," a woman says on the other side of the call.

"Speaking," I say in response, still unsure who is calling.

"This is admissions from Orange University in Boston. I hope I'm catching you at a good time? I apologize for calling later in the day like this," she says.

My heart rate ticks up.

"It's no problem at all." I try to even out my breathing.

"Well, I know you submitted an application for our sports medicine program. It's a highly sought-after major and we had a long waitlist," she says.

I stay quiet, hoping she'll continue explaining.

"We actually had a slot open up last-minute. Classes haven't started yet and I wanted to call and let you know as soon as possible. I know you're currently at Singer University in Connecticut, correct?"

"Um, yes, but I'm majoring in kinesiology," I stumble out.

"That's okay. I can see from your transcripts that many of

your classes fulfill both majors. Many students here double major in kinesiology and sports medicine. You don't need much to finish off the requirements for both," she explains while my head is spinning.

"Oh, well, that's good news. Would this affect my graduation date? Do I have to take an extra year of classes to graduate?" I ask.

"The way our classes work with the two majors, you might need to take a few extra classes, which could possibly mean an extra semester, but I could have the counselor take a closer look at your courses and give you a better idea of what things would look like. You'd likely walk in the spring, then graduate later if you needed a few more classes. But we could get more specifics later, if you decide to accept our program," she explains.

I try not to yelp with excitement. I can't believe this is happening. "Oh, um, alright. How much time do I have to decide?"

"I believe Singer is on the same schedule as Orange University and has a late start, correct?" she asks.

"Yes, school will start after Labor Day." It's one of the few universities that starts late in the semester, which was one of the reasons why I chose it. I love ending late and starting late in the semester. Many universities start earlier in August.

"I know I'm giving you a lot to think about right now. Take a few days and give me a call back. If you decide to attend, we'd love to have you. And I know you'll have to get things figured out, like sorting out housing and also get things in order at your current school," she says.

I have roommates I'd have to leave behind. What would I say to my friends? I know they want what's best for me, but it still hurts to move away from them. What will I tell them if I decide to leave? I feel sick just thinking about it.

Then my mind goes to Myles. How would he react?

Would he understand? My stomach sinks at the realization that he won't be understanding in the least.

"I appreciate this opportunity. I'll let you know as soon as I decide," I tell her in response.

"Wonderful. I'll email you so you have my contact information." She rattles off my email to confirm it.

The moment I hang up the call, I take in a deep breath, and I swear, I think I may throw up. What in the actual fuck is happening?

Without thinking twice, I pull up my contacts and call my mentor at the internship I've been doing this summer.

"Hey, Baylee. You driving back?" Farrah answers.

"You won't believe who just called me!" I nearly scream into the phone.

"Um, who?" She sounds weary.

"Orange University! I got accepted!" This time I do scream. I can't contain my excitement.

"Shut the fuck up!" Now she's screaming into the phone too.

Farrah and I had an instant friendship when I started this summer at Conn Physical Therapy. She isn't much older than me, but she specializes in sports PT and is one of the reasons I want to go into the specialty. She was one of the cheerleaders to get me to look into applying to other programs and now, here I am.

"I know! You're my first call." I'm beyond excited right now.

"You're going to take it, right?"

"I mean, there's a lot to consider, but I have to, right?"

"Baylee, you have to! You're a natural. You're so good with patients and you deserve this. What's holding you back?" she asks.

"I mean, I have my roommates, and I don't know..." I waver.

"Your roommates will understand. I know it seems scary,

but Boston is your hometown. You'll do great. Talk to your roommates and explain your passion for this specialty. I doubt they'll keep you from pursuing it. Anything else keeping you from going for it?"

"Well, I mean, I have a boyfriend in Connecticut." I bite my lip, embarrassed that's one of my reasons.

"Ah, there's always a boyfriend." She sighs. "Well, you explain to him what's going on. I doubt he wouldn't be supportive."

She clearly doesn't know Myles, because he's probably the least supportive person I know.

"Yeah, of course," I say, lacking the enthusiasm I'd hope to have in my tone.

"You deserve this! I'm so proud of you for going for this, Baylee," she says.

"Thank you, Farrah!" If it weren't for her, I wouldn't have known I could apply for it this late.

"Of course. Let me know if you need anything from me but just know you're going to be great."

We hang up and I can't help the excitement coursing through my body.

I look in my rearview mirror and pull over to the side of the road. The moment I stop my car, I put on "Make Way" by Aloe Blacc. As soon as I hear the song through my speakers, I start to belt the lyrics, and I feel invigorated. Does it mean I know what I'll do? No. But I feel completely excited by the fact that I have options for my future.

For the last few months, I've felt like a darkness has come over me, but now, it feels like life is pumping through my veins for the first time. It's almost like I left my childhood home that fall day and I've been living in a state of limbo ever since, waiting to find the sunlight. But right now, I feel energized.

I will admit, I'm slightly scared about how I'm going to break this news to Myles. The thought of telling him about this brings a sense of fear over me that I can't quite put into words, but I'm trying not to focus on that. That's probably why I never told him I applied to begin with. I'm trying not to think of the vile words he might say in response to my confession.

I rock out to the song in my car, screaming the lyrics, feeling my nerves start to even out. Everything will be okay. Something about this song makes me feel better. This is good news, and I know my friends will understand when I tell them. I'll put Myles's reaction on the backburner for now. I'm only focusing on how amazing this is for me.

The moment the song ends, I put my turn signal on and get back on the road. The rest of the drive home is uneventful. The closer I get back to campus, the more at ease I am about telling my girlfriends. Myles is a completely different obstacle that I don't feel remotely ready to face.

CHAPTER 3

Tucker

WALKING INTO THE GYM, I'm immediately comforted by the sounds of the exercise machines and people talking. I went on another abysmal date last night and I've been itching to come in here and tune out the chatter in my mind.

All I think about after a terrible date, like the one I had with Allegra yesterday evening, is Baylee. I compare how much better it would've been had I gotten to sit across from Baylee in that bar instead.

Then my anger gets to an all-time high when I think about Rios and how I want to pull his head out of his ass for not seeing how miserable his sister is in her current relationship. After my horrible date, my mood was made worse when I saw yet another picture of Baylee, all prim and proper, at a party with her fucknut boyfriend. He looked like the smug bastard he is, his hand possessively on her side, while she had that strained smile, her clothes once again conservative. Her hair pulled tight in a ponytail, not one hair out of place, no loose tendrils like she used to wear when she studied at the kitchen table back home. No semblance of the person I knew so well. Then my mind went to the fact she would be happier with me.

Pushing the door open to the weight-room area and grabbing a towel, I walk toward the benches, grabbing the weights I need to start my workout routine. I put my headphones on, and lose myself in the music.

After nearly an hour, I've punished my body enough with the weight workout I've put myself through, so I decide to finish off on the treadmill. I warmed up on the way over with a light jog from my place, so a walk on the machine will help bring my heart rate down before I head back home.

I'm a few minutes in when someone comes to stand next to me and taps my arm, I look over to find Kennedy and River.

Pulling my headphones off, I greet them, "Hey, didn't expect to find you both here."

"We just got here..." Kennedy begins.

"You just get here?" River asks me.

"Just finishing," I say.

"Dang, I could use someone to spot me," he says.

"Why don't you call Clay?" I ask in return.

"He's wiped, Ella kept him up last night. I called on my way over and he was going to stay home and maybe workout later," he says.

I look down at my watch. "I can spot you for a bit then I'll have to head home and get ready to help my mom before taking her to her appointment."

"Perfect. Let me warm up," River says, kissing Kennedy on the cheek.

She rolls her eyes, then hops on the machine next to me, pushing the buttons and starting a brisk walk of her own.

"So, how are things going? You liking the gym so far?" she asks me.

"Yeah. Thanks again for hooking me up with this spot. It's a perfect distance from my place."

"Of course. Jerry owed me a favor. I'm glad he extended that family discount to you." She winks at me.

Kennedy scared me when I first met her. Her confidence is quite intimidating, even for me. She still has her moments, and when I see her interacting with River, I see why they compliment each other. They push each other's buttons perfectly.

"How's the team coming along this year? I watched the game last night. It was close," I tell her.

"They're going to give me an ulcer," she breathes out. "But I love the thrill." She smiles.

She's the CEO of the Boston Gaels baseball team, and she's in the thick of the season. I'm amazed she has time to be at the gym right now, although there's no game tonight. She probably needed a moment away from the office. Or River told her to take a break from her desk and all the emails she has to send.

"I heard you were on a date last night." She wiggles her brows.

"How did you know—" I question then realize, "Abby told you."

"Yep. She also said you're wasting your time on the wrong girl."

"Of course she did. *She's* wasting her time talking about that. I'm not going to chase *that* girl." I press the button to increase my speed. My light walk forgotten, and a jog now needed.

"Sorry, but Abby's right on this, Malloy. You're just wasting time. I think the perfect girl is right under your nose and you're being stubborn." She looks over her shoulder, then brings her gaze back to me. "I know you care about Rios, but he needs to stop being such a baby about this and realize that you're good for his sister. If he cared about you, he'd realize you're what's best for her too."

"His sister is with someone else. Why doesn't anyone realize this?" I say, a little more clipped than I had wanted to be.

"Hey, I'm on your side here," she says, putting her hands up, "but you're my friend. I want you to be happy."

"Why does everyone think I'm miserable?" Fuck. Do I look like a sad puppy or something?

Kennedy stops the treadmill. She stares at me until I do the same. See, she's fucking intimidating. She's giving me those god damn scary eyes that make me want to cower in a corner.

"Malloy, you and I both know I won't beat around the bush. You're being stupid with all this. I'm not going to sit here and act like I need to hold your hand. You're a grown man. Fuck, you're older than me. So, you do you. I'm going to say this once—I hate repeating myself—either you go chase the girl or deal with the consequences. Make the decision now though. If you never tell her how you feel, you can't be sad that she ended up with someone else. Do you understand that? If you don't go after her, you may not be the man she stands next to forever. And, if that's the case, you need to move the hell on. Understood?"

I nod, because what the fuck else am I going to say?

"Good. Now go spot River because I don't need him breaking a nail and crying about it later. He gets very needy," she says then goes back to her machine, this time bringing the speed up to a higher-paced jog.

Now *that* was Marissa energy.

I've been excused by "CEO Kennedy," who I know commands the room. She takes no shit and I know she's right about Baylee. I need to start being more receptive to these dates and being a little more aware of the fact that Baylee has moved on. I need to do the same. I've made my choice to smooth things over with Rios and let Baylee live her life in Connecticut. She's with that boyfriend who has pulled the life out of her eyes, and that's her choice. This life I'm living is my choice.

I move over to River, finding him on the rower, he slows

down when he sees me. He juts his chin, ready to start his weights. The minute we start his workout, I decide to let go the final strings of Baylee in my mind. I can't keep living my life with her in my heart when she let me go long ago.

———

A few days have passed since my talk with Kennedy, and it's my shift at the firehouse. River and Clay have reunited and the smile on River's face is infectious. The twins feed off each other. River is more of the clown between the two, louder and more inappropriate. But from the stories I've heard, both were rambunctious as kids. Having both in the same station is an interesting dynamic, to say the least.

The moment I walk in, I hear the laughter in the kitchen. I know River is up to something, or most likely a bet of some sort is transpiring. The Nichols brothers are always wagering on something. Hell, I'm guilty of it, even outside of the firehouse. I'll now bet things with my mom and Eric whenever I can.

I walk in and my attention is pulled by both River and Clay.

"Malloy, please tell me you haven't watched all of the latest season of *Love is Blind*?" River pleads.

Clay looks over, a smile sliding across his face. He knows I have because I binge watch it at his place with Abby every single time it releases. It's ritualistic at this point. We don't miss any episodes together.

I decide to play it cool. "Um, what season is it again?"

"Ugh. The one with Derek and Shawna. The chemistry is unreal," he says.

"I haven't, no," I say, scratching my beard.

Fucking right I've watched it. Those two were off the charts with chemistry. It was surprising they had the ability to keep the show going the entire season, it was pretty obvious they were getting married. But, they managed to keep us hooked. If they didn't end up together, I would've been pissed. Abby and I stayed up until the late hours to finish the season. We were committed to see it through.

"I need to make a bet those two don't last six months," River declares.

"Oh, you're on," I pull my wallet out and slap money down. Clay gives me a knowing look, my eager bet proving I've seen the season.

Everyone starts chiming in. The guys start yelling about the couple, passionate about the two in the relationship. We all have sides, Clay siding with me, pushing his brother's buttons just as much as me. Soon we're shouting about how we want to see their happily ever after written in the stars.

We hear a throat clear, and we look over to find our captain standing at the opening of the kitchen and sitting area next to another firefighter we don't recognize. We stand straighter, ashamed that we were just passionately arguing about a reality TV couple. Not only that, we were putting bets on their future outcome like we knew them personally. It's embarrassing.

"Gentlemen, I would like you to meet our new probie, Tyler Hunter." Our captain brings his hand to the newcomer's shoulder.

It'll be good to have someone new and I won't be the new guy anymore. Although I wasn't technically a probie, I was still new to the station. Plus, with the tension bubbling with Rios, it made for some discomfort nonetheless. This will be a welcome change.

We walk over to introduce ourselves and the moment I lock eyes with our newest member to Station 10, I realize he looks familiar. I've seen him before. For a few beats, I can't pinpoint where, but then it clicks.

Abby showed me his photo, although he was shirtless and his tattoos were on display last time I saw him, his face is hard to forget. She's going to shit a brick. Maybe I shouldn't warn her, especially because Clay will be none too happy to know his ex-wife-now-girlfriend-soon-to-be-fiancée has been drooling over the new probie on the internet.

I put my hand out. "Nice to meet you, Hunter. Or should I call you *Huntsamillion*?"

"Oh, you're a fan." He chuckles, not even bothered that I recognize him from his social media profile.

"What's he talking about?" River latches on to this tidbit immediately. Of course he does.

"Our newest member is an international sensation," I say. I can't help it. This is too good to be true. I guess in a city full of people, I did find Abby's little crush.

"Yeah, I've been outed." Hunter runs his hands through his hair, his smile easygoing, although a blush does creep onto his cheeks. River is going to eat this shit up.

"I run a little social media account. It's gained traction through the last couple years. I was in the military and in that time I was using it as a way to connect so I used to post videos. I guess it took off," Hunter explains, shrugging.

"So, what? You're like famous?" Clay asks.

"Do you mind if I take a quick selfie with you to send to a friend? She's going to freak," I say.

"No problem," Hunter says.

I snap a quick picture and begin typing out my message to Abby. I'm about to send it when Clay starts to piece things together.

"She? Who are you sending that to? Who's your friend, Malloy? How did you know about Hunter?" Clay's no fool.

I just smile at him and Clay starts to look over at our newest probie.

"Oh, come on. Really? Abby follows this guy on social media?" Clay asks.

River starts laughing. "Don't worry, Clay. She still loves

you. She has our Ella with you." That earns River an elbow to the gut, yet he still laughs.

River points to our newest recruit. "I like you already, probie. You're pissing my brother off and you've been here five minutes. This'll be fun. Ten bucks says Abby will be here by lunch to see you in person."

That has us all laughing, and I have no doubt River will be richer by the end of shift.

CHAPTER 4

Baylee

"MANDY, do you have that little black dress you bought when we went to that cute boutique on Main Street last weekend?" I yell from her closet.

"Yeah. You need to borrow it tomorrow night?" she responds from the kitchen.

She's making margaritas and I've been counting the days left to spend time with them. Myles is working late and I can't help but feel the relieved he hasn't asked to hang out tonight. I've been avoiding telling him about the call I got from Orange University last week. I'm running out of time and I've already accepted the transfer, but he still doesn't know about my move.

I've started packing my few belongings, but I've avoided having Myles over at my place, opting for his apartment whenever we hang out. He doesn't care to be surrounded by my friends, so he doesn't ask many questions, which works in my favor right now. The furniture isn't mine to take, so all I have are clothes and a few books to move back to Boston. Luckily, all that will fit in my compact car.

"Yes, please," I grumble.

"Don't sound too excited, princess," Mandy says as she

walks in with the dress on a hanger, margarita in her opposite hand. "I had it hanging in the laundry room." She smiles.

I sigh as I reach for her dress, eyeing the margarita. "Sorry, I just don't really want to go out to be around all those stuffy assholes tomorrow night."

Mandy pulls the dress away from my grasp and hands me the margarita instead. "Why don't you take this instead to ease your frustrations a bit and come hang out with us."

"I like that idea," I say, grabbing the offered drink as she moves out of her room and into mine to lay the dress on my bed.

A smile stretches across my face as the realization hits me that I can relax with my roommates tonight since none of us have plans. Tomorrow, I have to play nice with Myles and his coworkers, while my roommates are headed out for the weekend for a concert. They'll be gone for two nights with a few others in our apartment complex to see their favorite musicians on a summer tour.

We live off-campus, in a portion of housing that is university-owned but feels more like apartment buildings. It gives off that independent vibe for us without the dorms, although we still feel that vibrance of university life.

Because school's still out for us at Singer and we live in a very university-rich town, it's very quiet here in the summer months. Most of this complex is semi-dormant from June until late August. It's half-filled for now, but in a few days it will start to fill up. Once the semester begins, there won't be a quiet hallway around us.

After my call with Orange University last week, I came home and couldn't contain my excitement. My roommates could sense something was up and I was bursting at the seams to tell them. Despite knowing I'd be parting ways with them, they were pushing me to go. They know how much I've fallen in love with the sports side of physical therapy and this would really help me in the course of my career.

That doesn't mean we weren't all a bundle of crying fools once the high wore off, because we love living together. We vowed we'd stay in touch. I've lived with them since sophomore year and all of them told me I couldn't pass this opportunity up, explaining that this was part of my future. As much as I thought I was going to take days to think it over, the decision was made right then. They made me call the next day to start putting things in motion.

My parents are the only other people I've told up to this point. I made them swear not to tell my siblings because I didn't feel like being harassed on our text thread as to why I'm making this decision so close to graduation.

I haven't figured out housing yet, but if needed I can move in with my parents. I put my name on a waitlist at school for housing if something opens up, but the likelihood is minimal of something opening up this close to the semester starting. I'll start apartment hunting, but I have something bigger I need to figure out first.

My stomach hurts at the thought of telling Myles I'm leaving. Yes, I'm a chickenshit and I've never been this person in my twenty-two years on this planet. I'm being an absolute coward about this whole thing right now and I know why—Myles overreacts about everything.

I don't know what's switched between us, but he wasn't always like this. Recently he's just so tense. No matter what I do, he's on edge and I've noticed I seem to be the only one to push these imaginary buttons that take him to another level. I'm probably overexaggerating the reaction he'll have, but I don't want him to dim the light I have from my acceptance into this program. I want to bask in this glory a little longer before he might blow it up for me. The problem is, I'm running out of time. I don't think it would be right to tell my boyfriend I'm transferring schools as I'm driving off with boxes in my backseat. I doubt anyone would take that very well.

I got myself into this program with the hard work I've put into my grades at Singer. But since being with Myles, I feel like he's just pulling me away from my dream of becoming a physical therapist. I might be irrational in my thinking here, but I've felt like he's insinuated on more than one occasion that I shouldn't even work if we were to end up together. But what really worries me is that when I hear him speak about me to others, saying I'll be his future doting wife, I don't correct him. I just stand there and take it.

The Baylee pre-Myles would never take that shit. Little by little, Myles is pulling me apart and muting me. And I have no idea how he's making me into this version of myself. I see it happening right in front of my eyes, but it's like I fear he'll lash out if I speak against him.

The longer I'm with him, the more I find myself cowering, scared to push his buttons. He'll look over at me sometimes with his icy-blue eyes that once captivated me and reminded me of a clear blue sky but now feel like a cold plunge into frigid waters, and I find myself shuddering. They rake over me and no longer bring me comfort.

He'll now lean into me and degrade me with his words instead of telling me how much he loves me. I long for the nights he used to tell me how much he couldn't wait to get home and kiss me all over. Instead, he'll find ways to remind me why I need to cover myself so others won't look at me, because I'll draw the wrong kind of attention. He demeans me, calling me attention-seeking and a show-off.

I feel a shiver come over me as I get into the hallway toward the kitchen. I shove the thoughts of Myles to the back of my mind, hoping I can finally have a night where I don't let his words consume me, like I find myself doing most days.

Pulling me out of my thoughts, Mandy finds me in the hallway and grabs my hand, "Let's go sit down and chat. It's been a long week and you've been working a ton. You deserve to celebrate your win with us."

I'm walking along, and the minute I sip her drink, I hum my approval. This one is strawberry and it's my favorite of all her margarita mixes. I follow her down the hall and sit once we reach the kitchen island. Mandy continues to serve more drinks for our other roommates, Alexis and Brianna.

"So, where's the dinner tomorrow?" Brianna asks while looking for some snacks in the fridge.

"That swanky restaurant near the school," I say between sips of my drink. "The one with all the nice cars lined up every time we drive by."

"Descansi's? Someone's fancy," Bri chimes in.

"How are things going with him? Did you tell him yet?" Alexis asks as she brings her own drink to her lips.

"No." I drop my head down.

Each of them look at me, shocked at my confession.

"I know, okay? I'm stalling," I tell them.

"Bay, sweetie, this isn't like you. What are you afraid of?" Alexis asks.

"I don't know. I mean, Myles is a bit intense," I finally confess.

I met Myles at his fraternity party on New Year's Eve. The girls and I decided to go out last minute and I wasn't really looking to meet anyone. Even though I had vowed to cut him off cold-turkey after overhearing him agreeing to that date, I continued to text Tucker on and off for months with no response after last fall. Following another unanswered text on New Year's Eve, my roommates convinced me to go out. Tucker's silence had been deafening, and I won't act like I wasn't heartbroken. But that was the last time I reached out to him.

When the girls suggested going out to welcome the new year, I drowned my sorrows and irritation in alcohol and dancing, meeting Myles in the process. It felt fun and carefree at first, something I loved between Myles and I. Not only that, everyone in my family loved him, including Danny. I thought he was what the universe was supposed to bring for me. Like it was kismet that Tucker and I didn't work out; because Myles was my destiny in the end.

In the beginning, he brought all the new-relationship flutters. The thrill of a new boyfriend came with the hope of something unfamiliar. The butterflies were appealing with every turn. He and I went on dates and he seemed to love everything about my opinionated personality. I was full of sass that he welcomed. Even the way he looked at me made me feel alive. When he picked me up and looked over at me, I felt the heat in his gaze. And when he listened to me talk about the future, he acted like he was excited about my plans of becoming a physical therapist. At least, he never voiced concerns when I talked about wanting to pursue a career down that path.

But as time moved forward, my strengths became my downfall to him. His words of affirmation in my ear transformed into whispered slights and jabs to bring me down a peg. He started to dim the things I thought he loved about me. I can feel the way he judges my outfits with the way he trails his eyes down my body, processing how he can find words to use against me, instead of lifting me up. And for some reason, instead of shying away from him like I would expect, I'm becoming more attached. Like I crave him, even though he's the opposite of any man I've ever been attracted to previously.

The shine of our relationship is wearing off and what I'm left with is someone that seems more interested in showing me off to his friends and coworkers, than one that loves who I truly am. Now, I'm feeling like he just wants to parade me around, trying to make me into something I'm not. The skin he would run his fingers along, causing goosebumps along my flesh early on in our relationship, he now asks me to cover when we go out. He tells me I'm an embarrassment and a slut, words I'd previously have kicked a man in the balls for uttering to my face. Now, those words paralyze me, stuck deep inside me in a way I never thought possible.

I still remember the first time he said them to me. The way he stunned me as he whispered them in my ear when we sat at our table at the restaurant. I felt immobile, convinced I had heard him wrong, my limbs numb as I processed the harshness of his words, holding back tears. I expected my body to stand up and throw my drink in his face and declare our relationship over.

Instead, I sat there like a statue and when the server arrived, I plastered a smile on my face and ordered my meal. The satisfied look on Myles's face confirmed he expected me to comply. Disgust spread through me that I allowed him to treat me like that. From there, I accepted my fate.

Embarrassment has washed over me since then. I fear what my friends and family might think if they ever found out what their strong Baylee has fallen victim to. I keep his jabs my little secret, like an addict's. I tuck his remarks below the surface, where no one can hear or see. *I hope I hide it well.*

Since that day, I've tried to keep him happy with the clothes he asks me to wear. If I keep him happy, his comments are minimal. If we have a good night out, then his attitude remains jovial and things feel like they were in the beginning. Those are the nights I want with us. I've never been silenced, yet I've allowed him to do this to me. *How did I become this girl?*

I'm sitting with my drink, once again lost in thought, when I'm pulled back into the conversation around me.

"You know you can break up with him if you're not happy, right?" Bri says in return.

Brianna isn't one to stay in a relationship longer than a week it seems. She never stays committed longer than that because she feels this is the time in our lives to experience everything. I tried to keep up with her for a bit, going on a string of double-dates before finally caving. It was exhausting. I don't know how she does it. Looking back, there's a part of me that wishes I had stayed on that track. Instead, I'm stuck in this cycle with Myles, dreading what will likely be a messy breakup.

"Yes, oh wise one," I tell her while I cheers her with my glass in the air. "But it's not all bad." The face I make as I utter the lie gives me away.

The three of them give each other a look that I catch. "What was that?" I point at them.

"What?" Alexis says.

"I saw that look you gave each other. Is there something you need to say to me? What is it?" We don't play this game with each other. I hate that catty shit some girls play, talking behind each other's backs and keeping secrets.

Mandy hangs her head. "We've noticed that you've been a bit more reserved with him. You're just different, that's all."

"What do you mean?" It seems I haven't been hiding things as well as I thought.

"Baylee, we love you, you know that. But since you've been with Myles, you've just been a little off," Bri explains.

"Yeah, like you're in pain when you're with him," Alexis agrees.

I want to burst into tears. It feels like I'm going to burst at the seams if I don't let this out.

"And you dress so conservatively with him. It's sort of weird. It's not you, Baylee. I mean, you've got this sick style I've always admired, but now, you look like a Stepford Wife. It's creeping me out. You only do it around him," Mandy says.

My mouth hangs open with this confession and Mandy soon backtracks. She isn't usually that blunt, so it's sort of shocking to hear her describe me like that, even though I'm well aware of how I've been dressing lately.

"I'm sorry, okay? But it's true. You can't say you don't see it. Look at pictures and tell me you don't see it. I'm surprised you want to borrow that black dress. It's more revealing than anything you've worn with him lately. Then again, you'll likely put some cardigan over it and make it prim and proper to ensure it shows little skin when you're around Myles and his people. You used to have an edge about you, Baylee. But with him you've let it go. Like you're embarrassed of who you are, or something. Or he's made you feel wrong about who you are. Is that it?" Mandy asks.

It's hard to confess because embarrassment coats my skin right now. But if I don't tell them now, I'll never have the courage to do so.

"Don't be mad. We just thought you should know how we see it from the outside looking in. You're, like, the coolest person we know. And we don't want some guy to dim your light, Bay. You need to know we love you," Bri says, grabbing my hand.

I smile and nod, unable to talk over the frog forming in my throat. This hurts so much, knowing I've been carrying this whole thing on my shoulders, and I can't do it any longer. I look away and that's when the first tear falls.

"Oh my gosh, no, Baylee, don't cry." Alexis makes her way over to comfort me by putting an arm around my shoulder.

I finally find my voice. "There are some things about Myles I need to tell you," I start, but then I just let go.

Between sobs I tell them everything, from the beginning of the relationship to all the horrible things Myles has said to me in our time together. I word-vomit, confessing from that first night at the restaurant and how I felt stunned, to all the other times he's made me feel less than. And with each confession, I see my friends break with me.

By the end of my story, I could hear a pin drop in my apartment. All three of them are crying with me, my sadness their own with my words.

"Oh Baylee, why didn't you tell us sooner? We didn't know it was this bad," Brianna asks.

"I wish I could say it was because I was being strong. But I think it was because I didn't want you to think less of me. The longer I stayed, the more trapped I felt. At first, I thought it was a one-off. But then, little by little, I thought maybe a part of his words were true. Maybe what he was saying about me was the reason Tucker didn't want to be with me," I whisper.

"I never thought I would be this person," I admit. "I've never seen myself living in a life where a man would treat me like this. I was always the person my friends saw kicking ass, no matter what part of life I was in. And here I am, letting a man walk all over me," I confess.

With that, Mandy scoffs. "Myles is no man to belittle a woman like that, Bay."

"So, let's get you back to taking over the world. It starts now," Alexis says, drawing circles on my back.

"How so?" I look up at her.

"Let's start with that little black dress," Mandy says, her smile growing across her face.

CHAPTER 5

Baylee

I ROLL down the window of my car, feeling that warm August air hit my face, hoping it brings some relief to my nerves as I make my way to the restaurant the next night. But, nothing is making me feel better about this dinner.

After I confessed everything to my roommates, I had a wave a relief wash over me. I felt like the old pieces of me were coming out as the plan came together for tonight. But the moment I started this drive, my resolve started to waver and now I'm feeling nauseous with the thought I have to face Myles. I've broken up with guys I've dated before, but with him it's different. He has this inexplicable hold on me. Instead of feeling like his words repel off me like droplets of oil on my skin, they seep into me and cling onto the depths of my soul. It's like he's got a hold on my psyche in a way I can't dislodge.

I can feel my pulse racing, and not in the way I look forward to on a date, with anticipation and exhilaration, but in fear that something horrible is about to happen. It's taking everything in me not to turn this car around and go back to the comfort of my apartment. Packing my stuff and simply moving to Boston to start at my new school sounds more appealing than confronting Myles right about now. But Mandy made the point that cutting off ties is best. Saying goodbye to this life with him is necessary because he'll always have this hold on me if I don't end things with him now.

I know she's right. It has to end tonight. I'll have to walk tall, find that inner Baylee I know is still inside, and stand up to this person I've called my boyfriend. I can't do this anymore.

Alexis made me realize this relationship is killing me from the inside. It's taking parts of me and stripping me. It has pushed me to seek a life outside of Connecticut without even telling Myles, because I wanted an out. Had I been happy, I would've been straightforward with Myles when I applied to these different programs from the start. But I went behind his back and looked for an out. I knew deep down I was unhappy, and I was looking for any excuse to leave.

I turn into the restaurant parking, seeing the valet attendant and stopping in front of the gentleman to give my key and grab the stub from him. I can see his smile of approval at the little black dress the moment I step out of my car. It's confirmation that I made the right choice.

I took charge with this black dress and matched it with killer heels, much like I would've before meeting Myles. From the front, this dress looks modest, but the moment I turn around, I know the attention I'll get will set Myles off. It's form-fitting, with a plunging backline, revealing the delicate firefly tattoo on my shoulder. The dress hits right above my knees and paired with heels it shows off my toned legs.

Tonight it's about seizing control of myself again. Fuck Myles and the thoughts of what he'll say. The days of letting him hold power over me are no longer going to restrain me. I'm taking control of my life and walking away from him and all the horrible things he's said to me. His hurtful words stay with him after tonight, I will no longer carry them with me.

I walk through the entryway of the restaurant and I'm immediately assaulted by the chatter of diners inside. Myles is an accounting major at our university and has his sights set on becoming a financial broker once he graduates in the winter. He only has this next semester until he finishes his degree. He hopes to work at the office where he's been interning after he graduates. Myles comes from an affluent family here in Connecticut. His mother is a lawyer in the state and opportunities have always been handed to him, versus worked for. I doubt he'll have any trouble getting whatever he wants after graduation.

I make my way to the front where the host greets me with a smile.

"Hi, I'm here for the dinner for Grace and Jance Financial Group," I tell her.

"Oh yes, they're in the private room down back to the left," she explains, pointing in the direction through the double doors.

I smile and begin to make my way over. There are a few glances my way by diners as I walk by and I simply smile, my head held high.

The moment I approach the room filled with associates from his firm, I spot Myles. I can feel myself shake a bit at his presence, but I feel a little more at ease since his back is to me as he's deep in conversation.

Someone he's speaking to looks up and locks eyes with me and says something to Myles. Right then, Myles turns his gaze over to me. The easygoing smile that was on his face turns to stone when he sees me, his eyes rake me over from head to toe, taking in my outfit. I keep my head up high, walking over to him.

The moment I reach his group, I plaster a smile on my face, forcing myself to greet him. I can tell he's angry, his eyes continually roaming over me.

I move my cheek toward Myles and greet him with a hug and kiss.

I whisper in his ear, "Good to see you, sweets."

"What are you wearing?" he whispers so only I can hear him. I try not to let his words sting, but it's hard not to feel hurt that of all the things to be greeted with, this is how he starts our interaction. Not even a "hello" or a "good to see you."

Pulling away, I wipe the little bit of dark red lipstick from his cheek that rubbed off on his skin. "Oops," I say on a wink.

I turn and introduce myself to the group. Some look young enough to be fellow interns like Myles. At first, Myles remains silent, probably internally seething, but he finally pulls his head out of his ass and starts to take over introductions to his colleagues.

"Well, if this isn't the stunning Baylee." An older gentleman makes his way over to our group. "I'm Conrad Gontry, I'm this guy's boss." He thumbs over to Myles.

"Oh, well it's a pleasure." I go to shake his hand, but he pulls my hand to his lips. Myles has moved his hand to my lower back and I feel his hand stiffen around my waist, his fingers digging into my skin.

"I've heard great things from Myles about what an amazing woman he has by his side. He didn't emphasize how stunning you are," he says, looking anywhere but my face when he says this. The discomfort is climbing. So, we can add douche to the boss's resume.

"That's very kind. Thank you," I say, trying to step further away from Mr. Gontry without being a total ass, although he's a close second to my boyfriend in taking that award tonight.

"If you'll excuse us, I'm going to grab a drink for Baylee." Myles doesn't wait for an answer and steers us away from the group, his grip on me only intensifying.

As we get closer to the bar, I expect us to order something, but he maneuvers us so we veer right, where we move away from the crowd and no one can hear our conversation. The moment we're alone, there's only fire in his eyes as he turns me to face him.

"That was a bit rude, no?" I comment.

"What the fuck are you wearing, Baylee?" He completely ignores my question.

"Excuse me?" I look down, making sure nothing is out of place.

"What the fuck is this dress?" he bites back.

"Normal," I counter. Yes, I'm pushing his buttons.

"Like hell it is. Everyone is looking at you like you're their next meal," he says.

"I look good," I say, a small laugh slips, only making Myles angrier.

"Baylee, don't you see the way my coworkers are salivating as you walk by? You're supposed to look like my future wife, not like someone that would get on your knees for any of these guys!" he whispers.

"Excuse me?" What. The. Fuck.

"You heard me. You look like you're giving it away." This asshole has the nerve to not even look sorry. "That's not a half-bad idea. Maybe I should offer you to Mr. Gontry whenever he wants you to solidify my job."

We stare at each other for an extra beat. I'm waiting to see his words click, hoping he has a heart somewhere in that hollow chest of his, but soon he just stalks off, leaving me in this corner without a care in the world.

I watch him move toward the bar, greeting another coworker in the process, as if his words didn't just gut the person he claims to love. I wish I could say I feel the sting of tears, but all I feel is anger. I pull in a breath, steel my spine and walk over to Myles.

"Excuse me," I interrupt. Myles and his colleague look over.

"Yes, love," he says, as if he didn't just insinuate I'd suck dick for anyone in this place. Fucking asshole.

I tamper the desire to roll my eyes. "Do you mind if I just pull him away for just another second?" I address the gentleman across from him.

The man nods and gives me a small smile. Myles looks annoyed by my request but complies and turns toward me.

I plaster a smile and move my hand along his lapel to smooth down the fabric, hoping to show myself off as a caring girlfriend having a conversation with him, instead of the seething one I will be in about a second.

"Myles, baby," I begin. Myles looks at me, already appearing bored by whatever I'm about to say. "I want you to know that's the last time you ever speak to me like that, because you will never see me again after this. We're done. I hope you fuck off. Have the life you deserve."

Myles's face distorts and I see the anger move along his features as he processes my words. He continues to stare at me and I'm well aware he hates to make a scene. I lean in and plant a slight kiss on his cheek, barely touching his skin. When I pull away, the smile I give him is full of satisfaction. To anyone watching, it just looks like I'm saying my good-byes and leaving the dinner early. No one would guess I've just broken up with my boyfriend.

I move along the room and the relief rolling off me is beyond anything I can explain. Each step away from Myles feels like years of my life restored. I thought a part of me would feel some sort of pain from walking away from him and our relationship, but all I feel is tremendous relief that we have parted ways. I know I did the right thing. Did I make it a bit dramatic by doing this at his work event? Probably. I had planned to do it after the event so it wouldn't be awkward for him. But no one speaks to me like that. That was demeaning and uncalled for. What he did tonight was unnecessary and humiliating. So, I returned the favor.

I make my way back outside and feel the summer breeze flow through my hair. It's freeing in a way I never expected. I take a moment to enjoy it as I take in a breath and realize my newfound freedom from Myles Stempler.

I get my stub to hand to the valet and it's only then I realize my hands are shaking. The adrenaline pumping through me is taking its toll. I pump my hands, hoping the rush I'm feeling from all that went on between Myles and I will pass by the time I get home. I can finally put everything behind me when it comes to my relationship with Myles. I'm ready to move forward with the new stage of my life that awaits me in Boston as I look upon my career at Orange University.

I retrieve my car and make my way back home fairly quickly. It's eerily quiet on my walk up the stairs to my apartment. I miss my girls, but they'll be back soon enough. When they return, I'll begin my move to Boston. Now that I've cut ties with Myles, I can begin getting situated at my new school. It's all surreal, things are truly moving in a new direction for me.

I walk through my door and lock up behind me. Closing my eyes, I lean up against the cool surface of the door and marvel at how much things can change in the course of a few days. I never imagined things could be so different in the span of a week. I feel lucky I can move, not only because I get to take a step closer to conquering my dream toward sports medicine and my path of physical therapy but pull out these claws Myles dug in me. I've allowed him to sink them in too deep for far too long; that's finally over tonight.

I never really took the time to realize Myles was emotionally abusing me with his words. I think, to some degree, I knew he was controlling, but I didn't label it as anything more. I guess I didn't want to come to terms with the fact that I could be a person in such a relationship. It's proof that anyone can fall victim to an abusive situation, no matter their personality. He truly pulled me in then flipped a switch, and as time passed, I fell deeper and deeper. I let his words mask themselves as love.

I want to be angry, but I also have to realize I gave excuses for his behavior. I think with time, I allowed myself to believe this was what I deserved from another person and I forgot what a proper relationship should look like.

I push myself off from the door and throw my keys into the bowl nearby. I turn on the lights and go into the kitchen to get some water. I grab a water bottle and begin to walk through my living room, taking in the calm of my place, longing for someone to talk to about how my night went. Once my roommates hear how everything went down tonight, I think even they will be surprised by Myles and his ugliness.

I'm about to take another sip of my water when pounding begins on the other side of my front door. I'm startled and drop the water out of my grasp, spilling the opened bottle onto the ground.

Myles's voice sounds next, the volume growing steadily. I rush to grab paper towels, more concerned with cleaning the water up than talking to my ex-boyfriend. He's not worth my time right now. I'm hoping he'll give up and simply go home.

Instead of calming down and walking back to his car, the pounding gets worse, the volume of his voice escalating with each bang of his fist against the wood.

"Baylee, open this damn door," he commands.

I stay silent. I don't feel like talking to him. It might be juvenile to stand on this side in silence, but I also don't feel like speaking to him at the moment. I'd rather wait until the dust settles and have an adult conversation. Obviously, he isn't rational right now and needs some time to relax.

It seems he disagrees with the stillness from my side of the door and continues, "Baylee, goddammit, open this fucking door and let me in. I know you're in there, I can see the light through the blinds."

Why do people think that getting more verbally aggressive is a way to get their point across? I roll my eyes and continue to clean up the water, hopeful he'll leave me alone.

Unfortunately, Myles is stronger than I imagined and continues to pummel his fist against the door. Soon he ceases and I think he finally relents and walks away. But a second later, he comes back with a vengeance, this time using what I imagine is his shoulder to slam into my front door.

"Myles, stop! What the fuck are you doing?" I drop the items I'm using to clean up the water spill and walk closer to the door. "Go home. We're done. Nothing you say here is going to change that!"

It seems that was the wrong thing to say because instead of answering with words, he slams into the wood with more force. I start backing away, my heart rate spiking as I realize he's unrelenting at this point. He won't stop until he crosses that threshold.

I realize he's going to succeed soon. He's going to break the lock and I have no idea what he's going to do once he gets into my apartment.

I won't stand here and let him walk all over me. I won't permit him to stand over me and use his physical presence to scare me, much like he was using his words to quiet me all these months. Enough is enough. I will stand tall when he comes in here.

I grip my phone, ready to call the police in case I need help, even though I doubt Myles will do anything physical against me. He hasn't once shown me that he would physically hurt me. He's only ever used his words to push me down. He wouldn't hit me, would he?

It isn't until he finally breaks the lock that I see the malice in his eyes. I realize how wrong my own assumption was because this isn't the Myles I knew even an hour ago. This man is a beast, a monster. He's panting, looking at me with this wild way about him, his hair disheveled, his eyes more animal-like than anything I've seen in him before. They hold something that makes him look like someone I should run from, rather than toward, and I wish I had prepared myself for a fight.

The blue that once drew me into his eyes is completely gone and now all I see is a person that makes me want to call for help. Something snaps in me and my fight-or-flight instinct kicks in. I turn to run, but I'm too slow. He grabs me by the arm. The moment his grip connects, I cry out.

"Where the fuck do you think you're going, *princess*?" He pulls me violently back toward his chest, my back slamming into him. He's nudging his nose into my hair, breathing me in. I try to pull away from him, but he's holding me so close, giving me no ability to free myself. He's going to leave a mark.

"Myles, you're hurting me," I tell him.

"No fucking way I'm hurting you as much as you're hurting me, sweetheart," he seethes. "I fucking gave you everything and you just left me like that tonight. Like I'm the trash on the bottom of your shoe?"

Now he's walking me forward, dragging me with him to meet his long strides. Once we get to the wall on the other end of the living room, he turns my body and slams me against the wall. My head hits the drywall, causing an indent.

"Fuck," I cry out.

"Don't be a little bitch, Baylee!" he yells in my face, caging me in with his arms. "You walk in that restaurant, in that dress, showing off your body, hoping to be treated like a dirty whore, so I'll treat you like you should be tossed around a little bit. You know you like it rough," he throws at me.

It's hard to focus on his face with the instant tears forming. What the fuck is he saying to me? And all this from a simple dress I wore?

He grips my arm again and the sting is instant. I can't move, frozen in place. My head is pounding and all I want to do is fall to the ground and curl into a ball. My phone fell out of my hand when he slammed me against the wall, and I feel completely helpless right now. The old Baylee never would've been this helpless. Where is she now?

"You think I'm going to let you walk away from me after I wasted all this time on us? No fucking way, Baylee. I groomed you to be mine. There's no way you're getting rid of me that easily. But it seems you need a little reminder that I'm as good as you'll get," he whispers into my ear.

I can't help the whimper that escapes my lips and I turn my face away from him. I hate how scared I am right now, because I want to show him he doesn't affect me. Somewhere deep down I find my last resolve and turn my eyes to meet his. I won't let him feel my fear, he doesn't deserve it.

My eyes connect with his and I steel my spine and stand as straight as I can.

"Myles, maybe it's time for you to clean your fucking ears because like I said before—we're fucking done. I'm not your fucking girlfriend anymore. FUCK. YOU."

If I thought Myles was pissed before, I was wrong. His eyes become lifeless orbs before me and things move faster than I could've imagined. He lets go of my arm, but I can't react fast enough to move out of the way. Before I can register what's happening, he balls his hand into a fist and punches me in the stomach.

The last thing I remember is the wind being knocked out of me and I fall to the ground. I cough a few times and blink heavily. The exhaustion takes over and I can't fight it any longer. I try so hard to keep my eyes open while Myles breathes heavily over me. I finally relent and let my eyelids close. Maybe this was all a nightmare, and when I wake up I can go back to a life where I never dated this monster.

CHAPTER 6
Tucker

IT'S BEEN A LONG DAY, but I can't complain about it because it's the closest thing to normal I've had with Rios in a long time. He came over tonight and we hung out like old times. Slowly, I think we'll finally get our friendship to what it once was. I can only hope he'll start to see his sister and I had nothing going on between us.

I've known Rios most of my life. We grew up together as neighbors, going through our biggest moments together, and he has been my ride or die for as long as I can remember.

We went through so much, from little league, flag football, high school dances, and then starting at the fire academy together. He was the first call after I heard about my mom's diagnosis. Spending these last few months feeling like our friendship wasn't going to survive this hardship felt like my body was missing a limb.

Abby talks about Baylee and I needing to explore this thing between us, but she doesn't realize that I can't envision my life without my best friend. I know so many see Rios as this terrible person, but he's been the guy I call when I hear the worst news in my life. I just don't understand my life without him in it.

Much like my shadow, he's been by my side, no matter what. There's loyalty between us. I may have been curious about where things could've gone between Baylee and I, but I've only known my life with Rios in it.

I walk through my apartment, still finding boxes in corners because I have yet to fully unpack. I've been here a few months, but life has been busy between shifts at the firehouse and taking my mom to appointments, so unpacking boxes is the last thing on my mind. Plus, if I have extra time, I'd much rather soak up the nice weather while Boston hasn't frozen over yet.

I'm brushing my teeth when I hear the faint sound of my phone. I rush to grab it, concerned it might be my mother with an emergency. I finally find it in the living room and see it's from the last person I'd expect. I press accept and put the phone to my ear.

"Hey, you okay?" I ask into the phone.

At first, I think she dialed it by accident because she never calls me, until I hear a hoarse, faint version of her voice.

"Tucker? I need you." Her voice cracks at the end as if she's holding back a sob.

"Where are you?"

"My place," she croaks.

"Stay right where you are. I'm leaving right now." In a rush, I grab my things, not even turning off any lights.

———

Luckily, it's summer, and it's the middle of the night because there's no traffic. I make it to Connecticut in record time. I pull up to her apartment complex, and her light is dim but on. She's lived here for the past two years. Thank goodness she hasn't moved. I helped her get settled here when she and a few of her friends found this place after moving from the dorms.

I park my truck and lock up, running to her apartment. I'm getting ready to call her to come unlock the door when I see it's already open. It's then I realize the lock is broken.

I walk frantically into the apartment, my heart pounding, the whoosh of the blood flowing through my ears all I can hear.

"Baylee, it's Tucker. Where are you?" I call, taking in the scene in front of me.

The apartment is in shambles. The living room light is knocked down, and some of the chairs are tossed. She hasn't called out to me in response, but I hear a slight sniffle coming from the back room.

I try to keep my breathing calm because my blood is still rushing through my ears. What happened here tonight?

I finally go back toward the room that was last hers. When I push the door open, I find her in a corner, her knees pressed up into her chest, her hair a mess, and her arms hugging her legs into herself. Her mascara is running down her face as if she's been crying for hours.

What. The. Actual. Fuck?

"Baylee?" *Who did this to my girl?*

"I didn't know who else to call."

I run to her and crouch in front of her. I push her hair away from her tear-streaked face.

"Baylee, tell me what happened?" I try to suppress the anger I feel creeping up my spine.

She looks too fragile right now as I run my hand through her hair. She closes her eyes and leans into my palm and all I want to do is pull her into me and take away her pain. The more I take her in, the more questions keep piling up in my head.

"I've never seen him like that before," she says, as if she's talking to herself, almost like I'm not sitting in front of her.

"Baylee, baby, look at me." I try to get her eyes to fully

focus on me. It's then I see her fingers trembling as she moves them along her shins. "Tell me what happened."

"Myles—I broke up with him. He… he got so mad." Tears well in her eyes and I cup her cheeks in my palms hoping she feels safe enough around me to tell me what happened here tonight.

"I shouldn't have pushed him, but I didn't know he would get so angry." A sob breaks loose.

"You didn't do anything wrong," I tell her as I watch the tears slowly fall down her cheeks.

"I told him it was over at the restaurant. I thought I could walk away, but he came after me. He forced his way in here," she says, and it takes everything in me not to stand up and go after this fucker. I want to kill him with my bare hands.

I'm not a violent person, but this sorry excuse for a man made Baylee feel unsafe when all she wanted was to break things off. He's a coward. I take a deep breath and let her continue.

"I've never seen him so furious before. Then he grabbed my arm. At first I thought that was as far as he'd go. But then he wouldn't let go, even when I told him it hurt. He pulled me further into the apartment and pushed me into the wall. It was so hard, Tucker. He's never done that before. But I was so stupid." She starts to sob as I pull her into me, and she balls her fists into my chest.

I rub her back until I feel her calm down. I kiss the top of her head and soon she regulates her breathing, pulling away from me and continuing.

"The way he spoke to me, telling me he wasn't going to let me go so easily. He was just saying such hateful things, I couldn't let someone talk to me like that. So instead of taking it, I pushed back and told him to pretty much fuck off. It was the wrong thing to say and he punched me in the stomach." Right then she brings her hands to her face and cries harder.

I knew something was off about this guy she was dating,

but never in a million years did I expect this confession. It's taking everything in me to school my expression. If I allowed myself to truly show her how I'm feeling on the inside, my face would be murderous. But she's seen enough tonight.

I slowly pull her hands away from her face, but she forces her gaze downward.

"Baylee, look at me," I tell her.

She shakes her head, embarrassed to let me see her.

"Baylee, please let me see you," I plead.

"I can't. I'm too embarrassed. I can't believe I let things get this bad," she says, still shielding herself from letting me see her face.

"Bay, you called me and I'm here to help. Please, look at me," I say, keeping my voice calm.

She finally looks up at me and those deep, dark eyes meet mine. Even with her mascara marring her cheeks, she's still the most beautiful person I've ever laid eyes on. And all I want to do is make her feel better.

"I'm sorry, Tucker. I'm sorry for calling you all the way over here," she says.

"Don't ever apologize to me for that. I'll always be here when you need me," I tell her. "I need to take a look at where he hit you. Can you show me? Are you comfortable showing me?"

"Mmhm," she mumbles and nods.

I slowly get up and reach my hand out for her to take hold. I help her up. Once standing, she pulls her dress up and I can already see the bruise forming on her abdomen. The dress has no sleeves so I can see the mark from where he grabbed her upper arm and some bruising along the shoulder from where it connected to the wall. There's no blood on her head where she hit the wall, but they'll do a more thorough assessment at the hospital.

"We need to call the police, Bay, then get you seen at the hospital to make sure you're cleared. The sooner everything is official, the faster they'll get an arrest warrant out for him," I explain.

Her eyes go wide, dropping the dress, and she wraps her arms around her waist.

"Baylee, you didn't think this was something we weren't going to report, did you?" I look up at her.

"I just didn't think about it, Tucker," she says as her eyes take in the room around her. I can tell she's starting to feel overwhelmed at the thought of everything that's going to happen from this moment on.

"You're a few steps ahead of me in all this," she continues. "I'm still trying to catch up. I passed out from him hitting me and when I woke up he was gone. He trashed my apartment after I lost consciousness, and I'm just putting some of the pieces together. Myles comes from a prominent family here in Connecticut and I'm scared. What if it's his word against mine? What if he does something else to me?"

The fear in her eyes nearly cripples me. I've never seen her this way before. Baylee has always been a pillar of strength whenever we tackled things throughout the years. She's always been the person to stand tall against any obstacle. Obviously, nothing has ever been this big in her path, but I've never heard her sound so small. And that just makes me feel even more angry at what Myles has done to her. He's muted something within her, and I wonder how long this has been going on.

"I won't let you go through this alone, okay?" I reassure her.

She nods, but I can still see the apprehension in her eyes.

"Do you want me to call your family? I can have them meet us here," I ask.

"No, I don't want them involved just yet. Can we wait until we get to the hospital first?"

"Whatever you want. You're in charge here. I'm going to

call the police now, okay?" I tell her, pulling my phone out of my back pocket and showing it to her.

She nods and I bring the phone to my ear. I make the call and it feels like the minute I finish explaining to the dispatcher what happened, everything moves at lightning-speed.

I walk with Baylee to the kitchen, shielding her so she doesn't need to look over at the area where she was attacked. We choose to sit in an area that won't disturb the crime scene. It isn't until we walk through the living room that I really take in the force of the violence in front of me. The hole in the wall where he shoved her brings my blood to a boil all over again and I can only imagine how scared she must've been.

Once there's a slight knock at the door, I greet the officers and have them speak to Baylee where she remains shielded from the mess Myles left behind. She'll have to walk them through what went on earlier, but I'll keep her from looking at everything longer than she has to. I stand behind her, blocking her view of the living room the best I can until she is forced to walk through the events of the night and show the officers what happened.

At one point, I make a move to give her some space, but she reaches for me to stay, so I stand next to her while she retells exactly what happened throughout the evening. She begins with the dinner with Myles at a restaurant for his office and the moment she starts to repeat his vile words, I have to hold back my reaction. Luckily, Baylee can't see the reaction on my face, because I'm having a hard time keeping my features neutral at the moment. This asshole better be found after tonight because if he steps one foot too close to her, he may not be standing straight again.

Once Baylee gets to the point of her story where she's explaining everything that went on in the apartment, she begins to move through her living room, doing her best to explain how Myles attacked. Some of her memory is a little hazy due to the fact she lost consciousness, but she does a good job keeping her composure, although a few tears finally come loose at the end.

"Ms. Rios, I think we have everything we need here to file our arrest warrant. If we need anything else, we'll contact you. Here's my information. If you think of anything else, please don't hesitate to reach out." Officer Tamos hands each of us her card, a sad smile gracing her features.

"Also, we'd like you to make sure you stay somewhere else tonight. Have you contacted your roommates to let them know not to come back? That lock will need to be replaced," Officer Tamos explains.

"Oh my God, I forgot to let the girls know." She brings her hand to her face.

"It's okay. We can let them know once morning comes. They won't be coming back yet. We'll head to the hospital and once we have you checked out and cleared, we'll call them," I tell her. She gives me a small nod.

Officer Tamos seems satisfied with that plan and moves toward the front door. "Also, make sure you get this lock fixed as soon as possible. We will get things moving to get the warrant out for Mr. Stempler, but I'd feel more comfortable knowing this is repaired."

"Yes, I'll get some calls out to companies while Baylee is getting seen at the hospital."

"Great. And you'll have somewhere to stay, Ms. Rios?"

Baylee is looking over at the hole in the wall, lost in thought.

"Baylee, did you hear Officer Tamos?" I ask her.

"Huh?" She pulls herself out of her thoughts.

"You have a friend to stay with while you get the locks changed?" Officer Tamos asks again.

"Oh, um, I'm moving, so Myles won't find me here anyway," she says, shocking me.

"I see. Well, make sure to still get this fixed soon for the safety of your roommates." Officer Tamos looks over at me, leaving me stunned while I look over at Baylee, this time I'm the one left without words.

The officers say their goodbyes and I walk them out. Once they leave, I set myself in motion to gather some things. Baylee is still moving slowly, probably now that the adrenaline is wearing off, she's feeling sore all over.

"Maybe we should gather some belongings. We can always come back in a few days and grab a few more things too. But for now, some things for overnight essentials would be best. I think whomever you're staying with probably has a few things you can borrow, just tell me what to grab for you and I'll throw it in a carry-on or something," I tell her, moving toward her room.

I realize I'm moving toward her room and she isn't following. I come back out to the living room and Baylee is still staring at that wall.

"Baylee, we need to get you to the hospital. Come show me some stuff I can grab for you. You don't have to lift a finger. Just a few items are fine. I bet your friend has whatever else you need. Then your brother or I can drive back and grab a few more things for you before you officially move again and get situated wherever you end up," I explain.

This move was news to me. Then again, I barely talk to Baylee anymore and Rios never talks about his sister to me, so I shouldn't be so surprised. I'll let her tell me more as she chooses. I turn and make my way to her room, hearing her footsteps following this time.

I walk into her closet and find her carry-on luggage easily. Pulling it down, I bring it to her bed and unzip it, waiting for her to guide me in what to grab. I was so distracted I hadn't noticed the few packed boxes around her room. She must've been preparing to move prior to all this happening with Myles.

"Okay, let me know what I should start putting in here.

You can sit down and I'll do all the heavy lifting," I tell her. I want to get her to the hospital as soon as possible.

"Um, just some of those dresses right there." She points to some items hanging in the closet, so I go ahead and begin pulling items off the hangers. From there, she continues guiding me and I fold and place items in the luggage. Little by little it fills up. She gets up to get her underwear and toiletries. Once the bag is full, I close it up.

"Okay, is there anything else you want to grab before we head out?" I ask her.

She grabs a change of clothes and places it in a tote. "I'll change once I get the all-clear from the hospital staff. I assume they'll need me to keep this on until they evaluate me," she explains, pulling her arm around her middle again.

I simply nod, keeping my anger below the surface because I still have to compartmentalize my feelings right now. I can't let my mind wander to what Myles did to her tonight.

"Alright. Then we'll go to the hospital. Did you let your friend know we'll be headed their way after we're done at the hospital? I know it'll likely be a few hours, but it's good they're aware." I don't know what time of night it'll be once we're done over at Connecticut General, but I have a feeling the sun will be rising. I'll have to let the Rios family know what happened here sooner rather than later.

"Um, yeah, about that," Baylee begins.

"Do you need your phone?" I ask. I realize then I haven't seen her with her phone.

"No, it's not that. My move. Not many know about it. I, um"—she looks down—"I'm moving back to Boston."

"Oh. I didn't know." This is completely out of left field and has my head spinning.

"Yeah, it's sort of a new turn of events. But it's a great opportunity with school for me. I'm transferring. It just happened within the last week. It has nothing to do with what happened tonight, although it's perfect timing. And, yeah, um, I don't have housing figured out yet. I have most of my stuff packed up." She motions with her hand around her room.

"Okay, so are you going to stay with your parents?" I ask.

"That sounded like a probable plan at first, sure." The way she isn't looking at me makes my heart rate uptick.

"Okay, what am I missing, Bay?"

It's only then she looks up at me and the determination in her eyes is the first time I see that a piece of the strength Baylee possesses is still in there.

"You're the friend I want to move in with, Tucker."

CHAPTER 7

Baylee

WHY DO hospitals all have the same feel to them? A coldness laced throughout the halls. I sit in the gurney, waiting on my nurse to come back into the makeshift room, and the beeping on my monitor leaves me feeling more alone here than when I woke up in my apartment.

Unfortunately, Tucker had to stay in the waiting area while I was being assessed back here. I don't know what a difference it would've made though because he was a statue after I dropped that bomb about staying with him.

I know, maybe I shouldn't have sprung it on him like that. But what was I supposed to do? Wait until we were here and my family was surrounding me? I mean, that seems like the wrong time. Actually, no one trains you how to react when your ex-boyfriend physically attacks you and your life is completely catapulted into this new dimension. This wasn't supposed to be my life.

I reacted rashly, but living with Tucker is probably the best course of action. I can't live with my parents right now; Myles will find me there. And there's no way I'll stay with Danny. He'd likely be a nightmare if I stayed with him. If I thought he was protective before, now he'll be one hundred times worse. Plus, Tucker will act like I'm a normal human being at least. He won't treat me like a delicate piece of porcelain. I need to live my life as normally as possible. I want to move to Boston and continue to tackle my life and forge ahead toward my goals. This isn't going to derail my plans.

As much as I was pining after him, Tucker has no romantic feelings for me, and I'll just have to put whatever I felt for him aside while we're sharing a space. I can do this as I adjust at my new school. We'll be fine together. This will be a good test of wills for me.

"Okay, Ms. Rios, good news." Dr. Berkett walks around the curtain. "Your X-ray shows no rib fractures, which is always a good sign. You have bruising, which will take a few days to subside."

I wrap my arms around my middle. "That's good news."

"Like we discussed, we're waiting for someone to come down to take you for a CT scan. The ER is a bit behind tonight, but they should be here soon to take you over." Dr. Berkett is busy looking through my electronic chart, while the nurse moves through the room grabbing supplies.

"Um, can I have my friend come in from the waiting room?" I ask.

"Yes, I see no problem in that now that we've done our assessment that should be fine," the doctor says.

"Thanks." I grab my phone to text Tucker.

"Once we have results from the CT, I'll come by and speak to you. It will most likely be a while." Dr. Berkett gives me a small smile and heads back out of the room.

I'm scrolling through my phone for a while when I hear a familiar voice behind the curtain.

"Baylee, it's Tucker. Can I come in?" He sounds so shy right now.

"Yes, I'm decent," I call out.

He moves the curtain open and soon his hulking frame is taking over the opening in front of me. It's amazing how large

Tucker Malloy truly is. No matter where he is, he turns heads. Even here, I can see the nurses at the station looking over at him. It doesn't hurt that he's easy on the eyes.

With that ginger hair, he has a sexy Viking way about him. He's got a thick neck, with muscles trailing down his shoulders and arms. Years of firefighting, carrying gear and heavy equipment up flights of stairs, have only added to the beauty that is Tucker Malloy. I better be careful or I'll start drooling. If I look past him, I bet the nurses are doing just that.

I better get ahold of myself because if I'm not careful, I'll be where I was months ago, falling right back into my crush on him. No. I'm turning over a new leaf. This is about focusing on my career goals and finishing out my degree. I'm getting my shit done so I can move forward. I'm saying *fuck Myles* and all the shit he put me through, not just tonight, but throughout our relationship.

"You doing okay?" He looks up at me. The worry etched in his eyes is so genuine it's almost like I could misconstrue it for love.

"No broken ribs. I'm waiting for a CT scan right now," I say.

"Alright." He brings his lips to a tight line, like he's holding back from saying more. "Listen, about what you said earlier. Are you sure staying with me is best, Bay?"

"Yes. I accepted a transfer to Orange University. I would stay with my parents, but I don't want Myles looking for me there now," I explain.

"And your brother?" he says.

"In a one-bedroom apartment? No thanks," I throw back.

"Understandable." He chuckles.

"Plus, I do not need that kind of big brother protection breathing down my neck. But if you don't want me around, I'll find another way. There's no university housing available, but I can try and find some other place to stay last minute," I explain.

"No, it's fine," he says, scratching the back of his head, looking around the small room. "I have an extra room with a bed. It's okay. We'll make it work. I'll just have to figure out what to say to your brother."

"Why would Danny give a shi—" I'm about to inquire about my brother's objection when I hear commotion in the hall and then the curtain swings open to my parents' and brother's gasps greeting me.

"Oh, my sweet girl!" My mom comes toward me, tears in her eyes.

I gave Tucker permission to let them know I was in the hospital once we got to the waiting room. I guess they started their drive the moment they heard. My mom and dad come running toward me, while my brother stays back, his face hard as stone. He looks over at Tucker and they exchange a look I can't decipher.

What is that about?

It's just my parents and Tucker in the cramped space, but I'm feeling suffocated.

My mom pulls away and looks me in the eyes. "What happened? Tell me who did this to you?"

That's another thing… I didn't let Tucker tell them who did this to me until they arrived. I didn't want them to have all the information until they got here just in case they overreacted. Which, apparently, they would have.

The emotional roller coaster is hard to contain and the tears begin to well up. I blink, trying to keep them from falling from my eyes, but I fail miserably.

"Myles," is all I choke out and my mom gasps.

"I'll kill him," my dad seethes.

"Mr. Rios," Tucker puts his hand on his shoulder, "we spoke to the police and they're handling it right now. Let them do their job. Let's focus on Baylee please, try not to stress her out more."

"Why? Why would he do this to you, sweetie?" My mom has tears coming down her face now.

"I broke up with him and he just lost his mind," I explain.

"Don't worry, we'll get you all fixed up. Then back to Boston and home. Okay, Baylee?" My mom looks at me like she'll make it all better.

"Mom, it's okay. I have a plan. I'm, um, not going to stay at home anymore," I tell her. I look down and fiddle with a string that's come loose on the blanket in my lap.

"What do you mean?" my mom says.

My brother chimes in at the same time, "What are you guys talking about?"

"I forgot to tell you, Danny." I look over my mom's shoulder and up at my brother. "I'm transferring to Orange University in Boston. It happened last week. That was sort of part of the reason I was breaking up with Myles. And, well, yeah, then this happened." I shrug.

I look back at my mom. "But I'm not going to stay at home anymore. I'm going to, um"—my eyes swing over to Tucker then back at my parents, bouncing between them—"to stay with Tucker for a little while. I think it's best until things settle down a bit."

My parents look at one another but stay silent.

I look over to Danny and he's just taking it all in. His eyes bounce around from person to person, arms crossed at his chest. Why does he look to be fuming at Tucker right now of all people? Doesn't he understand I was just attacked and I need to stay somewhere that Myles won't look for me?

"Malloy, can I talk to you *right now*?" My brother doesn't wait for a response and stalks out of the room.

Tucker looks over at me and quickly follows Danny out without a word. What am I missing here?

"Why does Danny look so upset at Tucker?" I ask my parents.

"He's just upset you're hurt. We were all so worried about

you when we got Malloy's call," my mom says, pushing my hair aside, inspecting my head as if she's going to find something the doctor and nurses may have missed.

"Mom, I promise I'm fine," I assure her, although I know deep down I'm more shaken up than I'm letting on.

What Myles did to me is anything but fine, although I can't let my parents know how deep this goes for me. Myles has been chipping at my psyche little by little for months, but what he did to me tonight has stripped me to my core. And if I sit too long with my thoughts, I don't know how I'll break down.

The curtain opens and a gentleman emerges with a soft smile.

"Ms. Rios, I'm Jackson. I'm taking you to your CT scan. Can you tell me your full name and your date of birth before we head out?"

Jackson walks up to the computer in the room and scans his badge to log in. I assume he's looking at my chart.

"Hi, um, yes." I pull my sheet over my legs tighter. "Baylee Rios, date of birth November twenty-sixth, two-thousand-three."

"Great. Okay, I'll wheel you over and your family can wait for you here and we'll be right back." He unlocks the gurney while addressing my parents. My mom nods at Jackson and my dad squeezes my hand.

"We'll wait for you right here. Don't you worry, we aren't going anywhere sweetie," my mom reassures me.

"Love you, Baylee." My dad kisses my head.

"Love you." My mom kisses my hand.

I swallow down the lump forming in my throat. The emotional roller coaster that tonight has been for me is new and I try to let go a little of the tension I'm holding in my shoulders as I'm moved through the little room.

As Jackson opens the curtain all the way, I see my brother and Tucker in a heated argument, hushed voices exchanged between the two of them, and I can't help how my brows furrow at the interaction.

The minute my brother sees me coming by, he halts all conversation and looks over. Tucker looks over too, irritation evident in his demeanor and it takes everything in me to not tell Jackson to stop moving so I can ask what in the world is going on between them. Why in the world are they arguing right now? What could provoke a fight between these best friends right now of all times?

CHAPTER 8

Tucker

I WATCH Baylee's gurney roll away to her CT scan and once she's out of view, I bring my eyes back to Rios's menacing glare. The person I once used to see as my best friend is nothing but a shadow of himself now. It feels like years ago we were sitting on my couch playing video games instead of just a few hours. I was trying to forge a path back to our friendship; but after the asshole remarks he just threw my way, I'm fucking done trying to play nice with him.

"Honestly, Rios, fuck off. If Baylee wants to stay with me, I'm not turning her away. I shouldn't have to prove I'm a good person to you of all people. It's not my fault you're too stubborn to see that nothing is going on." I rub the space between my eyes, hoping to stop the throbbing headache I can already feel clawing its way through.

"Like hell it isn't. Why the fuck did she call you then and not me?" he whispers, hoping to keep anyone from looking over at us as we remain outside Baylee's ER room, where her parents are waiting for her. I really hope they can't hear him. Everyone remains clueless that Rios and I aren't on the best of terms since last fall. I'd like to keep it that way.

"Maybe because you're a pain in her ass and she didn't want you breathing down her neck," I throw back.

It feels good to tell him exactly what I'm feeling. For so long I was holding things back in an effort to smooth things over with him. However, I'm completely over this friendship, because Rios is being a prick on all levels. There's something freeing being able to finally say what's been on my mind all this time.

"She's staying with me and that's final," he orders.

"You know what? How about you stop acting like she's a child and talk *to* her and not over her. I'm not dealing with you and your fucking tantrums. You've been a pain in my ass for too long. I won't interfere with your relationship with Baylee, but I'm done trying to fix ours. Continue being the asshole. You seem to fit the role so perfectly," I say back.

"She'll stay with me. And when I bring it up, you better give her the out or this friendship is over," he tells me.

Right then the doors open and Baylee's gurney comes rolling back. I straighten and give her a small smile. She eyes us again, sensing something isn't right between us. Rios and I have never been ones to fight. Even as kids, we always got along, so this is unusual for us.

Months ago, when Rios forced my hand to take Abby on that date, Baylee was in the dark to the truth behind the whole thing. No one filled Baylee in on the fact it was never a real date and that I was never interested in Abby romantically. To this day, she probably thinks I was interested in some way, when in reality I was simply trying to save my friendship with Rios. I never confessed, instead keeping my distance.

The moment she gets wheeled into her room, Rios rushes back in and I slowly follow behind. I lean against the wall, watching from afar, as the family interacts. I feel like this would be a good time to excuse myself, but if Baylee is staying with me I need to drive her back into the city.

As if reading my thoughts, Rios chimes in, "Baylee, you're staying with me."

It takes everything in me to keep from rolling my eyes. Why is he such a selfish prick? If there's one thing his sister does poorly with it's authority. I swing my eyes over to Baylee and her eyes narrow.

"Says who?" she challenges her older brother.

"Says me," he orders.

"Danny, last I checked I have a dad and he's right there." She points to their father to her right. Her dad snorts and it's hard to keep a smile from forming on my face. Even after the night she's had, that fire is still in there. *Thank fuck.* Somehow, it confirms that Baylee will be okay after all this.

"Why would you stay with Malloy? You'll be more comfortable with me," Rios protests.

"I absolutely would not. Your apartment is small and you don't have a spare room. Mom, didn't you say Tucker has a spare room at his new place?" She swings her gaze toward her mom. Mrs. Rios nods and Baylee looks back over at her brother. "Listen, I'm a big girl and I'm more than capable of making this decision for myself. I'm not asking for permission. I'm telling you I'm staying with Tucker. What's the big deal?"

I can see Baylee's ready for a fight. That Rios stubbornness runs deep, and the fact her brother is fighting her on this is just more of a reason she's going to resist. He's being an absolute ass and he has an agenda of his own here. But, after what Baylee went through tonight, I wouldn't mess with her. She's taking her power back, and I love to see it.

I'm leaning against a far wall, watching everything unfold between the Rios clan, trying to let them have their space. But, of course, leave it to Danny and his asshole tendencies to bring me right back to the fucking center.

"Tucker, tell Baylee she can't stay with you. Problem solved," Rios says in front of everyone.

Rios, like his sisters, was always this force to be reckoned with, while I was the easygoing friend. We jived from the moment we met as kids. But right now, I'm looking right into my best friend's eyes and I can't think of a reason I want our connection to continue. Everything leading to this moment is in the past; making sure Baylee feels safe is my purpose now.

This man in front of me isn't the Daniel Rios I considered my best friend all these years. This isn't the guy I would run into a burning building with. This isn't the man I consider a brother. He isn't the person I look at and remember laughing with on the couch for years over dumb shit. All I see is jealousy and anger swimming in those brown irises. I see someone that only wants to be rid of me for reasons I still don't comprehend.

Smoothing things over between us is the last thing I want now. So, I swing my gaze over to Baylee and simply say, "Nope, Baylee is coming home with me. I've already got all the things she needs to spend the night at my place. I guess you just need to grab the rest of her belongings from her place to get her officially moved in, Rios."

And that right there is the last nail in the coffin on my friendship with Daniel Rios.

CHAPTER 9

Baylee

"WELL, THIS IS IT," Tucker says as we walk into his apartment.

I'm fighting to keep my eyes open after being up all night. I take in the open concept of his space. It looks nothing like I'd imagined, yet it's exactly somewhere I can see Tucker Malloy living.

The kitchen is to the left of the front door, with a moderate-sized island in the center. He has four barstools tucked to one side where I envision him sitting in the morning while eating breakfast. It's so tidy, with sleek cabinets and state of the art appliances. Nothing like the bachelor pad I imagined on the drive over, with dirty dishes scattered about.

My car will get dropped off at my parents' house tomorrow when Danny comes back into town. He agreed, begrudgingly, to return to my apartment to meet a locksmith in a few hours to get the door fixed and collect the rest of my packed belongings for me. I don't want my car left here in case Myles decides to look for me. Even if the police put a warrant out for his arrest, it will take a few days to take effect.

I walk further into Tucker's place and find a few boxes of

his own he's probably still needing to unpack. To the right in his living room is a large couch where I imagine him sprawling out, his large frame likely taking up the whole space and watching television or playing video games, much like he did so many times in my childhood home. My mind wanders to a shirtless Tucker in gray sweatpants and my heart flutters. I can feel my cheeks flame and I quickly look away, hoping he can't read my mind.

Behind his TV there's a wall with exposed brick that brings this whole place together. Something about it screams Boston and it might be my favorite thing about this place. It immediately looks like a place I'd pick for Tucker.

"Bay, did you hear me?" Tucker is closing the door behind me.

"Huh?" I swing my gaze, finding him looking at me tentatively.

"I asked you if you want a glass of water before I show you to your room." He juts his chin toward the kitchen.

"Oh, sure." I tip my smile upward slightly. I don't know why I'm shy all of a sudden.

"Alright." He moves into the kitchen to grab a bottled water.

Once he gets one for me and himself, he's moving ahead of me with my items, while I trail behind him. I'm taking everything in, wondering how my life has brought me here. Months ago, I would have butterflies multiplying in my stomach at the thought of sleeping down the hall from this man, while I'm currently crying inside at the realization that my life is literally in shambles right now.

I'm a victim today, part of a club I never wanted entry into. I'm living a nightmare life in comparison to what I pictured when I got that call from Orange University last week, because I let someone put their hands on me and shatter something inside of me. I'll have to learn how to pick up pieces of myself and I have no idea where to start.

I'm once again lost in thought when we stop in front of a door, and Tucker must sense it.

"Baylee, I know you're probably feeling a lot of things right now, but you're not in this alone. I won't let this guy take you away from us." His words blanket me, as if they're finding a way to envelop me in a hug.

I look up into his green eyes and I feel the emotion reflected in them in the depths of my soul. This connection right here is what I want to capture in a bottle and bring with me when I want to crumble. Because I know this isn't going to be the only low moment I'll feel in this hell I've found myself in.

I start to blink rapidly, hoping to stop the tears from falling. Of course, I fail and one escapes down my cheek and with a swipe of a thumb, Tucker grabs it.

"Let's get you situated." He opens the door, and the guest room reveals itself.

It's pretty bare, with white walls, a simple nightstand and a television hung on the wall. The bedding is a light blue with matching pillows. The light fixtures on either side of the bed are gold, and he has two baseball-themed art pieces hung on the wall.

"I didn't know you were a baseball guy." I look over at him, chuckling.

"Yeah, that's courtesy of Kennedy. She gave me those as a housewarming present." He smiles.

"And she's a baseball fan?" I give him a questioning look.

"You haven't kept up with everyone on your brother's squad?"

"I've met a few of them, but not really." I shrug.

"Kennedy is River's fiancée and she's the CEO of the Boston Gaels," he says matter-of-factly.

I lift my eyebrows. "Wow, you don't hear that every day."

"Yeah, she's a ballbuster." He laughs in response.

"Well, I didn't realize River got engaged. But knowing him, he needs someone like that." I laugh. River is a handful.

"That's for sure." He sets my stuff down on the dresser. "Alright, well I better get going. I will be back a bit later." He reaches into his pocket. "Here's an extra key, and I'll text you the alarm code. Will you be okay while I'm gone?"

"Uh, where are you going?" I can't help the panic laced in my tone.

He winces. "I have to take my mom to her treatment. It's an early appointment. I'll be gone a few hours. But I'll have my phone with me."

Shoot. I forgot Carolyn had an appointment at the hospital today. "Of course. No, it's fine."

"Alright. You have your own bathroom and there's soap, extra toothbrushes, and anything you might need under the sink. Towels and such are there too," he explains.

"Thanks Tucker. Really, I appreciate it," I tell him.

"No problem. I have leftover pizza in the fridge if you want some. But make sure to get some rest. I'm just going to freshen up then head out. I'll be sure to lock up and let you know when I leave."

"Okay, thank you. But don't worry about me. I promise, I'll be fine." I try to stand up straighter to prove it.

"Baylee, you don't have to do that," he says.

"Do what?" I ask.

"Act like you're unaffected. It's okay to not be okay around me." He looks at me.

I look at him and realize that I want to let go so badly with him. But last time I almost did that, I nearly gave him my whole heart. I wanted everything with him and if I had gotten that, who knows where I'd be. One thing's for sure, I wouldn't be here, bruised and battered in this way.

Instead, I stand taller. "Tucker, I'm going to be fine. Thank you, though."

Tucker must realize a wall has formed right then.

"Ok. Call me if you need anything."

He turns and leaves the room.

I walk myself into the restroom and pull out everything I need for a shower. I turn the water on and let the steam engulf the confined space, slowly taking over the mirror in front of me. Before the reflection is fully covered by steam, I see the bruises that have truly taken over my body. I try to close my eyes in hopes I can shield myself from remembering how horrific these last twelve hours of my life have been, but those lifeless blue eyes take over my memories.

Myles left his mark on me—on my body and in my mind. He has permanently left scars in my memories and now I feel robbed of so much joy. It's as if the beauty of life's potential is tainted. I just hope he hasn't left his mark permanently on my soul. Maybe as I move forward, I can erase each piece of ugly with a moment of happiness.

———

I wake to the smell of garlic, and my stomach immediately growls. I can't remember the last time I ate something. It takes me a minute to figure out where I am. This mattress feels like I'm lying on a cloud. I turn over and stretch out, my muscles stiff.

That's when the memories from earlier come flooding back... Myles and the attack... my call to Tucker and the trip to the hospital. Everything feels overwhelming. I'm in Tucker's apartment and my life is no longer what I thought it would be.

I look over at the clock and it's four-ten in the afternoon. I groan thinking about my roommates who are probably sick with worry. We exchanged a few text messages before I finally succumbed to sleep earlier. My brother updated me with some short messages when things were getting handled at the apartment. I'm relieved the lock was changed without any issue. He also told me he found someone to come and fix the damage to the wall. He promised to drive back out to Connecticut later in the week to supervise that repair for me as well.

My roommates were given a brief explanation, and they wanted to come straight home, but I didn't want them driving back yet. With the apartment still unsecured and Myles out there, I thought it best they stick to their plans until it was safe to return.

I reach over and grab my phone to find missed texts from the girls, along with a few from my family checking in on me. I also see a missed call and voicemail from a number with an area code from Connecticut, which I'm hoping is from the police department.

I skip the texts and immediately put the phone to my ear to listen to the message:

"Hi, Ms. Rios, this is Officer Tamos. Please give me a call back when you get this. Thank you."

Unfortunately, she didn't leave much else to hint if they were able to speak to Myles. Maybe she can't leave details in a message. I'm too anxious to wait another second, so I immediately call her back. The moment I hear the line ringing, I feel my heart pounding. I place my hand over my chest, hoping I can calm myself down.

"This is Officer Tamos," she answers.

"Hi, this is Baylee Rios. I'm returning your call," I say, my voice a bit shaky.

"Hi, Ms. Rios. I'm glad you called. I assume you got my message?"

"You can call me Baylee. And yes, I just got it. I'm sorry for missing your call."

"That's fine. I assumed you had a long night after you left the apartment. I received the report from the hospital. I was happy to see you didn't end up with a concussion."

"Oh, um, thanks. Yes, I'm relieved. I'm okay. A bit sore and still shaken," I tell her.

"That's to be expected. I'm filing the information for the arrest warrant. That will likely take at least few days. Keep that in mind. You're staying in Boston, correct?"

"Yes," I tell her. The unease knowing Myles could just be anywhere is infuriating.

"Be vigilant of your surroundings, Ms. Rios. I did pay a visit to Mr. Stempler today and he was agitated with my questions. But he's aware he isn't allowed to leave the state. He has also been informed that you're pressing charges against him," she explains.

"You didn't tell him where I am, right?" I can't help the panic in my tone.

"No, I didn't tell him your whereabouts, I assure you."

"Thank you," I say weakly.

"Once I have more updates, I'll call you. But if you have any questions, or you see anything that makes you uncomfortable, you give me a call. You understand?"

"Yes, thank you, Officer Tamos."

"Alright. I'll let you go. Please rest up. Take care, Ms. Rios."

I say my goodbyes and the minute I hang up, I lean my head back on the headboard, closing my eyes and feeling the weight of the world on my shoulders.

I try to shake off the feeling of pain and dread that has been there since the moment Myles barged into my apartment and throw the covers off me. The moment I sit up, the soreness along my torso reminds me I can't move as fast as I'd like. I stand slowly, wincing, and make my way to the ensuite bathroom.

When I'm finished in the bathroom, I make my way out of the guest room and down the hall. I hear movement in the kitchen and soon I'm greeted with a naked torso and Tucker in gray sweatpants. Even in my battered state, I can't help the internal groan I'm holding back. I might be hurt, but I'm not blind nor dead. This man is gorgeous. I watch his toned muscles flex as he mixes the items in front of him on the stove.

It isn't until I get closer that I realize he has headphones on and what looks like an apron tied around his waist. His back is still to me, so he hasn't noticed I've entered the room and I'm enjoying the view too much to get his attention. I pull up one of the barstools and decide to sit down. May as well soak up the hot chef while I can. My eyes do another perusal while he's turned away.

"What a dirty bird," Tucker whispers.

Um, what now? My pulse races as my eyes nearly bulge out in panic. Can Tucker see me through the reflection on one of his appliances?

I'm relieved once he seems to continue with his cooking and my ogling isn't the reason for his outburst. But then he stops mixing and seems to be focused on whatever he's listening to. Is it a podcast or something? It's definitely got his attention.

There's a Bluetooth speaker to my left and I begin fiddling with it. Without realizing it, I accidentally turn the speaker on and whatever Tucker is listening to with his headphones is now connecting to this Bluetooth speaker in front of me.

It feels like I'm listening to a porno "*...oh, you fuck me so good, Anton...right there. Fuck me harder with that hard cock. Touch my nipples, like that. Oh yes! I'm going to come! Yes! Yes!*"

My eyes go wide and I look over at him, amusement etched on my face. He swings his head over as it registers what's going on.

"Oh my God!" Tucker says, pulling his headphones off.

I start laughing. That prompts me to grab my side because the pain is sharp, but even with it, I continue to laugh. Is Tucker listening to a smutty book?

"Baylee, what are you doing up?" Tucker yells over at me. His face is fucking beet red.

"What? Was I supposed to stay asleep until you came to my room with a tray or something?" I'm laughing so hard that I'm wheezing and I have tears streaming down my face. I've known him my whole life and he still finds ways to surprise me.

"*Fuck, Robin, you're so fucking tight...*" the audiobook continues and it's just too much. The volume is on full blast too, so it just makes this whole thing even more comical.

"Fuck, where is the god damn off button on this speaker!" Tucker exclaims.

"Tucker, this might be the best thing ever!" I've fallen off the barstool and I'm crouched on the floor. I can't help it.

He finally turns the audiobook off from his phone and he places his hands on his thighs, heavily panting like he just ran a marathon, catching his breath. I'm bent over, still in hysterics because it's hard to imagine this burly man, that I've loved most my life, listening to a smutty book while cooking dinner. Now I'm laughing all over again. *Who is this guy?*

I'm wiping the tears from my face and soon I feel Tucker's shadow looming over me. I give him a big smile, the first I've had since he came to my rescue.

He continues to stare at me until I calm myself down. I finally catch my breath and get back up on the barstool. He moves his fingers to wipe the hair that has fallen across my face and I feel his warmth on my skin, I try to ignore how it lights me on fire, much like it did months ago.

I clear my throat and sit up taller on the barstool. I give him another smile. He's still standing close to me, with a stern look on his face. Did he feel that force between us like I did?

For a minute I think he's going to say something about it.

"Baylee," he begins.

"Yeah," I whisper.

"Not a fucking word about that damn book to anyone, you understand?" he says in a gruff voice.

I give him one of my sly smiles. "Oh Tucker, you know me better than that."

"Fucking hell. You're going to tell everyone, aren't you?"

"Abso-fucking-lutely," I fire back.

And just like that, I realize that maybe, by surrounding myself with Tucker, I'll start to get the pieces of myself back that Myles robbed from me.

CHAPTER 10

Tucker

FOUR FUCKING days I've had Baylee under the same roof as me and it hasn't gotten any easier. I can hear her moving around out there and I'm still sitting on my bed trying to kill time so I can possibly avoid having to interact with her. Yes, I agreed to have her here. But it's fucking awkward with her in my space. Because every time she's around me, I long to run my hands through her hair, or fucking touch her in ways that I shouldn't.

It was never like this between us, but now it's just painful to be around her. Granted, since the attack, I want to throw something across the room because that asshole hurt her and every so often, she'll move a certain way and I'll catch her wincing. That guts me to my core. Fuck, how I want to rip that piece of shit to shreds.

We still haven't gotten word that he's been arrested. Apparently, he's got people in high places because he's still walking free, as if he didn't punch a woman in the gut and leave her behind without a care in the world. Fucking piece of trash. But, we know that mandatory arrest will occur in this case, thanks to Connecticut law requirements.

Thankfully, he isn't a threat to Baylee right now and we've made sure she doesn't leave the house alone.

I ball my hands in front of me, my head hanging, my right leg bouncing uncontrollably as my mind wanders to that night. I've never been an anxious person. But thinking about the way Baylee looked that night, the fear in her eyes as she looked up at me, simply pulls something out of me. I can't help but wonder how things turned out this way and it keeps me awake at night. I should've done more, I knew something was wrong. I let my friendship with Rios guide me into ignoring the signs. I didn't listen to my gut, and I let life lead her in the direction of some creep instead.

"Argh," I grunt and stand. I'm fucking frustrated at myself and at life. It's unfair. I'm watching my mom go through treatment and now I'm watching Baylee go through something she shouldn't have to deal with.

I pace the space of my room, feeling like the walls are caving in and this feeling is so unfamiliar. How the fuck did this all happen in such a short amount of time? She was supposed to go off and figure things out with someone better than me. Life was supposed to be better to her. That's why I let things go between us. Instead, I let her walk into the hands of a monster.

"Tucker, are you okay?" Baylee knocks softly on the door, worry etched in her tone.

"Yeah, sorry, I can't find my favorite pair of socks." I roll my eyes at the stupidity of my comment.

What the fuck? Socks?

"Um, okay? Well, I made some coffee if you want some. I'm headed out. I have orientation today," she says. She sounds a bit hesitant.

"Do you need a ride? I'm headed to my mom's so I can drop you off on the way," I tell her. I forgot to ask her if she had someone taking her to campus today. We hadn't quite coordinated how things would work out once her classes started.

"Oh, uh, sure," she says. I really hate how hesitant she is all the time now. This isn't the Baylee I know. She was always so independent, even though she was the youngest of the Rios kids. Now there's a reluctance to her tone when she talks to me. Like she's treading carefully. How long has she been dealing with demeaning retorts from the person by her side?

I take a deep breath and walk to my door. When I swing the door open, Baylee stands there, her eyes going wide.

"You find your socks?" She looks down at my shoes.

"Yep." I've been dressed for an hour.

"Great." She clearly sees right through my lie.

I walk straight for the coffee maker, knowing I'll be aching for caffeine on a day like this after my sleepless night.

I fill up my to-go mug, and we grab our things and head to my truck. Once inside, Baylee starts messing with the music. She connects the Bluetooth to her phone and the minute the music starts, she sits back and I can feel her eyes on me.

"Just spit it out, Bay." I grab my aviators then look over my shoulder and pull out into traffic.

"I just want to make sure I'm not interfering on your time in case you need to get some smut reading in," she says very seriously, before she fully lets out a laugh.

"Motherfucker," I say under my breath. "How long have you been holding that in?"

"Let's see"—she starts counting out on her fingers—"four days."

She looks mighty proud. This interaction is the first since the attack where I see the old pieces of Baylee coming through. She's busting my balls just like she used to, and I honestly don't mind. But I won't tell her that, I'll let her think it bothers me.

"Okay, let me have it. Go ahead, ask me what you need to ask." I keep my eyes on the road.

"Obviously, I need to know when this started? I mean, come on Tucker, you don't come off as the smutty romance reader type," she explains.

"That's a bit judgy." I sneak a glance over.

"You needing to find a way to connect to the ladies?" She pouts.

"I have no problem in that department, thank you very much." I cough, making this conversation a bit uncomfortable.

"Okay, then what is it?" she pushes.

"Fine, I'm in a book club, alright?"

"What? Are you joking? Is it at the firehouse?" She laughs.

"No, it's with my friends Abby and Kennedy," I tell her.

"Hold on, didn't you go on a date with Abby? Isn't she with Clay? So, what? Now you're friends with someone you dated? And she's with one of the guys you work with? What a weird love triangle." She scrunches her nose.

"You have no idea what you're talking about." I wave my hand at her. "It's definitely not a love triangle. That would be weird." I shiver. "Abby and I were never romantic. Gross."

"I think she'd be offended if you referred to her as gross." She looks at me like I'm a chauvinistic pig.

"Um, no she wouldn't, I can promise you that. There was never anything romantic between us. She and I never saw one another like that. That date was sort of fake. From the second it started we were instant friends, and the rest is history. We connected with a deep-seated interest in reality-dating shows and now we have a smutty book club. Plus, I love her daughter. She's one of my best friends. Kennedy still scares me more than anything, but she's growing on me. Clay and River have become great people in my life. I've formed a little family around me outside of my actual family. It's become an incredible support for me." I can't help the smile that forms as I talk about the new part of my life I've built in the last year.

Silence falls over us and once I reach a traffic light, I look over to find Baylee staring at me.

"What?" I feel uncomfortable with her gaze on me.

"So, that date—it wasn't anything?" she asks.

"No, it wasn't anything. It was just two friends going out," I explain.

"I see." Her face goes to stone and she moves her body forward and any lightness we had built feels like ice.

"Bay, did I say something to offend you?" I ask her.

"It's green," she answers.

"Huh?" I ask in confusion.

The car behind me blares its horn and it's then I realize the light has changed to green.

I start to move through traffic again.

"Baylee, what did I say to upset you?" I ask again.

"I texted you," she says, just above a whisper.

"What's that?" I heard her, but I don't know what to say, so I need to buy time. I'm being a chickenshit.

We arrive at the university and she points to where she'd like to be dropped off.

"I can get you closer if you'd like," I tell her.

"No, I want to get out." She doesn't even look at me.

"Baylee, look at me." I stop the car at the loading zone.

"Tucker, listen, I appreciate what you're doing for me. But"—she takes a deep breath—"I texted you for months. I thought you didn't respond because you had something going on with Abby. I... um... I just feel stupid right now. I just... forget it. I appreciate the ride. I'll see you at your apartment."

She doesn't wait for my response and slams the door. Fuck. The thing is, Baylee has no idea how I felt about her. How I *feel* about her. That day in her parents' house, I almost said something, but Rios walked in and everything changed. I started to feel this attraction between us rise and I never got to act on it. He doused a dose of reality on it and then she ran off and I focused on my friendship with Rios.

That's what these last few months have been about for me. Then my mom got sick and that's been my only thought lately. When Baylee started dating Myles, I thought her life was headed in a different direction. I never imagined she was in an abusive relationship. This path is more fucked up than I imagined. How have things gotten this messed up? I honestly thought I was doing the right thing last year by accepting that date with Abby and letting Baylee go.

That's the thing, we don't have a Magic 8 ball to help us figure out if one simple decision will lead us in the right direction. My one decision led us down a path of destruction for her. She texted me for months and I left her unanswered because I feared what that would do to my friendship with Rios. The common denominator here has always been her brother.

Everything changed a few nights ago though. Rios has been giving me the silent treatment and I don't give a flying fuck anymore. I choose Baylee now and it's freeing. I know having her living with me is the right decision.

Myles never met me in the months he dated Baylee because I kept my distance. So, he won't connect us together, and he won't come looking for her at my place, hopefully keeping her safe while we wait for him to be arrested.

Laying hands on someone so precious is something I still can't wrap my head around. I can't let my mind go down that road, especially as I'm about to take my mom to the hospital for her treatment. I need to keep myself calm while I prepare for the hours ahead.

Before getting back on the road, I connect my phone to the Bluetooth and pull up my audiobook. Baylee was right, I have to finish my current read. Book club is coming up and I've got to finish *Beneath the Sheets*.

I laughed when we pulled this book out of the jar last month, but it is an addictive listen. Kennedy was the one that put this one in and she was giddy when it got chosen. Her eyes gleamed and I swear I almost gagged. I know she's going to be trying some of these fucked up positions with River. She overshares when we meet, knowing it makes me uncomfortable. It's messed up. Although I'm not saying anything because Kennedy is so fucking scary sometimes, especially when she gets riled up.

———

Days later I find myself at the firehouse, still unable to shake my car ride with Baylee. We were never together and yet, it looked like she was heartbroken over something I did to her. Like the realization that my date with Abby was fake broke something between us. I still can't figure it out. I'm lost in thought when River saunters in the kitchen.

"Let me get this straight, you have thousands of followers and you know your way around a kitchen? The ladies must be lining up at your door." He grabs an apple and looks over at our probie with a gleam in his eye.

He loves pointing out that our newest recruit has a huge social media presence when he can barely understand how to post a reel. How are we nearly the same age?

Hunter just smiles his easy-going way as he lines up the lasagna on the tray and continues cooking. He's still getting used to all the guys at the station, but he's quickly learning to tell River and Clay apart. Hunter is a man of few words, but so far, he's fit in well with the crew here. If he's not cooking, he's working out with us and helping around the firehouse.

"Hey, Malloy, we still good for a run tomorrow after shift?" River looks over at me.

"Yeah, that works for me. Your brother joining us?" I ask.

"I think so, after he sees his girls." He's scrolling through his phone while taking a bite of his apple.

His comment brings a pang to my heart. It's a reminder of how much I lack in my own life, because I have little to run home to after my own shift.

"You have room for another if I were to join you?" Hunter chimes in.

We both look up to see the probie waiting for a response. River and I swing our gaze to each other then back to Hunter.

We both shrug and I answer, "Sure, why not? But no groupies allowed. We run and don't stop for selfies with strangers, got it?"

"Yep, no problem!" He flashes his charming smile, something I know probably wins over hearts online.

Clay saunters in, the biggest smile on his face. Since reconnecting with Abby and having his daughter, this guy is always happy instead of sulking. I haven't known him long, but I have noticed a lightness to him now that his life seems to be coming together with the person he loves by his side.

"Hey man, how's everything going?" I ask him.

"Good." He's looking down at his phone.

"What's got you smiling like that, man?" River asks his twin.

"Ella's smiling at everything now and I swear it's the best phase." He turns his phone and it's a video of his daughter babbling and smiling at herself in the mirror.

It's hard not to react and soon we're all watching her in amazement. It seems she's doubled in size since I last saw her, even though I know that's not the case. I'll have to text Abby to make sure she brings her to book club so I can snuggle her.

"I think she needs some time with her uncle River. That girl adores me. Last time she saw me, she reached for me instead of this guy." He juts his chin over to his brother. "I swear she prefers me." He puffs out his chest.

"Fucking hell. How many times do I have to tell you? She

doesn't think you're her dad, Riv. You nearly yanked her out of Abby's arms. You barely give her space when you're around. I think even she's exhausted around you." Clay rolls his eyes.

"My dear, stupid, sad brother," River begins, reaching over and putting his arm around his brother's shoulders and bringing him into a hug, "you just can't admit your daughter loves me more. But it's okay. Once she can speak, she'll settle this once and for—"

As if we've conjured her up from thin air, Abby walks in with Ella in her arms.

"Hey, guys!" She's got a huge smile on her face.

Abby and Clay recently got engaged and I assume she's walking on cloud nine since then. For someone who only returned from California a year ago and was pushing Clay away, she's really settling into this life they've built back up again. I couldn't be happier for my friend. She looks free and settled, something I envy about her as I feel like my life has taken a turbulent turn recently.

"Hey, baby." Clay pries River's arm off him to make his way to his fiancée and daughter. "What are you doing here?"

Abby looks to Clay and gives him a quick kiss. "Oh, I was in the neighborhood, walking with Ella. The weather is so nice, and I thought we'd take advantage of it. I brought some snacks for you."

I see Abby's eyes lock on something behind Clay, and it registers why she's really here. I can't help the laugh that escapes; I know her motives and I narrow my eyes at her.

"So you were just in the neighborhood, huh?" I ask her.

"Yeah, Malloy, I was," she says.

"Well, give me my niece, then." River makes grabby hands toward Ella.

"Let me have my daughter first, man," Clay demands.

"Dude, you live with them. Let me have my time with her first." River's tone is no-nonsense while I keep my eyes on

Abby the entire time. Her cheeks flush and I can't believe Clay is oblivious to why she's really here.

Abby makes her way to the island in the kitchen while the Nichols brothers continue to fight over the baby. Abby stands next to me, and I continue to lean against the counter, watching her stand there. I know she's waiting for me to introduce her to Hunter. He's still putting together the lasagna.

Abby elbows me when she realizes I'm stalling, and I laugh again.

Because I have no intention of making this easy on her, I push a little more, "Oh, you want me to introduce you to our newest member at Station 10?"

"Yes, please." She smiles sweetly, although she's speaking through gritted teeth.

"Tyler Hunter, I would like to introduce you to Abby Morris, soon to be Abby Nichols, *again*." I emphasize the again part. "Abby, this is Hunter, our newest addition."

"Nice to meet you. You look familiar. Have I seen you before?"

I roll my eyes. She's fucking killing me, I snort, and she glares at me.

"Abby, cut the act. I told him I had a friend who knew he was famous online. Remember I took that selfie on your first day? This is who I sent it to." I throw her a Cheshire grin.

"You're demoted, asshole," she whispers.

"Fat chance. You love me." I wink at her.

"What's happening here?" Hunter asks about our exchange.

"He's a pain in my ass," Abby explains. "And yes, it's true, I do know who you are. Malloy doesn't let me get away with anything. He's lucky I love him... but not like that." She turns toward me and sticks her tongue out.

"Real mature for a mom," I tell her.

"Fuck off, Malloy." She turns away from me and toward

Hunter. "I follow you on my social media and it's really cool to see your workouts. I can't believe you ended up at this firehouse of all places."

Hunter watches us for a few extra seconds, probably thinking we're both lunatics, but then he smiles at us, and continues working on the food.

"Thank you. I appreciate it. Yeah, I left the military with a following. Once I got to civilian life, I needed something to feel like myself again and working out was really for mental clarity, so I continued with it. Never thought it would take off like it did. Joining the fire academy felt like another way to connect with a community here and now here I am. I appreciate the support."

"Maybe you should tell him when you watch his videos, Abs." I laugh as I grab a carrot and take a bite.

"Malloy, don't you have something else to do?" Abby smacks my arm.

"No, this is really the highlight of my day." I smile back.

"When do you watch my videos?" Hunter asks, with a confused expression.

"Yeah, Abby, when do you watch Hunter's videos?" River and Clay ask at the same time as they walk up to the counter, Ella cooing in River's arms. I guess River won the battle once again.

"I think this conversation is done. Clay, why don't you show me around? I don't think I've seen the firehouse since you came back from leave." She's already pulling Clay away from the kitchen, but not before she shoots me a murderous glare.

I throw a huge smile her way and another wink to solidify how much I adore her.

"Oh, but Abby, this conversation was just getting good. When again?" River won't drop it.

She makes her way back to put her belongings down on the chair, all while glaring at her future brother-in-law.

"When I'm breastfeeding. You happy now, you assholes?" She looks at me and River. "You're not an asshole, Hunter. You seem *absolutely lovely*. It was wonderful meeting you. Don't hang out with these dick pickles if you know what's good for you. They'll just corrupt you." She gives him a sweet smile. Then she looks over at River and I one more time and points at us both, giving us the middle finger.

"Abby, come baby. I'll show you around a bit. Maybe we can make out in a dark corner while River has Ella." He chuckles.

"Oh, sounds hot," she says. The minute she catches up to him, he slaps her ass and laughs.

As much as I give her shit, my heart squeezes because a part of me aches for a love as pure as what she has with Clay. I hope at some point I can find what she has. I long for a love that ignites all the corners of my life, even after it gets enveloped in darkness.

CHAPTER 11

Baylee

I'VE BEEN AVOIDING Tucker since that day he dropped me off on campus for orientation. Is it immature? Yes. Do I care? Absolutely not. I just don't feel like dealing with my emotional freak out with him right now. I don't want to have the conversation with him regarding how that rejection felt. It's on me, not him.

I get it, he didn't feel the same thing erupting between us that summer. It's embarrassing and I don't want to dwell on it. I assumed he was finally reciprocating my feelings back then and I was obviously imagining it. But then to hear that the date he went on was fake just set something off in me, I had to get away from him. The car felt suffocating.

So no, I don't want to face him and have him pretty much say, "Oh, Baylee, you silly, naive little girl, I don't see you like that. I just see you as my neighbor and my best friend's little sister. Please don't hate me. And you're living with me because I also feel bad for you that your sick, monstrous ex-boyfriend hit you and you need to recover." Blah, blah, blah.

Okay, I need to seek some help because I'm having full imaginary conversations now. But that's how I imagine

Tucker talking to me. He's a pretty sweet guy and I doubt he'd be demeaning in any way. I need to get out of this hole of self-pity I'm sitting in right now.

In all my years of crushing on Tucker, I never sat around and contemplated it like this. So why now? How is it consuming me this way? It all comes down to the timing of my relationship with Myles and the way he sucked out my self-esteem. This narrative I've written for myself is taking a toll on how I interpret the person I see reflected in the mirror today.

I'm walking on campus and today is the first time I haven't been looking over my shoulder. Officer Tamos called me last night, letting me know Myles was arrested. The judge signed the arrest warrant and I can finally breathe a sigh of relief. I'm still in shock how long it took for the warrant to go through, but with his mother being a big-time attorney in the state, I shouldn't have even questioned she would fight tooth and nail to ensure her son would avoid time behind bars. I should simply feel grateful an arrest was made.

I have to come to terms with the fact that Myles will likely be out on bail though. Officer Tamos explained the probability is high that it would happen quickly with his mother being motivated to get her son back to normal life. Luckily, he has to stay within the state of Connecticut, so being in Boston, I should be safely away from him. I sent a text to my family to give an update late last night. I also sent a text to Tucker separately, even though he was in the next room from me.

I make it to my class and I'm greeted by Jacob and Sydney. I met them at the orientation. They weren't new to the school, but they were running the program that day and we instantly clicked. It was simply lucky they were in my kinesiology class and were all in the same major. Sydney is also double-majoring in sports medicine so she's been helping me get acclimated into the university lifestyle and it's been an easy transition.

I can't ignore how much I miss my old roommates, though we've FaceTimed since I moved. They got back to the apartment two days after the attack. Danny was able to meet them there with the new keys. They let me know Myles hasn't shown up at all, nor have they seen him on campus. My brother had gotten an alarm system installed that week after the attack, getting some cameras put in place for their peace of mind. They're planning a trip out to Boston to come visit me in the next couple weeks and I can't wait. Because of everything that happened with Myles, I've decided to stay here and they've been understanding about everything going on. I know that with the charges I had to file I'll have to make my way back to Connecticut once we get closer to a hearing date, but I won't do so until I absolutely have to.

My brother left my car with my parents, but I've been able to either get a ride or use a ride share app to get around the city. All my things are now at Tucker's apartment, and I'm fully settled.

"Hey, how are you?" Jacob smiles up at me.

I grab a seat next to him. "I'm good. Trying to get back into the swing of things now that classes have started."

"I know. I want to throw my alarm across the room." Sydney moans.

"Well, maybe if you didn't go to every frat party." Jacob nudges her.

"You should talk. Your frat is one of the ones I go to every week." She yawns.

"You should come, Baylee," Jacob tells me. "They're fun. We have a house off campus and the parties are usually Fridays and Saturdays. Friday we have a home football game, and we'll host a party, then Saturday we'll just have something chill at the house. I'll admit, Friday will get a bit more rowdy though, so if you're wanting something more laid back, Saturday is probably the way to go."

"They're a ton of fun," Sydney chimes in.

I laugh while grabbing my items from my bag. "Yeah, I don't know." I still haven't told them everything that happened with Myles. I'm keeping it close to my chest.

"Please come. It would be fun to have you around," Sydney adds. "The parties are epic. You can join me and my girlfriends. Just let me know if you decide to come. You can always text me, I'll swing by your place and pick you up. I usually DD. I don't care to drink at these things."

"Let's just say, Sydney sort of had a rough freshman year with Jose Cuervo, so she would rather dance the night away instead. She saw the contents of that drink coming back up and it was not pretty—ow!" Jacob yelps.

"I thought we weren't going to talk about that ever again, Jacob!" she counters.

He looks over at me. "I never promised that. She looked like the exorcist that night." He laughs as Sydney shoots daggers at him.

"Okay, I'll let you know." I chuckle at their exchange.

Our professor walks in and we quiet down. It feels good to find my place bit by bit here, even if it's just with two friends in such a big university. I only have a year to get my classes done here and I'll soon begin another chapter, this time in my professional life. The bruises of my past are still healing and I honestly want to put that part of my life behind me. But as I move forward, I'd like to take the old parts of me back. I just hope I won't carry the broken pieces with me.

———

I'm walking back to the apartment and I'm totally wiped after the long day of classes. Luckily, I don't have too much work to do tonight. I'm just ready to change out of these clothes and get into pajamas.

As I get closer to the front door, I hear voices. I quickly

realize they're right in front of my door. I approach and the moment they see me, I notice their eyes bulge a bit.

"Um, hey." I get my keys out.

"Oh, hi! You must be Baylee," the brunette says as she moves a stroller by her side with an infant sleeping inside. She's short with long brown hair and stunning blue eyes. I look over and the woman to her side is tall and blonde. She looks straight out of a magazine. Her blue eyes are piercing and I have no idea who either of them are.

"May I help you?" I can't hide the bite in my tone.

"Yeah, sorry, we're waiting on Malloy," the blonde one says.

"Oh, um, he's not home," I tell them. I unlock the door, but don't hold it open to give them space to follow me.

"That's fine, we'll wait for him to get home," the blonde one says.

Okay, what in the world is happening? And who are these women? Does he date two women at the same time? Is he into people with babies now? *Not that I could blame him, they're beautiful.*

"I'm sorry. Can someone catch me up? Who are you?" I stand at the door.

"I'm so sorry. I'm Abby and this is Kennedy. This here"— she points at the sleeping baby— "is my daughter Ella." She smiles down, the love pouring out of her.

Oh, now I feel like an asshole. This is the famous Abby. She's breathtaking. And he had no attraction to this woman? That's surprising.

"Tucker didn't tell me you were coming over. Sorry, I wasn't expecting you," I explain.

"We have book club tonight. It starts"—Kennedy looks down at her watch— "well, now. But he probably went to get snacks because he's not prepared. Figures."

"Kennedy, retract the claws," Abby tells her.

"I'm hungry and River was being a pain in my ass. He

keeps giving me demands for the wedding. Who knew the groom could be so fussy." She rolls her eyes.

"Because you're marrying a high maintenance child," Abby says, and I can't help the snort that escapes.

I've only met River a few times, but that's an accurate description. He's incredibly high energy and I can only imagine him being a lot to handle.

"I heard that snort, I like you already," Kennedy says. "Now, can we come in?"

"Oh, yes. No problem. Sorry," I tell them.

"Thanks so much," Abby says.

"I hope you don't mind. I'm going to go change. I've been in classes all day. Make yourselves at home. Do you want me to get you anything before I go to my room?" I ask them.

"No, don't worry about us. We'll grab it if we need anything," Abby says.

"Okay. Just holler if you need me. I'll be right back," I tell them.

I'm walking back and I hear a quick "I like her a lot" from Kennedy, and a smile spreads across my face. I don't know why having Kennedy's approval means something to me. I barely said anything, and what I did say wasn't very nice.

After freshening up and changing into something a little more comfortable, I make my way back into the living room. The moment I reach them again, Abby has Ella in her arms, but it's the conversation that has me halting in my tracks.

"Okay, explain that again. You're telling me that they're injecting what *where* now?" That's coming from Abby.

"Oh, you heard it right the first time. They're injecting filler in their labia," Kennedy explains.

"Why? I mean, no judgement, but why?" Abby asks.

How long was I in my room? Is this what women talk about after having kids? And how destroyed does someone's pussy get after giving birth? Actually, I don't want to know. I may never give birth if I find out.

"Because some women feel like it deflates too much after giving birth and they want to plump that area up," Kennedy explains.

"I mean, Clay hasn't complained." Abby shrugs. "But now I'm going to ask."

I'm still standing here like a statue, frozen in place as they have the conversation, although they can see me. I'm not invisible, but I wish I was.

"Hi, Baylee. Did you know women are injecting filler in their labia after giving birth?" Kennedy asks me like we're lifelong friends.

I continue standing there, unable to form words. Damn it Baylee, you're not a fucking scared woman that shies away from conversations like this. Why are you being this way?

I finally find my voice. "No, I can't say I have."

"I guess the camel-toe is in. First nipples showing through the bra, now this," Abby says.

"Puffing up the kitty cat." I laugh. But I don't stop there, I gesture the words with a motion of my hands. Of course, I say this right when Tucker walks through the door.

Wonderful, this is a great way to start seeing Tucker again after my hiatus from us being around one another. Perfect. Absolutely beautiful timing.

"Ladies," Tucker nods toward us, "I see you've begun corrupting Baylee."

"Oh, I was well on my way to being corrupted before meeting them." I laugh.

I make my way over to the kitchen to help him unpack the bags of groceries he places on the kitchen island.

"May I ask what in the world you're talking about?" Tucker asks Kennedy and Abby.

"Yes, you may ask," Kennedy says.

"We were talking about how the labia deflates after childbirth and now some women are opting to put filler into that part of the body to plump it up," Abby says as she peppers kisses along her daughter's face.

"Fucking hell," Tucker says to himself. "Why do I hang out with you two again?"

"Because you don't have friends," Kennedy retorts.

"I could hang out with your significant others instead," he says back.

"You know they're not as cool." She flips him off.

"You're such an asshole, Kennedy."

"There's a baby around now, Malloy. Language." She double-birds him.

A laugh escapes as I watch this juvenile behavior.

"Can you two stop? We don't want to scare Baylee this early on in book club. She won't come to the next meeting," Abby says.

"She's not in book club," Tucker's quick to add.

"She lives here," Abby adds.

"Yeah, I live here," I tell him, grabbing the pre-made tray, giving him the bird as well.

"I fucking love her," Kennedy says.

"She hasn't read the book," Tucker continues to add.

"Yeah, but I did listen to a little bit between Anton and, who was it again Tucker?" I glance back at him.

He's squinting at me. "Robin," he says between gritted teeth.

"That's right, Robin. I heard that little romp in the sack. They were in a heated labial pounding of their own. She might need filling after that thorough pummeling. Though, she had some filler of her own, didn't she, Tucker?" I laugh.

Kennedy and Abby laugh and the redness that takes over Tucker's face is priceless.

"Fine, she can be in book club. But if River or Clay ask to join, I won't say no. I'll give them a pass." He points at Abby and Kennedy.

They both look unfazed. He then goes to grab Ella and she

gives him a big toothless smile. He snuggles her, and I think my ovaries explode at the sight of this big teddy bear of a man holding this tiny little baby in his arms. But then I remember my walls are up toward him at the moment. So, I push aside my feelings of lust even though this man in front of me has the ability to melt my insides at every turn without even trying.

CHAPTER 12

Tucker

THE LONGER BOOK club goes on, the more I see pieces of the Baylee I used to know shine through. I'd feel relieved if it weren't for the fact that when she looks over at me, I get a mix of irritation and attraction coming off of her. I'm feeling more uneasy as time drags on.

I'm usually all for these nights because I fucking love book club and teasing Abby to the point of seeing her squirm. She's always super uncomfortable talking about the sex scenes in these books in front of me. I don't know why; it's not like we don't talk about everything anyway, but this is her limit, I guess.

"Okay, Baylee, as our newest member, you pick out of the jar," Kennedy says.

Kennedy pulls out the phallic-shaped accessory and it gives Baylee pause.

"Is that a pickle-shaped jar or a dick? I can't tell." She's holding back a laugh.

Kennedy smirks. "Oh, it's a pickle. And it's skin-colored because River thought I would be too disgusted to use it when he gave it to me, but I had to double down and use it for book club, obviously. He's just bitter we won't let him in the club now that he has discovered we don't, in fact, read self-help books."

"I assume there's a story behind that?" Baylee asks.

"There is," I answer as I get up from the couch and hand Ella off to her mother. I start clearing the plates and taking them to the kitchen.

Baylee pulls out a piece of paper and I hear a squeal from the couch and I groan. It's going to be some sappy romance because it's an Abby-pick. I just know it.

"Don't be a party-pooper, Malloy," Abby says.

"I know the books you pick, Abs. Kennedy picks the darker romances and her book boyfriends are dirty. I like those ones. Anton was hot as fuck in bed. I could get down with what he was getting up to with Robin," I say as I toss stuff in the trash.

"Oh really, so you've done a few of those dirty things before?" Kennedy asks.

"A man never kisses and tells," I say quickly.

"Oh, fuck off. I bet you're the dirtiest of the guys in the group," Kennedy says as she starts to grab her things.

I keep my back to them as I load things in the dishwasher. I don't need to give them any ammunition. They hound me enough.

Soon, I hear them move on to another topic and it's safe to turn around. I continue getting things in order around the living room and kitchen.

"Alright, my place next time," Kennedy says.

"Great, I can't wait," Abby squeals.

I roll my eyes.

"Don't give me that, Malloy. I know you're going to love this one. It's an age-gap and it will be so hot, I promise." She has the audacity to wink at me, then she waggles her eyebrows as she looks over at Baylee. Fuck my life. Could she be any more obvious? She's going to make this even harder the next time we hang out.

I hug both of them goodbye then they wrap their arms around Baylee, saying how glad they are to have finally met her. I can see they're both in love with my new roommate.

Once the apartment is quiet, it feels like the tension returns between me and Baylee. I look over at her and right as I'm about to say something, she speaks.

"Abby's really pretty."

"She is," I respond, there's no point in lying.

She moves past me to the kitchen and opens the fridge to grab a water bottle. "And you're telling me you have no feelings for her?"

She twists the cap and takes a sip, watching me closely.

I cross my arms in front of me, confused where this is going.

"No, Baylee. Why are you not understanding that I have no romantic feelings for her?"

"Because you took her on a date and I really don't understand why you did that and didn't pursue her after that, Tucker," she insists, her tone cold.

"Because she loves Clay, that's why," I reply.

She rolls her eyes and caps her water bottle. She's about to walk away, irritation rolling off her.

"Bay, what's up with you? You've been giving me the cold shoulder for days and I don't get it. You're the one that wanted to live here, and I have no problem with that. Then you ask about my date with Abby, only to discover it was completely platonic. You proceed to get pissed after finding that out and close me off. Did I leave anything out? What gives?" I throw my arms up in the air.

"You know, this isn't you. I know you've been through something incredibly difficult and I'm trying to give you space. I also understand you and I are worlds apart in age, but you've never acted so immature before. I never saw you like this before, acting like a child. But if you think this is how you'd like to behave, go right ahead."

I begin to walk off, until she yells, "*I'm* acting like a child?! Are you fucking serious, Tucker?! After what I've been through, you're going to walk off after saying that to me?"

"You know what, Baylee? If there's one person who's going to treat you like a human being, it's me, and you fucking know it," I throw back. "I'm not going to treat you with kiddie gloves, Baylee. You know I'd walk through fire for you, but I also won't let you treat me like I've done something wrong. I'm here for you, but you're acting like I've hurt you, when all I've done is be right here."

"Fuck you, Tucker. You weren't there when I needed you," she throws back at me.

"What are you talking about? That night when you called, I was there in a heartbeat!"

She leaves her water on the counter and starts moving toward me.

"No, all those months I texted, you never answered. The silence led me straight into his arms." She begins pointing at me. "You were a coward, and now I know that despite all the years I put you on a pedestal, all I've been to you is Danny's little sister. So yes, maybe to you I'm acting like a child, but I'm hurt. I'm confused. I'm processing. While you were building a friendship with Abby, I was getting lost with a monster by my side. I was losing myself in a way I never imagined."

I'm stunned by her words. I wasn't expecting this type of rawness, especially after the lightness that came from seeing her laughing with my friends tonight.

"Baylee... I... shit." I rub the back of my neck.

"You know what? Forget it. I'm alone in my feelings anyway," she says, moving past me.

I grab her hand and she snatches it out of my grasp. "No, Tucker. Don't you see?"

I just stand there looking at her. I can't form words. Do I tell her how I felt all these months? I see her holding back the tears and I'm lost in my own thoughts when she opens her mouth and pours her heart out for me instead.

"Tucker Malloy, you've been the person I see each time I close my eyes. All these years, I've grown into this person people see as strong, self-confident, with the ability to walk into the room and feel like she can take on the world. But all I've ever wanted was to have you look at me as more than Daniel Rios's little sister. All I've wanted was to be your world. Because for most of my life, you've been mine. Who's the fucking idiot now?" She lets out a sad laugh and I think my heart just shattered on my floor.

"The weird thing is, though, I shouldn't even care about this"—she motions between us—"because I'm in a fucking mess with Myles right now. But living with you has really fucked with my head. Because I think I still love you. Fuck." She looks up at the ceiling. "I just said that out loud, didn't I?"

She bites her lip and looks back at me. "Well, I might as well admit it all, right? I'm fucking young and stupid, anyway. Yeah, I fucking love you. There. Fuck it. I'll stay here until I get this whole thing with Myles figured out if that's okay with you. Because I honestly don't have the mental capacity to deal with anything else right now. Then I'll move out. I hope you're okay with that."

She stares at me an extra beat and I can't help the fact I just stare back. I'm frozen in place.

I open and close my mouth, the words caught in my throat. I don't know where to start. I open my mouth again, about to say something when she cuts me off.

"I'm not sure what I expected, but seeing you stand there and not respond wasn't it. This feels eerily similar to your silence via text, but it hurts even more."

She looks down, takes a breath then whispers something to herself that I can't make out and walks off. The door slams and I flinch.

I stand there for some time in the empty space, processing everything she just said, still unsure what I should do. This whole time she hasn't just had feelings for me, but she has fully loved me. I've fucked this up and it didn't even start. I should've pulled her into my arms and kissed the hell out of her, but instead I left her with nothing. I'm such an asshole.

I turn off all the lights and make my way down the hall. I stand outside her door, I can hear her walking around her room, and I consider knocking. I hold my hand up but decide to let us have some distance tonight. A lot was said, and I want to give us some time to cool off. I need to figure out how to respond. Hopefully in the morning everything will look a little clearer.

Unfortunately, I barely sleep. I toss and turn most of the night and when I finally start to drift off, all I hear are Baylee's confessions. The moment I wake up, silence is the only thing that greets me. Her bedroom door is open, with an empty room to show for it.

I sigh and decide to make my way to the gym. I text River, Clay, and even include Hunter in the thread. Hunter is the only one that's available to meet up.

I meet him down at the park as it's still a cool enough morning. I get down there and he's filming a segment to post later to his social media page. He's got his jump rope out and the view of Boston Harbor behind him.

"Hey, man! Beautiful day out," I greet him.

"Can't beat it," he says, smiling from ear to ear. It's hard to find Hunter in a bad mood.

He's got his hat on backwards and no shirt, with his tattoos on full display. His basketball shorts are a bright blue today and his shoes match.

"Do you have shoes that match all your shorts?" I laugh.

"Yeah, pretty much," he responds. "Sponsors send me all sorts of stuff. You have no idea the random things I have sent my way."

"Have you ever thought of doing your workouts outside the firehouse?" I ask him.

"Huh, I haven't, actually. You think chief would be okay with that?" He looks over at me hesitantly.

"It can't hurt to ask. Start with the lieutenant and he'll go up from there. I mean, if it looks good for the firehouse, it might go over well overall." Anything that shines a good light on the house as a whole, I don't see the harm.

"Yeah, I might do that. Plus, my sponsors might actually send some good stuff to the house. I'll see what I can do," he says. "Thanks, man." He slaps my shoulder. "You want to go for a run?"

"Sounds good," I tell him.

We set a good pace, and I get lost in my thoughts. Soon, I look down and realize we've been running for forty-five minutes. Something about running by the water is relaxing and makes me forget about all the craziness in my life.

Before we know it, our run around the harbor is finished and we're both covered in sweat. The humidity is at a record high today, so I had to forgo my shirt early on during the run. While we stretch, I enjoy shade under the tree as people walk past us.

"You adjusting well to Boston?" I ask as I stretch my calf.

"Yeah. Still acclimating to everything, but I like it so far. Nothing like Vegas, though," he says as he takes in the harbor.

"No shit? I had no idea you were from Vegas."

"Yeah, I don't talk about it much."

"You have any family back there still?" I ask.

"My parents are there as far as I know. I honestly don't keep up with them. Haven't seen them since I left." Discomfort is evident in his tone.

"Damn, sorry man." I can tell this isn't something he's comfortable sharing.

"My old man isn't the best guy, and my mom didn't win any awards either. The minute I could leave, I did. Let's just say, they were just as happy to see me go and I never put much effort into keeping in touch," he says as we both make our way toward my truck.

"And you joined the military after high school?" I feel compelled to learn more about him even though I know he isn't really wanting to talk about his past.

"Yep. I just wanted out of Vegas, and to see the world. Getting an education was secondary. The military was my ticket to all of that. So, I took it, and the rest is history. Luckily, I was good at it. I met some really great guys too." He sighs.

"You didn't want to continue on in the military?" I hope he doesn't mind me asking.

"Nah, I was done. I got to a point where I knew I was done. I saw a lot, and it was time to come back to start my civilian life here," he says, a sad smile moving across his face.

"Did you have someone to come back to here?" I'm prying now.

"I had the idea of someone," he says.

"That sounds ominous," I say, nudging his shoulder.

"It does, doesn't it?" He chuckles as he looks off at the water, apparently lost in thought. "Alright, sharing time is over for today, Malloy." He turns toward me. "I know you're avoiding being home."

"Ha! I'd never do such a thing." I laugh.

"You're a shit liar, man," he tells me.

"You don't know me that well, Hunter," I throw back.

"You're not that hard to read. Plus, aren't you shacking up with Rios's sister? That sounds complicated." He crosses his arms over his chest.

"Understatement of the century," I confess. Something about Hunter tells me he understands complicated. "There's a lot to unpack between us and I just don't know where to start with it. And she sorta unloaded a ton of shit on me last night."

"Maybe you should go talk to her about it then," he says.

"I sort of froze when she did." I wince.

"Amateur," he says. "Women *do not* like that. How did she react to that?"

"Aside from walking off and slamming her door?" I confess.

"Ouch."

"I know. Beyond that, I wouldn't know. She had already left for class this morning." I look over to see him giving me an apologetic look. "Not good, huh?"

"I predict a lot of groveling is in your future," he says.

"You're probably right." I scratch at the back of my neck.

"And don't worry about any of this getting back to Rios. I take it from the seething looks he gives you at the station that he's not too keen on his sister hanging out at your place?"

I nod.

"I won't say anything," Hunter says.

"I appreciate it, although it seems we aren't on speaking terms anymore since she moved in. But she needed me, so I chose her over him and he's just going to have to deal with it at this point. I won't apologize for it," I tell him.

"I get that. Rios will get over it eventually," he says.

"I hope so. But I won't hold my breath. He's a stubborn ass about many things," I explain. "Also, if it's any consolation, you've got a family here with us," I say, putting my fist out.

He looks down, and for a moment, he just stares. Then he bumps it. I hope he knows he can count on me and the guys now that he's here.

"Thanks for the run today, man," he says as we both make our way through the park to the street.

"I needed it," I say, as I reach my truck.

Hunter walks toward a black motorcycle.

"I didn't know you had a bike, man." I wave a hand in its direction.

"It was in the shop and I just got it back." His smile doubles in size as he looks down, moving his hand along the leather seat of his motorcycle.

"I seem to be learning quite a bit about you today." I laugh.

"Yeah, I guess so. Have to enjoy it"—he gestures to the bike—"while I can. The winters here are a beast. I have the truck once the cold hits."

He pulls his helmet over his head, then waves at me and hops on, starting the engine. Soon he pulls into traffic, and I watch him ride off. It seems Tyler Hunter is full of surprises.

The moment I'm back in my truck, my mind is consumed by thoughts of Baylee and the look on her face during her confession last night. I was such a prick. My silence was a cowardly move, but I wasn't prepared to hear what she said. It's no excuse though. I should've said something back.

Before, when these feelings started to creep in months ago, I let the excuse of my friendship with Rios be the reason for me not to cross the line. But I obviously walked away from anything with Rios being mended now. That's no longer a possibility now that Baylee is living with me. He made that blatantly clear that night I told him to shove it when I told Baylee she could stay with me. I have no regrets with my decision. So why did I hold back last night?

I pull out of my spot and make my way back to the apartment. Maybe Baylee had a plan to pour her heart out to me last night and I was unprepared. But today I won't stand in silence. I'll finally pour everything out for her so she knows where I stand.

CHAPTER 13

Baylee

"IN TODAY'S SESSION, it's important to understand that what Myles did to you is not your fault," Dr. Nuys explains.

"Yes, but—" I start.

"No, Baylee, there is no but to add to that. I need you to understand that what Myles did to you is simply not your fault. Period." There's finality to her statement.

"Okay," I say.

"His behavior is his to own up to. Do you truly believe that?" she asks.

"Yes and no," I answer honestly.

"Okay, explain that for me please," she says.

"I understand that what he did was a choice he made. All the things he did to me leading up to that night, those were his fault. But on that night, I sort of pushed him and he physically hurt me because of that. I said things knowing it would get a reaction from him," I admit.

Dr. Nuys looks at me and I can tell she's processing what I just said to her.

"Baylee, I have met many in your position and you are not the first to say that to me. I understand what you just said and appreciate why you might feel that way. We all have pivotal moments in life where we're brought to these forks in the road, and we must make a decision."

I look down at my lap, having a hard time seeing past the fact that I knew very well I was pushing Myles that night.

"The thing is, Baylee, what Myles did to you was *his* choice. He chose violence. He did not choose words. He chose to be physical. I understand that in your mind you believe it was your words that pushed him over the edge. But he could have easily had a conversation. Instead, he chose to respond with force. So no, it is not your fault. The fault still lies with him. You spoke to Myles and he did not respond with words, he used his fist." She's calm as she explains. I can't help the tear that escapes down my cheek. I quickly swipe at my face.

"I'm sorry," I tell her.

"I don't want you to apologize. This is something that I expect you to feel emotional about. It's something that will take time to process. It might take years for you to speak about it without feeling emotional," she says.

"I feel like he took so much of me that night. Hell, I think he took so much of me for months leading up to that night," I admit.

"Well, let's talk about that then. What are things you liked doing before you started dating Myles?"

"Staying in with my roommates to watch movies. And I loved going out to parties with my friends," I say with a distant smile on my face.

"Oh, well, that sounds about right for a woman your age. Why don't you try going out this weekend? I bet you can find a party on campus to go to." She smiles.

"I don't know if I'm ready for that just yet," I tell her quickly.

"Do you have some friends here in Boston you feel comfortable going out with?" she asks, concern etched on her face.

"Yeah, I've made some new friends," I say.

"Then it might be nice to get out a bit."

"Well, I guess that's possible. I just don't know if they're going to a party," I tell her.

"Baylee, I bet your friends are going out. If not to a party, then to dinner or something. I bet they'd gladly go out somewhere. I'm not asking you to divulge what happened with Myles to them just yet if you're not ready, but going out with them would be something good to do. Having a new group of friends here is important," she assures me.

"Okay, maybe I will," I tell her, as I fiddle with my index finger.

"Good. I think this is a good place to stop for today," she tells me.

I've seen Dr. Nuys twice so far. Once I moved to Boston, she was one of the first orders of business my parents asked me to figure out. I thought it was going to be harder to find a therapist, but my oldest sister is a therapist, and she helped me set up the appointment quite quickly. She's highly recommended in the field and luckily had an opening.

Therapy isn't as bad as I expected. I thought I'd be lying on a couch, with her taking notes in a chair like I've seen in movies, but this is nothing like that. She sits opposite me, both of us in plush seats and it's a very comfortable environment. I feel relaxed with her, and she's been easy to talk to so far. I hope it continues to be an effective way to get my feelings out in the open.

"You're finally going out with us?" Jada asks me, shock evident across her face.

I get it. I've been pretty reserved since they met me at the beginning of the semester. We just started school, but each time they extend an invite to go out, I'm always giving them an excuse—I'm going to study or go home. But after last night's disaster confession in front of Tucker, the last place I want to be is home. Plus, once Dr. Nuys suggested this outing being a good idea, I started to get excited at the prospect of getting out a little.

"Yeah, why not?" I shrug my shoulders.

"Okay, awesome," Jacob smiles. "I can pick you up on my way over to Jada and Sydney's place. Does that work?"

Sydney and Jada live off campus, and apparently right near this house party that's happening tonight. The party seems to be something everyone is excited about to kick off the weekend.

"That works. I'll text you my address." I pick up my phone and start typing.

"Great. I get off work around six-thirty, then I'll get ready and pick you up from there. Sound good?" he asks.

"That's fine," I tell him, "I appreciate the ride."

"I'm so excited you're coming along with us," Sydney says. "There are so many cute guys at this party too." Her eyes get big, and she gives me a sneaky smile.

"Hey, I'm standing right here," Jacob says.

"I know." She gives him a look and nudges him with her elbow. They're constantly flirting, and I wonder if they'll ever address the fact that they're into one another.

I look over at Jacob and it's hard not to take in how attractive he is. The day I met him it was hard to look away. He's easy on the eyes, but once I saw him look at Sydney, it was apparent he only has eyes for her. The way he looks over at her, it's like all he wants is to make her happy. And from the way the air crackles between them, the chemistry is mutual.

Jacob is tall, with vibrant blue-green eyes that pop against his warm golden-brown skin. He's showing off his muscles in the warm weather that's lingering with the last bit of summer before the cold starts to creep in.

Sydney is equally gorgeous with her short black hair, which she has dyed pink at the ends, and a sleeve of floral tattoos down her left arm. The way she carries herself reminds me a lot of myself before I dated Myles.

We're hanging out in the quad before class, soaking in the sun on some benches and I'm trying hard not to think about my life before this. I still haven't divulged what happened with my ex-boyfriend and how everything unfolded with the attack. I really wanted to start fresh here, leaving that difficulty behind me. But I still find myself looking over my shoulder, fearing I'll see Myles and those cold eyes watching me.

I know he posted bail shortly after his arrest. I knew it was bound to happen, but I still held hope it would take longer than it did. Thinking about how he's free and living as if he didn't lay a hand on me really pisses me off. But life isn't fair, and I know I need to find a way to live without thinking about him every day.

He can't leave his state without facing more consequences to his actions. I know his mother will counsel him to be smart and I have to hope he's not dumb enough to do more damage to his reputation.

"Baylee, you okay?" Jada pulls me from my distant thoughts.

"Yeah of course." I smile.

"You sure? You look lost in thought," she says.

"Oh, sorry. Just thinking about this paper I have to write. Plus, I have no clue what I'm going to wear tonight. It's been a while since I've been to a party," I try to come up with a cover up.

"Oh, I bet you've got something you can wear." Sydney winks.

I give them a small smile, hoping it's believable. I look down at my phone and realize my next class is about to start.

"I'd better get going. Cunningham is not a fan if we walk in even a minute late. I swear she's got hawk eyes, even with that lecture hall being so big," I tell them, grabbing my bag.

"Oh, I know. I had her last year. I'll walk with you. I'm headed that way," Jada says.

"Awesome. I'll see you two later," I say to Sydney and Jacob. "Text me when you're headed over." I jut my chin to Jacob.

"No problem," he says as he takes a bite of his apple.

Hopefully, Tucker isn't home when I'm headed out and I can avoid the awkwardness. I honestly don't want to deal with him after I word-vomited and he didn't even say a word back to me. Standing there, opening and closing his mouth like a fish was enough. *Humiliating* is what it was.

———

I thought I was in the clear for the night, but I can hear Tucker moving around in the living room as I'm finishing getting ready right now. I just got a text from Jacob telling me he's on his way and I'm nowhere near ready. Fucking damn it!

I took too long figuring out what to wear tonight, but I didn't have my girlfriends here to help me out. I caved and FaceTimed my old roommates for help. Mandy was the only one home and she helped me go through outfits. After what felt like fifteen options, we finally found one that looked right for a house party.

We settled on a tight dark-purple dress, sheer black tights, black combat boots, and a gauzy crisscross long-sleeve black top. I did a smokey eye for my makeup and I step back, looking at myself in the reflection. I do a few turns and it's the first time since the attack—actually, since dating Myles—that I feel like the Baylee Rios I once was. I feel like the empowered woman who took charge of what I wanted.

I'm excited about tonight, which is a huge step for me. Dr. Nuys was right, I needed this connection with friends, and I think tonight will be good for me. I haven't been to a party, as a single woman, in quite some time. For months I've had a voice in my head, telling me I wasn't enough, because that's what Myles kept enforcing. I've had a man talking down to me, telling me I was inferior for so many reasons, making me believe all his horrible words.

After months with Myles, I adapted in the worst way for him. Little by little, he peeled away the best parts that made me who I am. He then formed me into a version of myself that became raw, hurting and constantly vulnerable. He knew exactly what he was doing while I was oblivious to his monstrous ways.

He may have knocked me down that night in my apartment, but when he showed me the ugliest side of him, I also proved that I can pick myself up. And little by little, I know that strong version of me is still inside this body of mine. I just need more time to get back to who I once was. And I will come back stronger. I just need to be patient with myself.

There's a ping from my phone and I look down to see that Jacob is stuck in traffic. I blow out a breath of relief. I'll use the extra time to add a little more to my makeup and avoid Tucker. Once Jacob texts me he's downstairs, I'll run out and my night will be drama-free. At least I can avoid Tucker altogether and have a little fun with my friends.

CHAPTER 14

Tucker

I'M out here waiting for Baylee to come out of her room and she's in there like a fucking hermit. Why won't she come out here? I even made extra food so she could have some. I know I fucked up, but she can't avoid me forever, right?

My anxiety causes me to flip between channels until I finally settle on a game to keep my mind busy. I was an absolute ass last night and failed on every level to communicate how I felt. I just need her to give me a shot to tell her what's going through my head right now.

Despite loving my favorite baseball team, I can't keep my focus on the screen. The Gaels are up by two runs, but I rub my hand down my face in frustration, because nothing matters right now except Baylee. I just want to see her and talk to her about everything she said. I waited for her after my run today, but then I got a call from my mom, so I was gone for a few hours unexpectedly. When I got back, Baylee was holed up in her room and she hasn't come out since.

Nothing is working out the way I wanted, but here I am, trying to make things right. I groan in frustration. This is my fault, but at the same time, she's not making it easier either.

Right when I'm about to get up and go to check on her, there's a knock on the front door.

I toss the remote aside and head to the door. Looking through the peephole, I see a guy I don't recognize.

"Can I help you?" I ask through the door.

"Hi. Um, I'm here for Baylee," he says hesitantly. I know this isn't Myles as I would recognize him from the photos on social media.

I open the door and find a tall young man standing before me.

"Yes?" I cross my arms across my chest, standing at my full height, blocking the doorway. I can't help the protectiveness. I've got a few inches on this guy.

"Hey, boss. I'm Jacob. I'm here to pick up Baylee." He looks up at me.

Boss? Who does this guy think he is?

"Okay. Is she expecting you?" I still haven't let him in.

"Yes, we're headed to a party," he answers.

"Oh really?"

"Tucker, stop it!" She comes up behind me, pulling me aside. "Jacob, excuse him. He's ridiculous." She smiles at him, then looks over at me and glares. "Tucker, I'm headed out. Don't wait up."

"What time will you be home?" I ask her.

"I don't have a curfew!" she throws back. "'Night."

Is she fucking kidding me? After what she's been through, she expects me not to worry?

"Baylee—"

"Tucker, I'm fine." She looks over at me.

I put my hands up. "Okay, fine. Have a good night."

I'm not her keeper. I close the door, pissed for a whole new reason. I lean against the door, hearing her speaking to Jacob.

"Who is that guy?" I hear him ask her.

"No one," she responds.

No one, huh? *I guess we'll see about that.*

———

I'm getting too old for parties, and I'm not even out tonight. But if I'm going to stick to my guns and do this right, I have to stay awake. Baylee isn't back yet; it's fucking late though. I forgot how easy it is to be in your early twenties compared to a decade older. I'm struggling to keep my eyes open. It's been a long week, coupled with the shit night of sleep I had, I'm dragging right now.

I was losing steam waiting on the couch, so I hopped into the shower in hopes it would wake me up a bit. Luckily it was just what I needed. I have a shift tomorrow and I tried to get some sleep while I waited for her. But it was pointless, because all I thought about was Jacob getting to put his hands on her all night while I sit around waiting like a fool for her to get home.

Wrapping the towel around my waist, I realize I forgot my phone out in the kitchen, so I make my way through the apartment to grab it.

I walk out and realize that I'm not alone. I was only gone a few minutes, but Baylee must've gotten home when I was in the bathroom. She's in the kitchen, grabbing water from the fridge. She's bent over in that tight dress, and fuck me, she's beautiful.

"Hey, Firefly," I say, using the nickname I gave her when she was younger. She was always trying, and failing, to catch fireflies in the summer months. She has always been so short, they flew too high before she could catch them. Her brother made fun of her for it, but I always helped her catch a few. The big smile she would beam up at me when I'd finally catch one and give it to her would instantly brighten my day, so I gave her that nickname pretty early on.

"Fuck." She slams the fridge and turns around. "Damn it,

Tucker. That's fucked up to do to someone that just went through something traumatic like I did."

"Shit, sorry." I put my hands up. "I thought you heard me walking in."

It's then she realizes what I'm wearing, or I should say what I'm not wearing. Her eyes go wide. I realize how well this plan came together. I hadn't planned it out this way, but a towel around my waist and her ogling my chest seems like a win, if I do say so myself. She simply stares, her mouth agape and her eyes mesmerized by the tattoos lining my chest and down a portion of my shoulder.

Her eyes peruse my upper body and move lower toward my happy trail, but she tries to recover when she snaps them back up to my face.

"Did you have fun?" I ask her.

She's biting her lip and nodding. "Mmhmm," is her only response.

"That's good." I smirk. "You need anything?" I move my hand through my wet hair, flexing my biceps in the process.

I see her eyes tracing my movements.

"Baylee?" I ask her.

"Yes?" she croaks out.

I walk toward her. She keeps watching me. At first, she doesn't know what I'm doing. When I walk around the island, she starts to walk backwards, and then I move closer. She walks back until she's against the fridge, then I lean my palms against the cool metal, caging her in—I make sure I'm not touching her though.

"Look at that," I tell her.

"What?" she whispers.

I lean in, bending down so I'm close to the shell of her ear. "From the look of those goosebumps on your arms and the way you're breathing—I'd say I'm someone."

I move my nose along her jaw, and I hear her breath hitch. Her eyes move down my body, scanning every inch of me, taking in the ridges of my abdomen, the deep V, leading to where I wish I could let the towel fall to the ground. But we aren't there just yet.

Finally, she brings her eyes back up to meet mine and the heat between us mimics the kind I'm usually putting out on a call. My eyes lock on her deep brown irises and her hands touch me just below my ribs. Fuck, it feels like she's going to leave burn marks along my skin.

"Baylee," my voice is just above a whisper, "my silence last night wasn't a way of telling you I didn't feel the same. You caught me by surprise. Last summer, it wasn't just you. I didn't just want a piece of you—I wanted all of you. I just wasn't sure I'd be able to let go once I had you. And I'm not sure if I got a piece of you now, I'd be able to let you go." I run my tongue along my bottom lip.

She tightens her grip on me, but doesn't say a word, so I continue.

"And Firefly, I've fucking dreamed of hearing you scream my name every single day since. But if you feel like this thing between us is over, you just lit a fire last night."

I push off the fridge, leaving her behind. I already miss her warmth, but I have to make her come after what she wants.

I smirk, seeing her chest rise and fall with her breath as I saunter off. I turn around, grabbing my phone in the process. In a spur of a moment decision, I decide to drop the towel, exposing my back to her. I hear her intake of break, but don't look at her to see her surprised expression. I can only assume it has the intended effect.

The minute I get into my room, I let the entire interaction wash over me. I look down and take in my erection and how fucking hard I am for this woman. Shit, I wanted her hands to travel south and feel how hard I was for her. I had to keep myself composed as I talked to her.

That outfit she was wearing was enough to make me

blow my load. That dress is tight as fuck, that sheer wrap she had on top of it did nothing but heighten the allure of the dress. Add that to the fact I wanted to rip those tights and put my fingers in her panties to see if she was wet for me. Damn it, I'll need another shower to rub one out at this rate. There's no way I'll be able to fall asleep without taking care of this.

I make my way to my ensuite bathroom and turn on the water yet again to get under the hot stream. The minute I get into the shower, I start to stroke myself. I close my eyes, imagining Baylee on her knees and it only takes a few strokes before my balls tighten and I'm climaxing. I orgasm and moan her name as I grip the tile. Fuck. I better get acclimated to my right hand because I have no idea if this thing between us is going anywhere.

I turn off the shower and towel off for the second time in the last hour. Once I get to bed, I close my eyes and drift to sleep faster than I expected. I dream about the deepest brown eyes and raven hair, and hope she'll put me out of my misery. Living like this feels like torture with her down the hall and still out of my grasp.

———

The next morning, I wake up early to head over to the station. I'm in the kitchen getting my coffee brewed when I hear the door to Baylee's room open. I'm surprised she'd wake up this early after what happened last night, but I school my expression before turning around to greet her.

"Good morning, Bay," I tell her as I take a sip of my coffee.

"Morning," she says, confidence radiating off her. That's the Baylee I've longed to see before me. I smirk behind my mug.

"Did you sleep well?" I say as I watch her reach up to grab a coffee mug.

"No, I didn't, Tucker. And you damn well know I didn't." She sounds aggravated.

I chuckle and she makes a sound of irritation but doesn't look over at me.

She's wearing clothes that she wore before douchebag Myles dated her—an off-the-shoulder shirt with her bra strap exposed, along with a pleated skirt and her combat boots. I can't help the way my eyes peruse her body. Every inch of her is perfection.

She swiftly turns around and catches me watching her.

"So, I was thinking," she says.

"Oh?" I say.

"Yes. Here's what's going to happen," she begins, "we're going to go on a date." I'm mid-sip of my coffee and begin choking. Baylee has never been one to beat around the bush, but I still didn't expect her to be so forward.

"Tucker, you okay?" She looks over, then comes to my side and starts slapping my back. I move my hand up and nod to indicate I'll be fine.

I finally stop coughing and once I calm myself down, she continues.

"As I was saying, you and I—a date." She brings her coffee to her mouth and takes a sip.

"Are you asking me out?" I ask her.

"Tucker, I think we're past that." She rolls her eyes. "I saw your ass last night. It's nice, by the way."

"Thanks?" I say in response, grabbing a napkin to wipe some of the coffee off the corner of my mouth.

"You're welcome." She smiles. "And nothing fancy please. You know I don't like that kind of stuff."

"Hold on. So you're telling me we're going on a date, and you're dictating where? I don't think so."

"Tucker, I—" she begins.

"Baylee, sorry, but—" I put my coffee down then walk over to her and grab her mug and put it on the counter.

I proceed to grab her and put her on the counter, I move her legs apart, using the opportunity to glide my hands along her thighs. Damn, her skin is soft. I use the pads of my thumbs to massage her thighs, and she moans.

I stand between her legs, then bring my hands up to brush her hair back and then cup her cheeks so that her eyes are on me.

"Baylee—yes, I'll take you on a date, but I dictate where we're going. I think I've known you long enough to know what you like." I give her a small smile.

"You don't know this side of me though," she says back, gripping my shirt with her small hands.

"That may be true. And likely we have no chemistry whatsoever," I tell her as I bring my face even closer to her, bringing our noses to touch. I can feel her breath on me.

"Maybe we should see if it's even worth a date then," she goads me.

"Not a bad idea." I take that as an invitation to nibble her bottom lip as I keep my hands on her cheeks. She's using her hands to pull my body closer to her.

But, in true Baylee fashion, she doesn't back down; she goes all in. She tilts her head and opens up for me. The minute our lips connect, it's like she's my next breath. It feels like all the reasons I gave myself for us not to be together melt away, because this is my only purpose in life. Our tongues intertwine and I deepen the kiss.

We both moan and I feel her bring her arms up along my sides, where I feel my muscles constrict when she glides her fingers up the contours of my abdomen. I want to devour her right here in my kitchen.

I pepper kisses along her jaw and move down her neck. She moans as I trail toward to her collarbone. If I had the time, I would rip this shirt and devour her, dropping kisses on every inch of her.

"Fuck, Baylee, I don't think chemistry is a problem," I tell her.

"No, definitely not a problem," she responds, then pulls my face back to hers. She kisses me again. I could lose myself in her for hours.

I have to pull myself from her and it takes everything in me to stop what we're doing.

"Bay, I have to go or I'm going to be late." I close my eyes and wish I didn't have to leave right now.

She's panting and nodding. "Okay. I guess it sucks to be you right now." She's laughing and looking down at the tent in my pants.

"Don't remind me." I laugh uncomfortably.

"At least I have time to take care of business before my class," she taunts me.

"Don't tell me things like that." I lean my head into the crook of her neck.

"Hey, I've gotta leave you with something while you're on shift." She laughs.

"That's evil, Baylee." I bite her neck softly. "I guess I'll see you tomorrow. It's a date, then?" I pull away to look into her eyes.

"Sounds good. I'm done at four." She bites her lip, looking shy all of a sudden.

I use my thumb to pull her lip from her top teeth. "Sounds good. I'll see you then. I guess you have to end things with your new guy, Jacob." I kiss her nose.

"Oh, Jacob was never interested in me." She hops off the counter and smooths her skirt.

"Yeah, right," I respond.

"I promise you, he isn't. He likes my friend Sydney. You are the one that got all alpha over me. It was super cute to see, though." She turns around and attempts to grab her coffee.

I move in, caging her in from behind. I sweep her hair to

the side, then whisper in her ear, "Maybe I'll have you pay for that later." I see her shiver.

It only registers then that I have to be careful how I speak to her after what she just went through with Myles, so I gently turn her around and make her look me in the eyes.

"Baylee, you know I'd never hurt you, right?"

Her expression changes as she looks up at me. "Tucker, of course I know that."

"This"—I point between us—"will always be equal between us. It'll always be about us having fun together, and always be a partnership." I run my hand down my face.

She pulls my hand away from my face. "Hey, Tucker, I know. You're not him."

"I'd never do that to you. Never. When I just said that, and I heard how it sounded, I just—"

She comes up on her tiptoes and kisses me. "You've never treated me like I'm fragile. Don't start now. Please, Tucker."

I nod. "You are the epitome of strength, Firefly."

If there's one thing I will never do it's treat Baylee like she's broken, because to me she's the strongest person I've ever met.

CHAPTER 15

Tucker

I CAN'T HELP the smile on my face as I walk into the station. Before greeting the outgoing crew for report, I head directly to my locker to put my things inside. I'm still grinning like a fool when I see Hunter on my way out of the locker room.

"What's got you in such a good mood?" Hunter sips his coffee.

"Nothing." I try to play it cool. "You just getting here?" Probies are usually here earlier than us.

"Been here an hour. No fucking way I'll be late. I got coffee for the captain, per his request and got one for myself." He holds his up. "So, back to my original question: Your good mood has nothing to do with your new roommate?" He eyes me and bumps my shoulder.

I stay silent as I keep walking toward the guys. I don't need to have this conversation with him and risk someone overhearing us. Even though I don't care if my friendship with Rios is over, I don't need to risk further animosity in the firehouse right now.

Hunter calls out before heading into the locker room, "Don't think this conversation is over!"

"I didn't think it was," I call over my shoulder.

I hear him laugh and push through the double doors into the apparatus bay, finding most of last night's crew gathered. I greet one of the guys from the previous shift, ready to get any updates from their shift.

It seems not much happened last night, so he doesn't have much to tell me. Luckily, aside from a few residential calls and a fire down the road that was easily put out, it was a pretty quiet night. Shifts like those are blessings and they seem to have had a good twenty-four hours overall.

Once I go through the details with him, I begin inspecting my personal protective equipment. Soon, River, Clay, and Hunter join me, checking their own PPE and getting their own updates from the previous shift on their way out.

We flow through our tasks easily, with Hunter mixing into our fire family as if he's been here all along. Rios, even with all the issues recently with Clay and myself, still works seamlessly in the mix, which is a relief. The minute we get to the station, we put aside our differences, a good thing in a position like ours. We need to have each other's backs, our ability to work together can be a matter of life and death very quickly.

The hours pass without a call, and soon we're famished. Hunter starts to prep lunch. Sandwiches seem to be the easiest thing to prep and one of our other guys lends a hand as well. I join in to help speed up the process and get the food finished up. Our captain is sitting in his favorite recliner, while some of the guys are watching a game on the television.

Something seems off and it's only then I realize it's too quiet. I turn to Clay and ask, "Where's your brother?"

He looks around and shrugs. "Probably talking to Kennedy. Don't ruin it. It's quiet in here," he answers. Our captain scoffs to himself.

I must've jinxed it right then, because not thirty seconds later River makes his way into the dining room.

"What the actual fuck is that shirt, Riv?" I hear Clay say behind me.

The whole room turns to look over immediately.

"What do you think?" River asks.

"What in the world does it mean, man?" I can't help but ask.

"UILF?" Hunter questions, completely lost.

"UILF!" River exclaims, as if repeating the acronym will help it makes complete sense.

We stand in silence, staring at him. His brother sits on the stool, waiting for the punchline as if this is a norm he expects from his twin.

"Out with it already, Nichols!" That comes from our captain.

"'Uncle I'd Like to Fuck', obviously," River says, with a shit-eating grin.

"Jesus Christ." I lean back against the counter with my arms crossed over my chest, and drop my head.

Clay stands and yells, "Are you fucking serious? I'm telling Mom!"

The rest of the guys start laughing, and it's absolute madness. I look up to see the guys taking photos, as if River is on a red carpet. I see him posing, flexing his muscles, acting like this is the moment he's been waiting for his whole life.

"Are you kidding, bro? I mean, dude, I was made for this role. This shirt is perfect. Come on! It's epic!" River starts.

"Dude! First off, that's just weird. Second, you're getting married! Did you forget that?" His brother throws his arms in the air.

"Kennedy doesn't care!" River responds.

Right then I pull my phone out and snap a photo and pull up my book club thread.

Your fiancé is a stud, Kenny!

KENNY

First off, I hate that nickname. Hard pass.
Two, are you fucking kidding me?

ABS

What's an UILF?

I'll give you a second to put two and two
together on this because it's coming from
River...

ABS

I still don't get it #mombrain

KENNY

Uncle I'd Like to Fuck. Can we swap, Abby?

ABS

HARD PASS 🤢

Clay's face is bright red. He's so mad. He
said he's calling their mom. I can't stop
laughing. BEST DAY EVER.

KENNY

Malloy, I'll take care of it.

KENNY

Also, Malloy, change my name on your
phone because I know you have me as
Kenny.

Hard Pass 😈

KENNY

I close out my phone and watch as the Nichols twins continue to verbally spar while finishing with the sandwiches.

"Does this happen a lot?" Hunter asks as he moves along in the kitchen.

"You mean, does River often make shirts with inappropriate sayings on them? No." I shake my head.

"No. Do they bicker like this often?" he asks.

"Not really. I mean, they're brothers. They usually bet on things. This is a new element to the relationship. I'm here for it, though." I laugh.

Hunter looks at them and back at me, laughing, but I can tell he thinks it's all a bit strange. I grab him by the shoulder and pull him in. "Welcome to the family, Bro."

He looks over and it's clear his smile is genuine.

Soon, I hear River's ringtone and he pulls his phone out of his pocket.

I expect it to be Kennedy calling him to ream him out for the shirt, but I'm surprised to hear him pick up and say, "Hey, Ma! What? No, I mean no disrespect... of course I love Kennedy. Ella is the light of my life. Yes, she's my everything. Of course I'm still getting married. I do respect women. Of course, Ma!"

She must say something to him and he hangs his head and rubs the back of his neck. Then he pulls his shirt off and throws it at Clay. The triumph on Clay's face says it all. We laugh at the look of defeat River gives us. He flips us off as he walks away toward the lockers.

The last we hear is a simple, "I'm sorry, Ma. I love you... Yes, of course, I would never do anything to disrespect you, Kennedy, Ella or Lola. You're my girls. Love you too. See you Sunday."

River doesn't get far before he runs back. "Snitches get stitches, you fuckers! I can't believe someone ran to Mommy on this one."

That only gets us to roar with laughter. Even our captain is laughing, trying to cover his face as best he can, but failing miserably.

———

I'm putting some equipment away from our last call when Hunter meets me out in the bay. We had a string of back-to-back calls. Some of the guys are inside, while some are checking equipment on one of the other trucks.

"Hey, man. Need some help?" Hunter asks.

"Sure, thanks." I hand him some equipment.

He's been doing tasks all throughout the firehouse. I don't know if it's his military background, but he's efficient. When I was at the station in Dover, our probie was always trying to take breaks. Hunter is the complete opposite.

"Okay," he looks over his shoulder, "spill."

I'd usually keep this to myself, but I feel a friendship with Hunter beyond the firehouse.

"I'm taking her out on a date." I smile.

"Nice. I'm happy for you man." He smiles. "I hate to bring this up, but what about Rios?" He looks over and finds Rios talking to some of the guys at the truck on the other end of the station.

"Our friendship is pretty much non-existent at this point. He made that clear when I took her in to live with me. I hate to say it, but I choose Baylee, even though it should never have come to that. He knows it could've been both our friendship and his sister. He's just too stubborn to realize both can exist." I grab a few things from the truck to check them off the list.

"I don't know him well, but I see what you mean." He nods.

"I tried, I really did, to keep myself away from her. But my life, doesn't make sense without her," I admit to him.

He stops what he's doing and looks over at me. "I completely get that."

"Yeah? You ever have someone like that in your life?" I ask him.

He shakes his head. "I didn't have to make a choice like you did between friendship and love. But I've had nights when I was away and dreamed of coming home and finding it. And I guess I've held hope that one day I'll still find it. I've had stirrings of love in the past, but nothing lasting. If I ever do get that type of love within my grasp, I wouldn't run from it. So, yeah man, don't let it go."

I'm about to press him further, but then we're interrupted by River, "Hey, Malloy, it was you, wasn't it?"

"What do you mean?" I come off as clueless as possible.

Since his mom called, he's been asking everyone who ratted him out to her about his shirt and it's been fun throwing him off the scent. We love watching him squirm.

"Who the fuck had my mom call me? I felt like a fucking teenager again on that call. She was fucking pissed! She threatened to take my dog!" He looks horrified. I have to bite the inside of my cheek to keep from laughing.

"Oh, no," Hunter finally says.

"I know, right? Pure evil from that little lady." He shakes his head. "My Lola!" He looks gutted. "Who would do such a thing?" He walks off, still baffled by the whole thing.

I look over at Hunter and chuckle quietly.

"He must really love that dog," he whispers.

"Oh, Lola is the fucking shit!" I tell him, all jokes aside. "I choose Lola over River every day of the week and twice on Sunday."

———

I make it home after Baylee has left for her morning study session. I can't help the disappointment that washes over me as I walk through my apartment. She hasn't been here long, but I'm already used to her presence in every part of my space.

I make my way through, putting my things down on the couch. My mom doesn't have an appointment today, so I use the extra time to plan out the date for Baylee while she's out of the apartment. I have something in mind, but there are a few things I need to get figured out. I pull out my laptop and sit on the couch with the sports highlights in the background.

Soon I'm lost on a website with a few options in front of me, when my brother's name highlights my phone.

"Hey, man, what's up?" I ask when I pick up.

"Not much. It's been a while. I thought I'd call to see how things are going. Sorry, we've been playing phone tag; I've been swamped at work."

"I understand. There hasn't been much to update you on from the last time we texted," I tell him.

"Yeah, I just feel bad." He sighs through the phone. I know the distance is weighing on him.

When mom was first diagnosed, he was torn and wanted to relocate back to Boston. His fiancée is from Ohio and after many conversations, he finally decided to stay back to continue his plans there. I promised him he was fine where he was and that if anything changed, I would call immediately.

"Ma's been doing well so far. She's in good spirits, even with all her treatments," I assure him.

"Yeah, she said as much when I talked to her this morning," he says. He still sounds unsure.

"What's weighing on you?" I put my computer to the side and take my phone off speaker and bring it to my ear.

"It's hard, man. This distance is more stressful than I imagined. I didn't expect to have her sick, I guess. I thought we'd have more time to tackle this stage, you know?" He sighs.

"I know." It's the only response I can muster.

"I feel like my mind is on my wedding, but it's also sort of mourning parts of my life that I won't get with her," he chokes out. "What if she's not here when we have kids?"

Fuck. I haven't let my mind wander that far ahead.

"Eric, you can't think like that. Right now, our focus is to see her participating in our lives. We live our lives in the present. She's here for us today and we focus on that."

"You're right, Tuck. It's hard though. My mind just can't help it."

Eric has always been a worrier. He's a planner and it's hard for him to stop that brain of his moving a hundred miles an hour. I get it, he wants to plan his life and envisioning a life where our mother isn't there is hard. If I let myself go there, though, it'll cripple me. So, I'll keep him grounded, at least until I feel like we need to worry about it.

"Listen, if I feel like things are getting bad, you'll get a call from me, okay?" I assure him.

"I know I will. I love you, little brother," he tells me.

"I'm taller than you, remember?" I laugh.

"By half an inch, you shit," he scolds.

"The ladies say size matters."

"Such an asshole." He scoffs. "Please let me know if you need anything. I'm here if you need me. I promise I'll drop everything, Brit and I will be there anytime."

I really love my soon-to-be sister-in-law. Her family is loud and welcoming and everything I've ever wanted for Eric. They've welcomed not only him, but my mother and I as well. Anytime we visit they're quick to pull us in for a hug and I'm grateful for the instant family they've been for all of us. I know he's got the support there, navigating all this while our mom is going through her illness.

"I know, I love you, man," I tell him. "And I got my tux fitting scheduled. I hope I don't look better than you up at the altar." I laugh into the phone.

My brother and I are spitting images of each other, however, I have my mother's green eyes, whereas he has my father's blue ones. I don't remember my dad, but I've seen a few photos my mom has in boxes. He wasn't around long enough for me to form memories with him, not that I care to know the guy. We did fine without him.

"You bringing a date?" he pushes for some information from me.

"I guess leave a plus one open, and see if I surprise you."

"Oh, that's promising," he answers with a little excitement in his tone. "Care to elaborate on this mystery lady?"

"Simmer down over there. I'm not saying anything to you because I know all too well you'll go off and tattle to mom. Last time I went on a date, you and Brit went off and told mom, and it was one date. No way am I saying anything this time."

I would rather not say too much before even going on a date. This is too new with Baylee, although after that kiss we shared, I'm hoping she'll come along with me. She already knows my brother and her parents are going to be at the wedding.

"Okay, I won't torture you, but I expect to hear more before the big day if you bring someone," he says firmly.

"Yeah, yeah," I tell him. "Give my love to Brittany."

"Will do. Let me know how mom's next appointment goes."

"Of course. Don't work too hard," I tell him.

"I'll try not to," he says, even though I know he'll likely work over twelve hours today alone.

I hang up and my thoughts gravitate to my brother's words about my mother missing out on big events in the future. I really am the type of person that focuses on the now. I try to stay positive, but it's hard not to linger on Eric's concerns over everything my mom will miss out on if this cancer takes over her body. I feel an ache in my chest as the pain of her illness consumes me.

I shove my fears aside, and pull my computer back onto my lap to get the rest of the date prepped for me and Baylee. Once I feel confident she'll love what I have in mind, I check the time and realize she'll be back soon from her study session. I want to make sure I'm ready before she gets home.

She's not into all the glitz and glamour, but making tonight special is something I want to do for our first date. Obviously, I need to step it up compared to what I did for Abby. I gained a best friend in Abby, but tonight is different.

I want forever with Baylee—my forever friend, my forever date, my forever *everything*.

CHAPTER 16

Baylee

TODAY'S STUDY session was long, and the caffeine wasn't cutting it. We went over so many notes and the content was packed with so much information. I'm exhausted after going over extensive notes. But the minute I get back to the apartment, I feel a flurry of butterflies and renewed energy at the thought that my date with Tucker awaits.

I turn the key in the knob and my smile is hard to contain. I bite my lower lip at the thought that I get to spend time with him. And it's not just as a friend; this is different, this is new. That kiss yesterday morning was out of this world. I felt it down to my toes and if I close my eyes, I can still feel the swipe of his tongue along my lips. Shit, I'm so turned on for this guy and we haven't done anything more than make out like teens.

The minute I walk into the house, it's so quiet that I start to wonder if he's even home. Damn it, did he forget? Disappointment hits me square in the chest, until I hear some rustling down the hall.

"Hey, Firefly," Tucker says as he comes out from the hallway.

My smile is instant as I see his wet hair and neatly

trimmed beard. Fuck, he looks delicious. *What would that beard feel like against my inner thighs? Focus, Baylee.*

"Hey," I croak.

"You alright, sweetheart?" The smirk he gives me confirms he knows the effect he has on me.

"Yep. We still going out, or are you too tired?" *Yes, that sounds completely indifferent. I'm calm and collected, like I haven't been thinking of this all day. Nope. This isn't a big deal.*

"Of course," he says as he walks by me and slaps my ass. I think he's going to leave it at that, but then he grabs me and I yelp in surprise. I can't help laughing when he pulls me into his arms. Instinctively, I wrap my legs around his waist.

"Baylee, don't act like I don't affect you," he tells me.

"You don't," I tell him, sounding completely unconvincing, even to me.

He's a millimeter away from my face. "Oh really?"

"Not even a little bit."

"So, if I kissed you along here"—he moves his lips along my jaw toward my ear, and I shift my head up to give him space to roam with more ease—"you wouldn't like that very much?"

"Oh, um, definitely not," I say above a whisper.

"And if I nip and lick you right here"—he grabs my earlobe and leaves open-mouthed kisses below my ear which is like a direct jolt to my pussy—"it must do absolutely nothing to you, huh?"

"Mmhmm." I can't form words anymore. I'm short-circuiting at this point.

"Admit it, Bay. If I stuck my fingers in your underwear right now, you'd be so fucking wet for me, baby," he whispers into my ear.

"Fine, you win," I tell him on a whisper, with a little hip thrust.

He nibbles on my ear one last time and squeezes my ass.

He then lets me down and tells me, "Good, now go get ready and then we're headed out. Wear something warm because you know it gets chilly at night even though it's warm during the day. September has a way of being bit a temperamental like that."

"Are you fucking serious? You got me all hot and bothered like that?" He lets go of me and I'm standing in front of him breathing heavy after he got me turned on.

"We have a date to get to, right?" he asks me.

"So, you're going to leave me like this?" I gesture at myself.

"I need to leave you coming back for more later." He winks.

"You know I can take care of myself, right?" I tell him.

He comes toward me and grabs my chin. "Oh, Baylee, don't you dare touch yourself because I'll know if you touch my pussy before I get a chance to." Then he gives me a chaste kiss and walks away.

"Has anyone ever told you how frustrating you are?" I tell him as he walks away from me.

"The longer you take, the longer it takes to get back and relieve yourself, Baylee," he has the audacity to say to me. Such a cocky ass.

I storm off to my room and slam the door. My body betrays me, and the butterflies triple in excitement.

———

I try to tamper my enthusiasm as I make my way down the hall forty minutes later. I slowed myself down as I got ready, but at one point I threw my makeup brush down and said *fuck it*. I've been waiting years for this moment. I'm not wasting another second before starting something with Tucker Malloy.

As I round the corner, I find Tucker sitting on the couch,

scrolling through his phone. The moment he hears me, he pockets it and stands up. He runs his hands through his beard and gives me a shy smile. Despite how cocky he sounded earlier, he's clearly a little nervous about our date. It's sort of endearing and I can't help the smile that breaks through my face.

"Hey," he greets me as if he didn't just see me when I got home.

"Hi." I walk toward him.

"You look beautiful." He grabs my hand and pulls me the rest of the way into his body, moving his fingers through my hair.

"You don't look bad yourself," I say on a whisper.

I have to crane my neck to look up into his deep-green eyes and I find myself lost in his gaze, biting my tongue to keep myself from professing my love for him. I think I've been in love with Tucker Malloy from the minute my heart started to formulate the meaning of the word. And since then, I've always used him as the model of what love should be.

He bends down and brushes his lips against mine. I want to deepen the kiss, but he pulls away quickly.

"Let's go, because if I had my way, we'd stay here and never leave." He grabs his wallet and keys off the coffee table.

"I wouldn't mind that." I giggle. What's wrong with me? I'm not a girl that giggles. I internally roll my eyes.

"Bay, we're going on this date." He squeezes the hand he still has in his grasp. "You warm enough in that?" He juts his chin in my direction.

"Yeah, I think so." I look down at my outfit. I opted for my black leggings and a sweater.

"Okay, let's go. We aren't going far, but I want to head out before it gets too late."

We walk out the door and lock up. We get into the elevator, but instead of heading down, he hits the button to go to the top level.

"Um, I think you're going to the wrong floor," I mention.

"Nope, we're going the right way, Firefly," he says, winking at me.

"Okay..." I give him a quizzical expression.

The doors open and he pulls me to a hallway that looks much like the floor we live on. There's a door at the end and once we reach it, he pulls it open.

I realize I haven't explored this building very much since I moved in. The top floor is a rooftop garden, and it is beautifully maintained. Being summer, the sun hasn't set yet and Tucker must have come up here before I came home from my classes. He has laid down a blanket and brought food up here already. There's even a cooler with drinks.

"Tucker, this is amazing." I walk ahead of him, taking in the space.

"I know you aren't one for all the glitz and glamour of the fancy restaurants, but I thought you'd enjoy something like this." He reaches his arms around my middle, resting his chin on top of my head.

I lift my head to capture his lips with mine. I immediately deepen the kiss, finding it hard to stop once I start when it comes to Tucker's lips anywhere near me. He pulls away, looking into my eyes.

"Baylee, I promised myself we would at least have one decent date together. Come on, let me do this for you. Please." He gives me a peck on the lips.

"Fine. But then I'm going to have my way with you." I pout.

"So bossy." He smacks my ass and moves us toward the blanket.

We take a seat, and he grabs some drinks.

"I didn't know what you'd want, so I have a few options. There's water, wine, beer, sparkling water, soda." He's looking at the contents of the cooler.

"You really thought of everything." I laugh.

"Well, I wanted to make sure you had options." He looks over at me.

"I appreciate that. I think a sparkling water works for now, thanks."

He hands me the can and grabs one for himself. "I kept dinner options simple too. I picked up sandwiches. I hope that's okay. I wanted something I could put up here earlier today in the cooler, so the set-up was easy while you were in class." He looks a bit nervous with this confession.

"Of course it's okay," I tell him.

"I got turkey for you." He grabs one for me.

"Did you—"

"Yes, I made sure they held the mayo and I confirmed there are tomato and provolone cheese instead of cheddar." He winks in my direction.

"Thanks." I smile at him.

"I know what you like," he tells me.

"I appreciate it." I forget Tucker knows so much about me that I don't have to explain these little pieces of myself to him. It's just known to him, much like I'm aware of his preferences like the back of my hand.

We eat in comfortable silence for a little while together, taking in the evening sky. As the sun starts to set, I look over at him and I can't help but comment how perfect tonight has been.

"This is really nice, Tucker. Thanks for doing all this." I wave at the picnic area he set up. "I'm surprised how romantic this is."

"Well, it's not like I haven't taken a girl on a date before, Baylee." He scoffs.

"I know, but still... it's me. I never saw myself being on a date with you."

"Is it weird for you? Being on a date with me?" he asks. It seems like, for the first time, a little bit of vulnerability is creeping in.

"No. I've dreamed of me being the girl on a date with you for as long as I knew what a date was." I crumple my paper from my sandwich and place it beside me. "But don't forget, I've always watched from the sidelines. I never thought you'd take me on a date."

He nods, then looks out at the view in front of us. He stays silent, as if he's processing what to say.

Finally, he speaks, "Yeah, I won't say I always predicted this happening between us. You and I were in different stages for so long. I can't lie and say I've fantasized about us together our whole lives, Baylee. You were too young for a long time. But last year, something changed. I felt it. I saw you in a different light and I haven't been the same. Now I want to explore what we could be."

"What changed? Why will you try now and not last year?" I ask him. I still don't get why he had to wait until right now to finally take this leap with me.

"Will you accept that I just had to pull my head out of my ass?" He looks at me. "That's the only explanation I can give."

"If that's the truth, then yes." The way his eyes rake over my body, I want to rip his clothes off and lick him all over.

"So, can I have my way with you now?" I blurt. Finding ways to let out pieces of myself again is freeing and fun. I think it's because Tucker makes me feel safe.

"I'm starting to feel like you're just after me for one thing, Baylee," he says.

"Oh, and what's that?" I ask, inching my body closer.

"A little release," he says, his eyes watching me eat up the space between us. He licks his lips, and I know he's not mad about the fact I'm getting closer to him.

"Well, a girl has needs." I shrug. "But I can just say goodnight and head downstairs and take out my trusty vibrator instead. If you think your little friend can't help me, that is. I mean, is he a micro-thing, is that it?" I pout while looking down at his crotch. "Oh no, Tucker." I gasp. "Do you have a micro-penis?"

Tucker moves so quickly that I'm laying on the blanket, my laughter the only sound surrounding us.

"Micro-penis? What the fuck, Baylee." He looks horrified. Right then he grinds his hips into me. "There's nothing micro about me, including my dick."

"I don't know. Maybe I need to see to be sure," I tell him even though I can feel the bulge against my thigh.

Shit, it is so long and thick. My pussy is getting wetter by the second in anticipation of him being inside me.

"I swear, Baylee, if you even think of calling me small or micro in any way again, I will fucking spank that ass." He brings his lips to my ear and nibbles on my earlobe. "Or maybe I'll put you on your knees and have to shut you up another way."

"Oh, fuck," I moan and I can feel my nipples harden with the mere mention of having that kind of control over Tucker.

"I know the thought of that turns you on, doesn't it, Bay?" He moves his lips along my jaw, his beard leaving a burn on my skin.

Soon he kisses me and there's nothing sweet about our connection. He deepens our kiss and I can't help the moan he pulls from me. I swear if this wasn't a shared space, I would be pulling his clothes off and fucking him right here.

"Tucker, if you don't take me back to the apartment, I won't care if we have an audience. I will literally take your clothes off right here and fuck you for everyone to see." I'm getting hot just thinking about it.

"No one sees this pussy but me, you understand me, Baylee?" He nibbles my collarbone.

Then he does something unexpected. He moves his hand up my calf and my thigh. It feels like every touch of his fingers along my skin is igniting a fire in my body. Then he moves that hand along the waistband of my leggings.

"How wet is this pussy for me?" he asks.

The dirty talking is only egging me on even more. I'm writhing beneath him. I bite down on my bottom lip. He's looking up at me, as if he's waiting for me to grant him access. I open wider for him, the only permission he needs, and then I watch his hand move beneath my pants.

I feel his fingers graze my sensitive clit and I can't help the involuntary lift my hips do when I feel him move along my folds.

"Fuck, Baylee, you're so fucking wet," he says. "I'm going to make you come, baby."

"Yes, please." I'm already so close.

He inserts a finger then adds another. The way he curls his fingers inside me, then plays with my clit, it's bliss. I see stars. I swear, no other man has been this good at playing with my pussy. I gyrate my hips while Tucker pumps into me, and I'm coming so soon while telling him how good it feels. I can't stay quiet and I don't even care.

Tucker doesn't seem to mind how loud I'm being. He's cheering me on, telling me how hot I am while I'm coming. It's unexpected, yet something I find completely in Tucker's character.

Once I come down from my high, I open my eyes and find Tucker inserting the two fingers he just had inside me into his own mouth.

"Mmm, I guess I don't need dessert anymore."

Damn, he's dirty and I'm completely here for it.

CHAPTER 17

Tucker

THE MINUTE we get back to the apartment, we toss everything from the picnic on the floor and Baylee pounces on me. She wraps her arms around my neck, with her legs around my waist. I palm her ass as I kiss her. We can't keep our hands or lips off one another.

I kick the door closed while I walk us deeper into the apartment. I'm tempted to find the nearest surface and fuck her right there, but I can't have our first time be just anywhere. I need to take my time with her. After I just had a taste of her while upstairs, it took all my self-control not to strip her bare and take her right then and there.

I walk us back to my room and the moment I'm close enough to the bed, I lay her onto the mattress. She stretches out on the mattress, her hair splaying across my comforter and I've never seen a more beautiful sight in my life. Fuck, she's stunning.

She pushes herself up and pulls on my shirt to bring my body on top of her. I decide not to give her what she wants so easily. She protests with a growl.

"Calm down, Firefly," I tell her as I toe my shoes off.

I grab the waistband of her leggings, and she bites down

on her lower lip. I pull her pants down, only leaving her panties on her lower half, exposing the goosebumps along her skin as I pull the fabric down. Next to come off are her shoes. Everything is thrown to the floor.

"You nervous?" I ask her.

She shakes her head as she moves her hands up and squeezes her breasts. Damn, she's so sexy.

"You'll let me know if you want me to stop?" I don't want to push too much tonight.

"I want all of you, Tucker," she whispers.

I crouch down to the floor. She comes up on her elbows so our eyes stay connected. I begin to plant open-mouthed kisses along the inner part of her ankles. She opens her legs wider for me as I trail up her leg.

"Tucker," she moans, the anticipation building.

"Yes, baby." I keep my eyes on her. "What do you want? Tell me."

"You. It's always been you." She keeps palming her breasts and pinching her nipples. She must be extra sensitive on her breasts. I'll have to keep that in mind.

I'm right at the juncture of her legs and I can see the wet mark on her underwear. I poke my tongue out and lick that spot. She moans and gyrates her hips. She's so fucking turned on and I'm so hard, I need to get these jeans off.

"Fuck, you're so damn hot right now, Bay," I tell her.

"You have too many clothes on, Tucker."

Getting her hot and bothered is exactly my plan.

I give her a sly smile and grab my shirt from behind my neck and pull. I hear a soft sigh from Baylee, and I won't lie how it feeds my ego.

I throw my shirt to the side with her pants and move to hover over her, stealing a kiss from her. There's nothing soft about the way we're moving now. Her fingers dig into my back, and I know she's leaving marks with her long nails. It only spears me on—I bring my lips to her neck and I suck hard, leaving my own mark on her that I know she'll see come morning.

I move lower and bring her shirt up and over her head. Her bra is black and lacy. I can see her nipples through the fabric and if it's even possible, my dick is getting harder through my jeans.

"Shit, Baylee, you're breathtaking." I bring my palm to her chest and squeeze her right breast.

She moans in response, arching her back and pushing her breast into me. Then I pull the fabric down, freeing the one breast. I bring my lips over the peeked nipple and suck it. I do the same thing to the opposite breast. She gets frustrated with the bra and rips it off entirely. I can't help the laugh that escapes.

She palms my face and brings my lips to hers and begins kissing me again. Soon she's fumbling with the button on my jeans and pushing the fly down. She uses her feet to push my pants down as we continue to make-out like teens. Now we only have our underwear separating us from being completely naked and I'm going to combust if I'm not inside her.

She continues touching me, her small hands exploring me, moving under the waistband of my boxers. The minute her hand touches my dick I can't help the intake of breath. I've been so turned on, any movement in this direction, I run the risk of blowing my load and embarrassing myself.

I feel her smile against my lips as she starts to move her hand further down my shaft. It's not until she gets closer to the head of my cock that she stills, which I was expecting.

"Tucker, is that—is that a piercing?" she asks. She doesn't sound horrified; that's something at least. She sounds intrigued.

She still has her hand on my dick and I can't help thrusting because it feels so fucking good with her hand wrapped around my shaft.

"Yes," I moan.

"I've, um, never been with someone pierced before." She smiles.

"Okay," I say. "Is that, uh, a problem?"

"No, I just don't know much about them," she says shyly.

"Well, it's supposed to be more pleasurable for you." I drop by head and kiss her neck. She still has her hand on my cock and she's stroking me and I'm really having a hard time forming words.

"Oh." She's squeezing me. "You're really big. Like, you'd probably hit all my spots without that."

"Bay, baby, I'm seconds away from blowing my load in your hand. I need you to stop for a sec or I'm going to bust before you even get a shot at this."

"Oh, sorry." She laughs.

"Don't be sorry. I got it a while ago and yes, I'm big, but I swear, it'll feel good. Does it freak you out?"

She shakes her head.

"Do you want to wait? We can do other things if you're not ready to do this tonight."

"No, I want to," she tells me. "I've wanted this for so long. Do you not want to do this?" She almost looks hurt.

"Baylee, I want this. I just don't want to push you or make you feel like you have to do this."

"Tucker, don't you get it? You're the only person I've ever wanted to do this with," she admits.

I look into her eyes and the genuine affection from her is palpable.

I lean down and capture her lips. There's nothing fast-paced to my movements. I'm slow and purposeful, knowing deep down she is a piece of my past, my present, and my future.

I move my kisses down her neck, collar bone, chest, belly, and navel. I'm then peeling her underwear down her body and throwing them over my shoulder.

I open her legs, and I swipe my tongue through her folds, while she grabs my hair and moans my name on her lips. I don't let her come, but I savor the feeling of her pussy against my lips for a few seconds, before I pull away.

I take my own boxers off, kneel in front of her, and stroke my dick as she marvels at the sight of me. She watches as the moonlight shines on the jewelry at the end of my cock, probably wondering how that will work inside of her. Her eyes are full of wonder and lust as I grab the condom that I threw next to us on the mattress.

I peel it open and roll it on. I bring my fingers to her center, even though I know she's wet enough. But I want to push two fingers inside her anyway, hearing her moan before my cock replaces my fingers.

"Baylee, there's nothing slow or gentle about how I fuck," I tell her as I move my cock through her folds once I move my fingers out of the way.

"What makes you think I want gentle?" she tells me.

That's my girl.

Without another word, I slam into her, and she grabs the mattress and yells out while I moan.

"Fuck you're so tight, Baylee," I tell her as I clench my teeth, breathing through my nose.

"Holy shit, I'm so fucking full," she says.

I pull out and watch myself push back in. We fit perfectly together. We find our rhythm and I look down and watch myself pump in and out of her. I can't believe how hot we look right now. I keep one hand on her hip, while another hand moves up to grab her breast and tease her nipple.

I angle myself over her and that slight change causes her to moan louder.

"Oh my, Tucker. Fuck," she yells. "Right there, it feels so good."

"Yeah, you feel it?" I bet the piercing is rubbing against the G-spot perfectly.

"Yes, right there. Keep doing that." Soon she's calling out my name and watching her come on my dick is probably my new favorite thing. Her walls constrict around my cock and I see her skin flush as she climaxes. Fuck, she's beautiful. I continue at this angle until she comes down from her high.

She opens her eyes afterwards and I continue pumping into her, knowing I can get another out of her. I lay back and have her ride me.

"Ride me to another orgasm, Bay," I tell her.

She rests her palms on my chest and starts gyrating her hips. I bring my hands to her breasts and pinch her nipples, watching how beautiful she looks from this angle. Then I can't help it and decide to sit up as well and pull one into my mouth.

"Fuck, everything is sensitive, Tucker," she moans. "Your dick is fucking magical."

I can't help the laugh that escapes. Then I pull her lips into a punishing kiss. She then pushes me down and starts riding me to find her release again. I can feel her tighten around me and she's chasing another orgasm. She arches her back, placing her hands on my thighs, throwing her head back and moaning. I pinch her nipple on one breast as I play with her clit with my other hand.

I'm not going to last watching her lose herself on me like this. It's euphoric. It's so fucking hot.

"Fuck, Bay, I'm going to come, baby," I moan.

"Tucker, fuck, you feel so good," she tells me as she rides me. Soon she detonates and her whole body begins to shake as she comes on me.

I take hold of her hips and begin to pump into her feverishly. I welcome the warmth that snakes down my spine and soon I'm following with my own orgasm, shooting my cum into the condom. My vision goes dark, my breathing labored, and Baylee lays her body onto my chest, sweat beading off both our bodies.

After what feels like hours, our breathing finally calms down and I open my eyes. I brush her hair away from her face and she lifts her head to rest her chin on my chest. Her eyes are sated, and she has a soft smile on her face. She carefully pulls herself off me and lays at my side.

"That was"—she turns onto her back and covers her face with her hands—"fucking amazing." Her shoulders start shaking.

Is she crying? Fuck. No.

"Baylee?" I hesitate and move up on my elbow.

It's only then I realize she's softly laughing.

"That was fucking incredible. Holy shit, your dick is—insane!"

"Um, thanks?" I say, even though it's slightly strange in a way.

"I've never come like that during sex before, like ever," she admits.

Huh?

She gets up and heads to the bathroom.

"Hold on, what do you mean?" I follow her, but she closed the door.

I talk through the door, "Baylee, what do you mean by that, exactly?"

She yells from the other side, "Exactly what I said. I haven't been able to come from sex alone. I usually have to like, you know, finish myself off."

I stand there, sort of baffled. I grab a tissue on the dresser to clean myself up and toss it while I wait for her. She opens the bathroom door and I pin her to the wall.

"So, you're telling me I'm the first person to make you come during sex with my dick?"

"Yeah," she laughs.

I move my mouth to the shell of her ear. "I'm sorry, but that sort of does things to me, sweetheart. I think we should do it again and see if it was a fluke or something." I waggle my brows and kiss her on the lips.

"Oh really? Maybe we should. I mean, it would probably be a good idea to test it out," she agrees.

"Yeah, let's start now." I grab her and toss her on the bed.

And I make good on my promise, and we test out the theory two more times. Turns out it wasn't a fluke. I do, in fact, have a magically insane dick, per Baylee Rios.

———

The last thirty-six hours have been magical. I'm trying to be quiet as I shower before my next twenty-four shift at the station. I hate that I have to leave Baylee, but it's part of the job. I've got my head under the water when I hear the shower door open, and hands move around me.

Soft open kisses begin to trail my back, then Baylee comes into my line of sight.

"Good morning," she says.

"Hey, baby, I'm sorry I woke you."

"You didn't really. I just moved over in bed and didn't feel you next to me anymore." She pouts and I kiss her.

"I'm sorry. How can I make it up to you?" I smile.

"Well, since you're going to be gone, I thought maybe I should give you a little something to help tide you over until you get back home," she says.

Before I can question more, she gets on her knees and soon her lips are opening around the head of my cock. Her tongue swirls around my piercing, then plays with the sensitive skin of my head.

She moves her lips to engulf my cock and before I can react further, she's bobbing her head to take me deeper. I can't keep my hands from running through her hair and my hips move of their own accord at a steady rhythm. Shit, her mouth is so warm and so tight.

She sucks me off so good. I look down and her eyes open to look up at me.

"I love your fucking mouth, Baylee."

She brings her hand to my balls, squeezing and playing with them. That combination and the way she starts moving faster with her mouth, I'm soon telling her, "I'm coming. You better move if you don't want me to come down your throat."

She stays where she is, and I detonate down her throat. It feels like the ropes of cum are nonstop and she takes every single drop proudly.

Once the last drop is swallowed, she stands up, and I bring her up into my arms, pushing her up against the wall and kissing her.

"You are perfection," I tell her.

"Our pieces fit together perfectly," she whispers into my ear.

And truer words have never been spoken. She and I fit together perfectly, indeed.

CHAPTER 18

Baylee

IF I CLOSE MY EYES, *I can still feel him inside me.*

"Earth to Baylee." Sydney snaps her fingers.

"Huh?" I turn my head to look over at my friends staring at me.

"Oh my gosh. What's with you this afternoon?" Jada laughs into her matcha latte. "Did you get laid or something?"

I turn my face toward the window, hoping the warmth in my cheeks doesn't give me away.

"Oh. My. Fucking. God!" Sydney yells.

"Shhhhh." My eyes bulge out when I look their way. "Be quiet. I don't need the whole coffee shop to hear you."

"Like they care. I bet half this joint got some on a Saturday night at a frat party." Jada waves her comment off.

"Who's the guy?" Sydney asks.

Neither of them know about my history with Tucker. All they know is that I transferred from Connecticut and that I'm from Boston. They know I'm living with a friend and that he's a guy.

"No one from school," I tell them. "You don't know him."

"Ah, so a friend?" Jada asks. "Like a friend with benefits?" She waggles her eyebrows.

"I don't think so?" I say, although it comes out more like a question.

"You better know for sure. I had something like that a while back, and it was definitely a sad state when I realized it was a friends with benefits situation, after I found him with one of my dorm mates a week later. Turns out we weren't official. I learned my lesson," Sydney tells me.

My coffee feels like a rock in my stomach. I'm not the type to date multiple people at the same time. I've always been a monogamous dater. Growing up, I saw Tucker date people in high school, but I know that's not quite the case as he's gotten older.

Fuck. Maybe I should have clarified this situation before we did anything intimate. I'm such a fool. I already had feelings going into this. I internally roll my eyes.

Jada and Sydney move on to another conversation; unbeknownst to them I'm reeling over here at the fact that I started something and I'm already in love with the person I just slept with. They have no idea how long I've dreamed of this with Tucker. Shit, they don't know who Tucker is to me. They really have no idea what my life is beyond school; we've only known each other a few weeks.

Once we finish up our coffees, we disperse, and I walk to the library. I have a study group to meet up with. Jada has a shift at a bookstore down the street and Sydney has a date with Jacob. Apparently, he asked her out. Fucking finally.

I'm walking through the campus, the library in my line of sight, when I feel eyes on me. I look over my shoulder, my skin prickling with awareness. The campus is quiet this afternoon, students simply moving about from their dorms to random areas with friends. Because of the late hour, it's pretty quiet on campus right now.

Still, that eerie feeling continues. I pull my phone out of

my pocket, just in case I need to make a phone call. The moment I reach the door of the library, I breathe a sigh of relief. Something about being in an enclosed space brings a sense of peace.

I walk through the doors and make sure to ask one of my classmates to give me a ride home instead of taking an Uber home alone. Something unsettling about that short walk from the coffee shop to the library has set off alarm bells.

———

I'm sitting on the couch early the next morning, wide awake. After I got home, I passed out on the couch. Once my study session ended yesterday, I got a ride and crashed immediately when I got home. The apartment was so quiet without Tucker, and I'll admit, he wiped me out with our sex-fest the night before.

He kept me up when he was off from his shift, not that I'm complaining. It was pretty memorable and I'm still pinching myself to make sure it wasn't a dream. Now I've fallen down a rabbit hole on my computer, lost in a search of piercings that I can't seem to get out of. This is fascinating.

I hear someone at the door and Tucker comes in quietly.

"Good morning," I greet him.

"Hey. I wasn't expecting you to be up." He seems surprised to see me at the couch.

He walks over and grabs my chin and plants a kiss on my lips as if he's done it hundreds of times before.

"Why are you awake already? You studying?" He juts his chin toward my laptop, unable to see my screen.

"Not in the way you think," I say as I feel my cheeks heat.

Tucker walks over to the kitchen to fix himself a cup of coffee. He's opening a cupboard for a mug.

"If you're not studying at this hour, what are you doing?" he asks, his back to me.

"I got curious about piercings after the other night. I mean, your dick is mesmerizing, Tucker. How am I supposed to go back to a regular one after yours?" I bite down on my lower lip, knowing he's going to react to my comment. That's exactly why I said it.

I avoid looking up, keeping my eyes fixed on my computer. He slams the cabinet and stalks toward the couch, eyes locked on me, arms crossed over his chest.

Innocently, I look up at him, blinking as if I didn't say anything offensive.

"What? Can I help you?" I say nonchalantly.

He grabs my laptop gently, knowing I need it for school, and places it on the coffee table. Then he proceeds to grab my ankles and pull me down so I'm lying flat on the couch. He cages his forearms on either side of my head, hovering his large body over me.

"Excuse me, but did I just hear you correctly? Did you just compliment my dick then proceed to discuss fucking someone else after me?" He pushes his half-hard dick into me and heat is already pooling in my core. Why is this so hot?

"Well, Tucker, I mean, you've sort of ruined it for me with other guys," I push his buttons a little further.

"Are you fucking serious, Baylee?" He brings his lips into the crook of my neck and bites right below my earlobe. I feel an electrical current down to my pussy. This man is sinful and delicious in all the right ways.

"Am I saying something wrong, Tucker?" I laugh and bring my hands into his hair, loving that I can now touch him in this way.

He pulls my hands out of his ginger strands and brings them above my head and pins them there. "I don't think so, sweetheart. I think we need to get something straight. You see, this pussy"—he pushes his cock into me to emphasize his point—"is all mine. And if I have it my way, you won't need to go back to a regular dick after this because my dick is all yours."

I moan as he rubs up against me. My sleep shorts are so thin that every movement against my center is sending jolts through my entire body. I'm panting and moaning as he gyrates his body directly over my clit, and I'm close to detonating already.

"I need you to fuck me," I whimper, I'm desperate for him.

"Oh yeah? So, you agree I'm all you need?" He continues at a leisurely pace as he thrusts against my center, kissing down my neck, his beard scratching my skin as he travels down my body.

"Yes, you're all I'll ever need, Tucker," I moan.

"That's a good girl," he tells me. Then he pulls away, letting go of my hands and sits back, as if he wasn't just about to get me off with the friction of our bodies moving against one another.

I groan from the loss. "What the hell, Tucker?"

"It was a long shift, Baylee." He rubs his hand down his face. Then he grabs my laptop off the table and opens it. "Plus, let me see this research you were doing."

I stare at him, completely perplexed by the turn of events. My mouth hangs open. He's gotta be joking.

"Are you fucking serious?" I yell at him, shoving him with my foot.

"Oh I am," he tells me, looking at the screen. "You think you can talk about fucking other guys and get away with it?" He smirks.

"You're an asshole."

"I'm actually not, and you know it. Many say I'm a giant teddy bear."

"They're wrong," I huff.

"Wow, you really took a deep dive into the pierced dick

pool here, Bay." He whistles. "This is intense." He turns his head. "This looks painful." He turns the screen toward me.

"Yes, I know. But your piercing doesn't look like a walk in the park either." My eyes go wide.

"Yeah, it wasn't. I was in my twenties, not much older than you, and curious. Probably stupid. Wanted to enhance the experience for my partner. So, I did it. Haven't gotten any complaints." He shrugs.

"Were you getting complaints before?" I ask him, shocked if he said he was. "I mean, you're not small."

"Well thank you. Keep the compliments coming, please." He smiles.

"Tucker, you know you have a huge dick. I mean, you're huge in every aspect. So, yes, Tuck, you have a gigantic cock. There, happy?" I roll my eyes.

"The eye roll isn't really necessary, but I love the gigantic dick part," he says, still looking at my computer screen.

"Are you really not going to take care of my needs right now?" I whine.

"No, because I think a lesson is to be learned here," he says as he puts his nose up.

A lesson, huh? I think two can play at this game. I take a moment for him to continue scrolling the images in front of him and for his blue balls to really settle in.

Then I stand up and stretch in front of him, reaching my arms up to the ceiling.

"Well, I guess I'll get ready for my day." I grasp the hem of my top and pull it over my head and off, revealing my breasts for him. It has the desired effect and Tucker's green eyes move from the screen directly to my chest.

He immediately closes the lid to my laptop and moves it next to him on the couch. I attempt to move away from him, but he's too quick and wraps his arms around my legs, pulling me into the space between his legs.

"On second thought, maybe you do need a little attention," he tells me.

"Oh really?" I laugh.

"Yeah." He captures one of my breasts in his mouth. The minute his tongue swirls around my nipple, I moan and I throw my head back. I'm incredibly sensitive in my breasts and it's a direct connection to my core. I move my legs to straddle him and he grabs my ass, squeezing it.

"I'm addicted to you already, Baylee," he says, his mouth traveling to my other breast. "I thought about you the entire time I was on shift."

I comb my fingers through his hair, and he uses his teeth to bite down before he sucks hard on my nipple. The sting only spurs me on to move my hips faster along his cock.

"I need you naked, Tucker. I need you inside me. I'm not kidding," I tell him.

He slaps my ass, and I take it as a command to get up again. He stands behind me and pulls my sleep shorts off. I don't have any underwear on, and he swears his approval behind me.

Without expecting it, he bends down and bites my ass, then quickly follows with an open-mouthed kiss. "You're perfect, you know that?"

"Mmm," is the only response I can muster.

"Bend over, hands on the back of couch," he orders.

I hear him rummaging to remove his clothing. I look behind me and see he's naked in record time. He's holding a condom in one hand, while he's stroking his cock with the other.

I lick my lips in anticipation of him entering me.

He sheaths himself and moves behind me, passing his dick through my folds. That simple movement is enough to cause shudders to pass through me.

He brings his lips to the shell of my ear. "You were made for me, Firefly. You take me so perfectly," he says. Then he slaps my ass, and the sting is felt straight to my pussy. He pushes my lower body down slightly, causing my hips to be slightly higher. Then he grabs my hips and lines himself up. Before I have enough time to process it, he slams into me.

We both moan at the same time. He stays seated in me for a second, both of us getting used to the feeling of how full he makes me. That fucking piercing hits in the perfect spot right away. This angle is downright intense. Without it, I have no doubt his girth and length would already be enough, but add that bulb at his tip, it feels like he's hitting my G-spot with every stroke.

The minute he starts moving, I swear I see stars. I'm white-knuckling the back of the couch and I hang my head, breathing through my nose, trying to last longer than a few strokes. It's not long and I'm already feeling my climax rolling through me.

He's pounding into me and I'm on the brink of coming. This man makes me feel like my skin and body are on fire from the minute he enters me. I've never felt this kind of need before.

"Baylee, I can feel you choking my dick again. Fuck, I'm going to come with you," he tells me.

The fact that I make him crazy in the same way he pushes me to the edge brings a power over me. I love that we have this chemistry together. He brings his hand onto my lower back, making sure I stay at the right angle. The friction against my G-spot is too much and I feel my orgasm building.

"Tucker, harder, right there." I match his rhythm, pushing my ass back against him, scared to lose my climax.

He increases his own speed, pumping in and out of me, the slapping of our skin and panting the only sounds bouncing off the walls around us.

"Your pussy is so fucking perfect for me, baby," he yells out.

Right then I detonate at his words and shortly after that I

feel him fill the condom inside me. His movements slow and I then feel his lips move against my spine, ascending until his lips reach my neck.

He grabs my hair to bring me upright. My head comes up and back, capturing my lips with his own and captivating me with a punishing kiss. I lose myself in him once again.

I've always loved him, but I somehow fall deeper. Tucker Malloy holds every part of me within his grasp and I never want him to let me go.

CHAPTER 19

Tucker

"WELCOME!" River opens the door and the smug smile on his face makes me want to bolt immediately.

I know he's most likely made a bet on how long it would take for things to happen between Baylee and I since she moved in. I can tell from the look on his damn face.

"You're such a fucker," I say under my breath and shake my head.

"Wow, Tucker. In front of two beautiful women. What kind of gentleman are you?" He turns his attention to Baylee. "Hey. Don't know if you remember me. I'm River." He extends his hand to Baylee as he opens the door for her to walk in. "And this is my beautiful Gabriella," he says as he holds her in his arms.

She flaps her arms around, her drool on full display as she babbles. "She says hello and she's trying to say dada," River explains.

I roll my eyes because she's not even six months old yet. I put my items down on the kitchen counter. Clay snorts from the corner, apparently giving up the battle at this point.

The minute the twins are near one another, I see Clay hand over a twenty.

"Motherfuckers." I point to both of them.

"I don't know why you even doubt us at this point," River says. "Isn't Uncle Malloy just a big dumb-dumb, Ella? Yes he is. Stick with me, I'll teach you the ropes." He blows raspberries on her cheek, and she giggles.

"Hi, I'm Clay, the better twin. We've met when you've come to the station before," Clay greets Baylee. She's just watching as the two Nichols brothers interact and I can see her brain try to take it all in.

I tried to warn her that whatever she has seen with them in the past is nothing compared to the two of them outside of the station. She laughed it off, but she's now getting the full Nichols experience. It's something else—especially River.

"River, are you embarrassing yourself already?" Kennedy says as she walks into the kitchen from one of the rooms. "Oh, hey, Malloy. Baylee, thank goodness. It's so good to see you. Clay, you owe me twenty." She waves her fingers at her future brother-in-law.

"You too?" I look at her horrified.

"Come on, Malloy. Don't judge." She gives me a look like I've got shit for brains.

Kennedy gives Baylee a hug. "I'm glad you could make it and I'm excited you're here. I hope you don't mind the craziness you'll see tonight. And don't judge me for the man I'm going to marry."

"Hey, I'm a catch!" River protests and Ella screams.

"Oh, yes, you're amazing," Kennedy says as she walks over to River and gives him a kiss. Ella watches their interaction, and Kennedy goes to grab the sweet baby from River.

"I don't think so"—he moves his niece away from his fiancée—"she hasn't had enough uncle time."

"River, you've had her the entire time she's been here," Kennedy protests.

"River, let Kennedy have some time with her," Clay interjects.

"You always side with Kennedy. It's so unfair," he whines.

"Yes, because this is preschool," he deadpans at his brother. "Let Kennedy have some time with Ella please. Pass the baby to her. 1… 2… there we go. Good boy, River."

Once he hands his niece over, River gives his brother the finger.

"So mature, Riv," Clay tells him.

Kennedy coos at Ella and sniffs her sweet head. "What is it about sniffing their heads?" I ask Baylee.

"Oh, they have the best baby smell," Baylee says. "I remember when Catrina was born, and I did the same thing."

Catrina is Baylee's oldest niece and everyone doted on her. Now that I think back, it's true, everyone sniffed her head too.

"Okay, I'm here. Sorry about that. Ugh. I promise no more work calls will interrupt me," Abby walks out of one of the bedrooms. "Hi, Malloy. Hi, Baylee!" She eyes our newest addition then swings her gaze to her soon-to-be husband.

"Sweetheart, you owe me twenty." She gives him a sweet smile.

"That's low. You of all people, Abs!" I protest.

"That's cute, Malloy. I still like to be part of the bet. You bet on Clay and I, remember?"

"I plead the fifth," I tell her.

"Okay, could someone clue me in. What the hell is happening?" Baylee finally chimes in.

"Oh, Baylee, first off, you're an outcast like Clay and I because you're not part of this posse that watches all the reality shows. You'll be an outside observer of their rituals. Just stick to me and Clay. Now that you're with us, we'll form our own trio. Don't worry." River winks at her.

She looks up at me, and I don't know if she's scared or honored to be included.

"Second, we bet on everything, and absolutely anything is fair game, including the two of you finally dating," Kennedy explains with a sly smile taking over her face.

———

"This shit is stupid!" I yell at the TV.

"I think it's cute!" Abby says as she takes another bite of her pizza.

"It's sort of playing with their feelings," Kennedy says.

"I'm here for it, you guys," that's from Marissa, who has joined in via FaceTime.

Loved and Lost is a new take on reality shows that's been added to our watch parties, and it's the first episode tonight. We've got all the necessary foods lined up in front of us: pizza, popcorn, cookies, brownies, pretzels, candy of different assortments and then salad. Kennedy told us we needed some vegetables because she has a wedding in a little over a year and she wanted to feel like she had something healthy in the lineup. Abby and I succumbed to the request, but the bowl remains untouched. Surprise, surprise.

The concept of the show revolves around people reconnecting with old loves and blindly speaking to them from behind closed doors. However, their voices are distorted and they don't know who they're talking to until they reveal themselves. So, even though they know these are people they once dated, they won't know exactly who they are until they reveal themselves at the very end the show.

"Dude, this is just a mind-fuck for the contestants." I point at the screen.

"Why is it a mind-fuck?" Abby asks. She's a softie for all these shows.

"Because they broke up for a reason. What if he was awful to her or vice-versa and now they're forcing them back together?" Kennedy says.

"Exactly," I agree with her.

"Yeah, I sorta see that point," Marissa chimes in. "This could get ugly real quick."

"Well, I guess we'll see. Maybe they vetted them for that," Abby counters.

"You know this shit isn't real, right?" River chimes in from the kitchen, where he's standing with Baylee and Clay. The three of them have really started their own little club.

The three of us turn toward them and can't help scowling.

"You know, no one asked you." I point at him.

"So hostile," Clay says. "You sure you want to be around such hostility, Baylee? I've got other friends I can introduce you to."

"You might be right. There's nothing *magical* about him." She gives me a smirk and winks in my direction.

"I feel like there's more to that, but it's probably dirty," Kennedy says.

"Oh, I love dirty things!" Marissa nearly yells from the phone.

"Of course that's all you heard." Abby laughs.

"Okay, this conversation is over." I grab my things. "The verdict is still out on this show, but of course I'll still watch the dumpster fire it will likely be. Bay, you ready?"

"Sure. Thanks for welcoming me in your crew," she tells Clay and River. I catch a wink their way.

"What was that?" I point in their direction.

"What?" the three of them question.

"I saw that. Why did you wink at them? You took a bet, didn't you? I know this game." I turn toward the girls. "Kennedy, Abs, there's a bet on us. I know it. They're ganging up against us," I declare.

"Spill, Riv." Kennedy crosses her arms across her chest.

"I'm a vault," he declares.

"Oh, this is going to be fun," Marissa eggs on from the phone.

Kennedy walks seductively toward her fiancé and strokes his cheek. Then she whispers something in his ear. I watch and can't help but smile. Clay rolls his eyes in frustration because he knows his brother will cave.

"No way, really?" River's eyes light up like a kid on Christmas.

Kennedy nods and kisses his cheek.

"Fifty bucks that Malloy will be the biggest fan of the show. Like he'll likely host the season finale party at his place and even do themed cupcakes and that kind of shit," River spills.

"What the fuck?" Clay throws his hands in the air.

"I didn't take the bet." River puts his hands up as if he's not guilty.

Marissa's maniacal laugh echoes from the phone. "This is the best night ever. I almost didn't hop on because I thought it was going to be a waste of time. You guys are sort of fucking crazy. You know that, right?" She continues laughing.

"River!" Baylee looks at him and I look at her.

"You took the bet against me?" I look at her horrified.

"Come on, Tucker. You know full well, you'll be heavily invested in this show. I heard rumors of a show you loved called"—she starts snapping her fingers, looking up at the ceiling—"*Road* something. Shit, what was it? It was before my time."

"Holy shit. *Road Rules*?" Clay starts laughing. "You liked *MTV Road Rules*? That show is ancient. How old are you, Malloy?"

"That was a fucking cool show, okay?"

"Okay, sure," River chimes in. Both brothers are laughing now.

"Yeah, well, I heard Tucker was really into that show. He's always been into these reality shows. So, no matter how much you act like you're not into them, I know you'll be all in by a few episodes. You're a sucker for this shit, Tuck." She gives me a megawatt smile.

I roll my eyes. "Whatever. You're all against me. We're

leaving before she outs me on more stuff from my past." I pull on her hand and make my way toward the door.

"Hey, Malloy, call me from your car phone and let me know you got home safely. Better yet, use your rotary phone instead!" Marissa yells.

"Fuck off," I respond.

I can hear everyone cackling as they close the door.

"I hope you're happy. I won't hear the end of that from the firehouse. Clay and River won't keep their trap shut." I look down at Baylee.

"Oh, I'm completely satisfied by that entire interaction." She looks up at me and smiles.

I bend down and capture her lips. Unfortunately, the elevator interrupts us too soon and I have to break away from her. I can't wait to get her home and lose myself in everything that is Baylee.

It's been two months since Baylee moved in with me, and a little over a month since we became more than roommates. We can't get enough of one another, and I won't lie, I've never been happier. She brings me a type of happiness I never imagined possible.

When I felt this connection between us last year, I honestly believed it would pass. Now that I'm with Baylee I see what I would've walked away from, and I feel like a complete idiot. She's added so much to my life and had I not taken this leap, I would've missed out on so much.

The fall season has kicked in with a cold front that we already feel to the core. I just got back from a trip to Connecticut to grab some winter items Baylee had left behind. Her roommates let her keep some of her jackets in the closet as she wasn't going to need them until later in the season, but I told her I'd make the trip out there to bring it back for her.

Baylee hasn't returned to the state, nor to the apartment, since that fateful night. There is a pre-trial set for later this month and she'll be headed back to Connecticut for that, which the attorney just contacted her about. Baylee has been incredibly nervous to return and I can tell she's hesitant to see Myles again.

I'm currently driving to my mom's place to take her to an appointment. Baylee had stopped by to have lunch with her parents earlier, but she has class, so I won't see her in our old neighborhood when I make it over.

I pull in and recognize the truck sitting in my neighbor's driveway. I take a deep breath, hoping my old best friend won't walk out right now. I'm not in the mood to see him. Even though we have shifts together at the station, I know he won't be civil outside of that.

He still checks in on his sister, but that's as far as his contact goes. The way his glances over at me at work have become glacial makes me believe he knows Baylee and I are an item. The way he has avoided me at work, I assume I'm the last person he wants to see. I know we need to clear the air, but today isn't the day. I'm here to care for my mother and nothing else.

I get out of the car and I'm striding over to my mom's place when I hear the neighbor's front door open. Out of habit I glance over and see Rios shooting daggers in my direction.

"So, it's true. You're really with my sister even though you know how I feel about it?!" he yells in my direction.

I cast my gaze down and breathe through my nose, trying to tamper my frustration. I just wanted to come over here and care for my mother. This wasn't about him, but of course he has to make everything about him.

"You already know the answer to that, Rios." No point in stretching this longer than it has to be.

"Some best friend you turned out to be, man," he spits back.

"Rios, you have some nerve. I stopped when you asked me to. I walked away initially. I did exactly what you wanted. I ignored my feelings for her the first time."

"Some good that did. I told you she was off limits!" he yells.

"Yeah, and you told me what a shit friend I was then, remember? You guilted me to believe she could do better. Then she walked into the hands of a monster!" I yell back.

"You're not good enough for her, Malloy. I told you to stay away from her. You were supposed to keep away from her. That's why I made you go on that date with Abby. So, you'd stay away from my sister!" Rios yells.

"I did stay away. For as long as I could, because you're my friend, I respected our friendship—" I'm cut off by the front door of the Rios household opening.

"What is he talking about?" Baylee walks out of the house, surprising me with her presence.

"Baylee, what are you doing here? You have class right now." I look over at her stunned.

She's looking at her brother, but the frustration she wears on her face is directed at both of us.

"Daniel, what the fuck is he talking about?" Her icy tone is full of anger.

"Baylee, I did it for you. He's a player. He isn't someone you can count on like that." He looks at her.

"What the fuck, man?" I hold my hands out. "What are you talking about?"

"Come on. All you do is go on dates left and right. You haven't had a girlfriend since high school," he throws at me.

"So what? Who are you to judge? That's why I can't date

your sister? That's why you forced me to go out with Abby?" I yell at him.

"You forced him to go out with Abby?" She looks at her brother horrified. Then she swings her gaze at me. "You agreed to that date because my brother made you take her out and you did it to please *him*? Like you bow down to him or something? What the fuck, Tucker? That's fucking pathetic!" she yells at both of us.

"Baylee, let me explain." I start walking toward her, but she puts her hands up.

"Please save your excuses right now. The ripple effect of your decision that day resulted in pain I now have to live with. I have scars embedded deep in my soul that I'll never know how to explain. And here I thought you didn't want me during that time, so I accepted that monster. I welcomed him because I thought that was what I deserved," she chokes out.

Fuck, her pain is my pain.

She hangs her head for a moment, then something snaps in her, and she pulls her shoulders back and looks at Rios, determination in her gaze.

"Shame on you, Danny, for making a decision you had no right making on my behalf. I stayed with Myles, partially because that's what I thought I was worthy of and partly because I liked that you approved of him. Damn, I'm so stupid. You're my brother, not my keeper. I know in your head you think that was a decision made out of love; but it wasn't, it was a selfish decision. Shame on you."

Then she directs her gaze back to me and the power of her stare feels like a dagger straight to my heart. "Tucker, I've felt like my heart has been yours since the day I understood what the power of love signified. I was willing to give it to you for years, and I was waiting for you to acknowledge me. I thought you saw me last year, I really did. But all you saw was his sister." She points at Rios. "Because if you saw me, you would've chosen me regardless of what my brother wanted, like you did in that hospital that night."

She doesn't give me a chance to speak. She turns around and walks back in the house and slams the door.

"Shit, she's pissed," Rios says.

I look over at him and I don't even acknowledge his comment with one of my own. I'm about to walk over to the Rios front door when I hear my own childhood front door open, and my mother calls my name.

"Tucker, come in here, son," my mother calls me inside and I oblige.

I don't even look back at Rios and stalk over toward my mother.

She looks a little more frail today, and I don't know if it's the treatment or if she hasn't been eating well lately. I'll have to ask her while we visit to see if the medication is making her ill.

The moment I walk through the threshold, she pulls me into an embrace, and it feels like all my troubles are less overwhelming in that moment.

"Hi, Ma," I whisper.

"It's good to see you, Tucker," she says into my chest.

My mother is much shorter than me. I inherited my height from my father, so I tower over her. But no matter how much taller I am, her comfort surrounds me in her embrace.

"Why don't you take a seat and tell me what's going on?" she tells me.

"First, why don't I get you a snack and some tea," I deflect.

"I already had my tea today."

"Are you sure?" I look down at my watch. She usually has her tea later in the day.

"Yes, Baylee came over earlier and had tea with me." She smiles softly. "Now, go sit."

The minute I sit down, I look over at her and I spill. I tell her everything about last summer, from my feelings about Baylee, to the fake date with Abby, and finally how things have evolved with Baylee now. Once I catch her up, I sit back, feeling the weight on my shoulders dissipating, yet feeling like Baylee may have walked away from what we just started together.

My mom sits next to me and pulls my hand into her frail one. Why is she so weak suddenly?

"Ma, what's going on with you that you're so much weaker than the last time I saw you? You don't look so good."

"The doctor just says I'm adjusting to this new medication they started me on." She pats my hand to reassure me, but it does little to comfort the unease that's creeping in. "Now back to Baylee. You need to tell her how you feel. You need to explain how conflicted you were last year, and how you really didn't want to lose a friend—how you didn't want to lose what was comfortable to you. That's understandable. She'll see both sides, son."

"But she's right to be upset. I wasn't honest when we started this up. I should've told her. I felt like that was between her and Rios. If I'd simply been honest with him and with her, she could've avoided all this with that asshole ex of hers." I run my hand through my hair.

"Tucker, you know there's no way you could've known that person would be so horrible to her. There's no way you could've predicted that for her." She moves her hand to my cheek.

I nod because I do know that in the logical part of my brain, but it doesn't make me feel better. I hope Baylee is still there when I get home and will hear me out while I pour my heart on the ground and beg for her forgiveness.

CHAPTER 20

Baylee

I GOT BACK to the apartment seething earlier. I tried to hang out with my mom a bit longer after I stormed away from my brother and Tucker, but I couldn't enjoy her company knowing he was next-door. I needed some distance, so I left and decided to walk around campus. The weather wasn't too bad with the sun shining this afternoon. Once it started to set, I had to head back though.

I had a session with my therapist that I asked to do virtually, because I didn't feel like sitting through it in her office. But she asked to see me anyway, so I begrudgingly went to her office and I sat there, arms crossed, until she pulled the information out of me. I know it was probably the best thing for me to be there, and I eventually caved and told her why I was so upset.

After letting out my frustrations, Dr. Nuys helps me make sense of the feelings going through my head.

"Tell me what's plaguing you about what he did, then we'll talk about what your brother did to you."

"I feel like Tucker made a decision for me and it led to me walking into Myles's arms," I say, anger laced in my tone.

"That's understandable. So you feel if he hadn't agreed to

that date with Abby, you would've gone out with him and avoided everything with Myles?" she asks.

"Yes," I say confidently.

"I see," she says, putting her notebook down. "So those are the only two options here?"

"I believe so," I answer.

"Have you ever considered a third option?"

I shake my head, confused by her question.

"Listen, Baylee, I can appreciate you seeing life with this scenario of two possibilities here. I see that your mind jumped to this conclusion that had your brother not intervened, your outcome would've been more positive. And yes, maybe it would've been, but there's a possibility it would've been completely different.

"I'd like for you to consider this ripple effect you're talking about. Because as much as I appreciate this two-scenario life you're talking about, I think we're not giving much weight to the fact that life is not two-dimensional and it's not simply about one thing or another; it's multifaceted. So, let's take another route. Let's take a route we haven't thought about and say he had stood up to your brother and not gone out with Abby, but hadn't gone out with you either. And you hadn't met Myles. What if you hadn't gotten to cross paths in this way like you are now. Maybe your road wouldn't begin together until ten, twenty or even thirty years from now. You went on to marry different people even." She leans forward.

"What I'm trying to say is, there aren't simply two possibilities here. It's not just that he could've stood up to your brother, then you and Malloy would've walked off together into the sunset, avoiding this whole thing with Myles. I think it's romantic to believe that would've happened. But honestly, Myles may have been part of your future no matter what. There's no way to know that for sure. But I think what's important is to understand Tucker wasn't ill-intentioned here.

He did this trying to protect his friendship with someone he loves—your brother. Unfortunately, he hurt you in the process."

A tear escapes down my cheek and I quickly move to wipe it. Why am I always crying now?

"I'm scared," I confess.

"Why are you scared, Baylee?" she asks me, concern etched on her face.

"Because with Tucker, I see everything clearly. I see my future. I've never felt more grounded with anyone before; I feel like he will help me be me again. But what if at some point he realizes what a mistake he made choosing me?" I look down at my lap and bite my lip.

"Why would he see you as a mistake?" she asks.

"Because for months, that's all I've heard from Myles and those ugly layers are sort of hard to shed," I admit. "But when I was with Myles, shedding the layers that made me strong was so easy when he said those vile things to me. I'm doing my best to let go of the ugliness that he plastered to me. But man is it hard sometimes, Dr. Nuys. I feel his words crawling on me sometimes when I look in the mirror. And they're so ugly. And when I heard my brother talking outside today, something about it felt like I was walking back in time, for some reason."

"First off, you're still who you were before Myles, Baylee. You're still fundamentally you. He didn't take that away from you. It's just harder to feel that person inside because his words hold a harshness to them that are easier to latch on to," she says. "This might be a hard question to hear me ask, but do you feel like your brother and Myles are similar?" I can see the concern on her face.

"No, I wouldn't say that," I admit. I've never seen similarities between Myles and Danny.

"Alright, that's good. But it seems the way your brother spoke about you today brought up some unwanted feelings.

That's understandable. Then let's talk a little bit about your brother now, that's something I think needs some attention. He isn't someone we've talked much about in our sessions before; tell me more about your dynamic with him."

"My brother never did well with sharing." I laugh, but it lacks humor. "Danny was always more selfish between all of us siblings. I think because he was the only boy, he sort of got away with things. I know I'm the youngest, but him being the only boy, he got doted on. He's spoiled, I hate to say. The older I've gotten, I've seen it more and more." I roll my eyes, embarrassed to admit this about my brother, because for so long I really looked up to him.

"Danny can't come to terms with the fact that I'm an adult." I shrug.

"Many big brothers have a hard time with that fact," Dr. Nuys says.

"Yes, I assume that can be hard for many. But Danny has to also realize that Tucker isn't a bad person. And that we can make decisions on our own. I guess what I don't understand is why he'd make his friend take someone else's ex-wife on a date to keep me from them. It's such a huge extreme, in my opinion. Tucker has never been inappropriate or rude to me or our family, so to push us apart in this way seems completely uncalled for."

"Your feelings are justified, it's a complete invasion of trust," she says in response.

"That's the thing. He's my brother, and someone I've leaned on in so many ways in the past. It feels intrusive and rude." It's hard not to be upset at this behavior from a grown man.

"How do you want to deal with him regarding this?" she asks me.

"Right now? I need space," I admit. "As you know, the pre-trial conference is coming up. I need to stay focused on that. Plus, I would rather smooth things out with Tucker. I'm supposed to be going to Ohio with him for his brother's wedding. I'd like to have something fun on the horizon right now. I feel like my plate is full at the moment. My brother can wait and hopefully think about his actions." Danny needs to simmer on what he's done. He's old enough to know better.

"That's justified. Just remember that he deserves a conversation too, Baylee. You can't just leave him waiting forever." She gives me a look and I smile.

"I won't leave him waiting too long, but he can sweat a bit." I smirk.

"There she is." She smiles as she grabs her glasses and phone. "Let's schedule our next session now before you head out. I want to make sure we have a few sessions before the pre-trial. It's important to meet up before you go back to Connecticut. I think you'll need it more than you expect. I want you to be prepared to face Myles."

Just the thought of seeing his face again brings a sinking feeling to my stomach.

"You're going to do great. I know it feels overwhelming, but hopefully you can have resolution in that pre-trial conference," she says.

"I just hope it doesn't go to trial." I sigh.

"I know. I hope the same for you." She reaches out and grabs my hand.

———

I got back to the apartment and showered. Now I'm listening to music as I go over a few of my notes on my laptop. The distraction isn't as helpful as I hoped, but it's better than the tub of ice cream I considered.

I'm about to close my computer and toss it to the side when I see Tucker walk into view at my doorway, nearly causing my heart to leap out of my chest.

"Fuck, Tucker! You trying to scare me to death?!" I rip the

headphones from my head. "Why must you do that all the time?" For such a large man he's a very quiet walker.

"Sorry, baby." He keeps his distance, his hands in his pockets, apprehension apparent in his expression.

I keep staring at him, waiting to hear what he has to say.

"Can I come in?" he asks.

"Yes." I push my computer to the side, along with my textbook and notes.

Tucker sits at the foot of my bed, keeping a distance between us. I can tell he doesn't know how to approach this situation.

"I, uh, fuck, I'm"—he runs his hands through his beard—"I'm so fucking sorry, Bay. I honestly can't tell you how mad I am at myself for fucking this up." The remorse he holds in his expression is evident, but I'm not going to let him off that easily.

"What exactly are you sorry for?" I ask him.

"I'm sorry I didn't stand up for what I wanted with you when it came to your brother right at the beginning. I should've told him I was developing feelings for you. I was a coward—I know that. I knew it then and I just let him take advantage of our friendship," he explains.

"Why did you do that?" I can't understand why Tucker just let Danny have that power over him.

"Honestly? I was scared," he admits, and I can't help but scoff. "I swear, Baylee. I was really scared. You have to understand this from my point of view. I've only known my life with your brother in it. Aside from my mom and brother, your brother and your entire family have been my constant. I didn't want to risk losing that. What if I tried this thing with you and it failed, and all of you turned your backs on us? And then finding out my mom is sick? I just—" He lets his head fall.

When he looks up at me again, I see unshed tears in his eyes and my heart nearly breaks.

"Baylee, I can't lose you." His voice cracks and I nearly crumble. "Then you called me that night and the realization hit that I almost lost you anyway. I stayed away and that asshole almost took you away from me."

He comes closer to me and he drops his head in my lap. I let the emotion in his words fully absorb because I realize that what Myles did to me has affected each person around me. He didn't just take from me, but he took from all those who love me.

"I'm still here, Tucker. I'm right here." I move my fingers through his hair.

"But because of me and my stupidity, he could've hurt you so much worse. I ignored you; I pushed you away. I was given this new shot with you and I don't want to take it for granted. I want to prove to you that you're everything. I'm sorry I let my fear push this away between us. It wasn't worth it." He looks up at me and those green eyes are full of so much pain and he pulls me in deeper.

"What happened with Myles is not your fault. It wasn't fair to put that on you. I see that now," I tell him.

"I'm sorry, baby, I never meant to hurt you. I thought I was doing you a favor, keeping you away from me. I never thought I was leading you into the arms of a monster." He closes his eyes, savoring my touch.

I continue to move my hands through his hair and there's no point in staying mad at him. I know deep down, despite my anger earlier, I'm layered with love for this man.

I bring my hands to each side of his face and he opens his eyes, our gaze connecting.

"Tucker, you didn't do this to me—he did it to me. He's the monster; not you, not me. This is on him, and it was wrong of me to put this on you. I'm sorry for doing that." I bring my lips to his, softly kissing him.

The minute we touch, he deepens the connection, coercing my lips to open for him. I can't deny him, my body automatically hums with anticipation. His tongue gliding in and his moan spurs me to utter a moan of my own.

"I thought you were going to leave me earlier," he admits, resting his forehead against mine.

"Never," I tell him between kisses.

"Baylee, my days begin with you," he tells me.

"My days set with you," I admit.

His lips come crashing against mine again, this time there's no softness to the connection. He starts to move his lips down my jaw to my neck. He brings his hands up my shirt and realizes I don't have a bra on.

"I love that you don't have a bra on right now," he bites down on my shirt, sending a zap of energy straight down to my pussy.

"Then you'll love what you find under my sleep shorts." I smirk.

"Fuck, Firefly," he moans as he moves his hands further south.

I move my hands below his shirt, touching the taut skin of his abs. I let my fingers trail to his back, and I skim my nails up along his shoulders as he glides his fingers through my wet center.

He pulls his fingers out of my shorts and pulls away to remove his clothing, while I do the same with my pajamas. He's left in his boxers, and I still can't get enough of seeing him like this in front of me. That happy trail has me salivating, and I just want to run my tongue down his sculpted body and watch him squirm.

"I need you naked," I tell him. "Lay on the bed so I can ride you."

"I like you giving me orders." He smirks.

I'm waiting impatiently on the bed in front of him, as he removes his underwear and sheaths himself in a condom, then he lays back on the bed. I'm so wet, I can feel it down my thighs.

"Baylee, come here, baby," he says.

I crawl over to him, but instead of facing him to sit on his cock, I decide to ease down in a reverse cowgirl. He grabs my ass and squeezes as I slowly sit on him.

"Fuck, you are so damn tight," he moans.

"Mmhmm," is all I'm capable of saying. The moment I'm filled to the hilt, I take a minute to get used to his size. The metal ball from the piercing hits a new spot in this position and I know the second I start moving, it's going to feel insanely different.

"Baylee, fuck, you need to move," he tells me. I can hear him controlling his breathing through his nose.

"Hold on, you're not small. I need a minute," I tell him. I need a moment to adjust to his size in this position, feeling incredibly full like this. I'm wholly aware of him everywhere and I'm simply trying to get used to him hitting every single nerve inside me right now.

I finally start to move, and I swear I can feel my orgasm already start to build. Shit, this is intense.

"Fuck, Tucker, you fill me so good," I tell him.

The more I set a rhythm, I swear I become possessed with need. I chase my orgasm in a way I've never done before. I have my hands on his thighs and begin pumping harder and faster. My orgasm comes over me, and I scream his name so loud, I'm convinced the whole neighborhood can hear me.

My body is spent and I doubt I can come again. But then Tucker moves me off him and puts me on my back. He brings my legs onto his shoulders and thrusts inside me. He's so fucking deep, I scream out yet again, arching my back and grabbing onto the sheets at my side. After a few thrusts, I'm already feeling like I'm on the brink of another impending climax.

"Give me another, Baylee." He's clenching his teeth, holding back from letting go. I can see beads of sweat on his forehead.

My breasts are bouncing, and I move my hands onto them to pinch my sensitive nipples. With the way he's thrusting into me at this punishing pace, the headboard is hitting the wall, along with the slapping of our skin and our moans bouncing off the walls is creating a symphony of sound. It's so fucking hot, it doesn't take much more for me to fall off that cliff again.

The moment I orgasm, Tucker's thrusts start to intensify, becoming more erratic. His moans are primal and I won't even lie—it's fucking hot to know I'm pulling these sounds out of him. He's moaning my name and telling me how tight I am, along with how much he can't get enough of my pussy. It's addicting to hear him worship my body like this and I'll never get enough of it.

Once we come down from the high, we're both panting beside each other on the bed.

"That was fucking incredible," I tell him.

"I know. The ladies say I have a magical cock." He winks.

I grab my pillow and throw it at his head as his laughter fills my room.

CHAPTER 21

Tucker

"THINGS ARE GETTING PRETTY serious with little Baylee Rios then?" Eric looks in the mirror at his reflection after the barber trims his beard a bit shorter.

"Please don't refer to her like that. It's creepy man," I say.

He smirks as he looks through the mirror at me. "I love fucking with you. Come on, you didn't think I was just going to let this slide?"

"You're such a dick," I say to him. Then I swing my gaze over to Franko, the barber, and say, "Maybe you should just shave everything off. I bet Brit would love that."

"Don't you dare. She had explicit instructions to keep this nicely trimmed." My brother rubs his ginger beard that looks too similar to mine.

"It doesn't matter, you'll never compare to this handsome specimen," I say as I stand behind him and do my own appraisal in the mirror.

"Fuck off, Tucky," my brother says.

"God, I hate that nickname." I roll my eyes.

"I know, that's why I used it." He laughs as he gets up from the chair and shakes Franko's hand.

We make our way out of the shop and walk to the car

outside. I can't believe Eric's getting married tomorrow. It feels surreal, although he's been wanting to marry Brittany for so long. They met back in undergrad, broke up for a year in the middle but ended up coming back together. My brother took his time proposing, mostly because he wanted it to be the right time with law school taking up most of his time and energy.

He's finally in a place he feels ready to start this phase of life. Now that our mom is sick, he feels like he's on the clock in many ways. Since our chat where he confessed that he felt like she wouldn't be there during the biggest moments in the future, I can't keep those thoughts from creeping into my mind too. I look at him and it's hard not to feel a pang of envy with the realization our mother will be present for him this weekend, whereas I still have so much up in the air. One of the women I love most in my life will likely not be by my side for so many future milestones and it's hard to wrap my mind around that.

I open the passenger door with this heaviness settling in.

"Hey, you okay?" Eric looks over as he starts the car.

"Yeah, just in my head a bit," I say, waiting for the car to warm up. The Ohio cold is starting to hit hard as fall is settling in for the season.

"Is it about mom?" he asks while he turns into traffic.

"Yeah, but she seems good this weekend," I say with a smile on my face.

"She does. I'm glad because she didn't seem too good a few weeks back when I saw her on that video call," he admits.

"Yeah, something about one of the medications she started wreaked havoc on her system."

"That's what she said. I almost flew home. You tell me if you need me. I mean it, Tucker. I'll drop everything," he says.

"I know you will. And I promise, man. You'd be my first call," I assure him.

"How is work going? Things getting easier with Rios?" he asks.

"Yes and no. At work we get through our shifts. We tolerate each other at this point. But the rest of the guys are great. We have a probie that I've gotten to know and he's a cool guy. The rest of the crew is awesome, they've been welcoming." Since moving from Dover, things have been nonstop in Boston, so I haven't really thought about my life at my old station. I barely connect with the old guys from my previous station aside from texting. It's strange how quickly I acclimated to this newfound routine as if it was how I was living all along.

"That's great. And how are things with Baylee? I know I was making fun of it being 'little Baylee' and all…but really, how are things going? Is it serious?" my brother pries.

"I mean, we haven't talked about it like that, but I think it is. The thing is, she's ten years younger than me, so I don't want to assume she's where I am, but yeah, it feels serious for me. She makes me feel grounded. Before her, all those dates I went on felt empty. But with her, she feels real. She feels like someone I can bare my soul to and it matters," I explain.

"Yeah, completely get that," he tells me.

"I thought it would be weird because I've known her since she came home from the hospital. Fuck, even saying that out loud is strange. But it's like that part of her life is separate from what we are now. I don't know how to explain it. But she's this strong, beautiful, confident person, and I feel this immense pride that she's choosing to be around me."

"Man, you should see your face right now." He laughs.

"What?" I look at him.

"You're a fool in love!" He smacks the steering wheel.

"You got that from me complimenting my girlfriend? How'd you figure?" I ask.

"Tucker, you are absolutely, head over heels, in love with that woman."

"Can we change the subject?" I say, looking out the window.

"See, you're shy. You used to do the same thing as a kid. You'd hide whenever you got embarrassed. Well, you'd get embarrassed like that too when you were shitting in your diaper, but I doubt that's what you're doing right now." He roars with laughter.

"I really hate your memory, Eric. Such an asshole," I mumble.

"I love you too, Tucker." He grabs my shoulder. "I love you so much."

I smack his shoulder. "You know I could still edit my speech tomorrow, right?" I remind him.

"I know. I can't wait to hear what you say." I see the twinkle in his eye. "Don't forget, payback's a bitch!" The cackle he utters is evil.

Why are brothers such a pain in the ass?

We get back to the hotel and as we walk through the lobby, I spot Baylee sitting at the hotel bar. I'm about to walk over to her when I see she isn't sitting alone. I notice my mom sitting with her. They're deep in conversation, both smiling, and it warms my heart.

I stand back and watch as they enjoy each other's company. My brother comes to my side after leaving his car with the valet when my soon-to-be sister-in-law comes up to us.

"I'm so glad you're both here." She seems out of breath.

"Brit, what do you think of my beard? Tucker almost made them shave it off," Eric throws me under the bus.

"Dick," I whisper to my brother.

"We'll have words later, Tucky." She smacks my arm.

"What is it with that nickname and everyone smacking me all the time?" I protest.

"Stop being a baby! I need you to help me," she whisper-yells. "I'm down a few helpers and we need to move a few heavy items for the ceremony. Can you guys come help me please?" She puts her hands in a prayer position in front of her face. "Pretty please?"

"As long as you don't call me Tucky again." I point at her.

"Deal!" She smiles and claps.

"I have terms, too," Eric protests.

"Oh, I know your terms." She waggles her brows as she moves closer and kisses him.

"Ew, gross." I scrunch my nose in disgust. "No one cares to hear about that. I have a sensitive stomach."

"Oh, please. I doubt it." He rolls his eyes.

I look over to see my two favorite women still talking to one another, and I decide to leave them be for now. I'll catch up with them later. I follow my brother and Brittany to the spot where the ceremony will be tomorrow, hoping I can catch up with Baylee soon.

———

Alright, I would rather Brittany have called me Tucky for the rest of her life. That was a lot of work, and my back will be killing me tomorrow. I'm wiped. At least I wore comfortable clothes to do manual labor today. I'm not regretting my cotton shirt underneath the jacket I had on. The gray sweatpants worked out with the cool weather, although they ended up being pretty warm in the ballroom as we moved heavy furniture around until Brit was happy with the configuration. Now, I'm walking back through the lobby, but I don't see Baylee anywhere.

I'm about to give up and head back to the room when I spot my mom sitting at the bar, eating a snack and sipping on some water. I decide to sidle up next to her.

"Hey, Ma, how are you?" I lift a hand up to the bartender and ask for a water.

"Hey, son. I see you were pulled in to help set up." She chuckles.

"What gave it away? The look of exhaustion or the sweaty shirt?" I roll my eyes.

"I assume you moved things around a few times?" She winks.

"Don't ask. Brittany seems happy though, that's all that matters." I shrug.

She brings her hand to my cheek. "You're a good brother, Tucker. I'm proud of you."

I can't help but lean into her touch and close my eyes. Savoring these moments has become my new obsession. As much as the doctor has given her years and not months, it doesn't mean I don't log all these memories into a special place in my heart, because I'm starting to understand how meaningful they are. This woman gave me all her best moments and the older I get, the more I realize how impor-tant they are. I won't take them for granted.

"I appreciate that Ma, thanks." I kiss the inside of her palm. "I saw you earlier with Baylee," I mention.

"Oh, yes. Mmhmm." She takes a bite of some fries.

"Is she okay?" I ask, wondering if something happened.

"Of course. That's part of our routine," she says.

"Your routine?" I ask, confused.

"Hasn't she told you?" Now she's the one confused.

"Told me what?" I take a long drink of my water.

"I assumed she would've told you now that you're together. We meet weekly for tea at my house. She's been coming over since I got diagnosed. She didn't have time to see me before this trip. And she wanted to have some time with me before her family arrives for the wedding later today and things get hectic, so we sat together earlier." She smiles. "It's our special time together."

"She's been doing this for months?" I ask.

"Yeah. Sorry, I thought you knew by now," she answers.

"It's no big deal," I wave it off. But it's a huge deal. Baylee took the time to come into Boston for months before we got together. When I ignored her, she still cared enough to spend time with my mother. When I gave her nothing, she still gave everything to someone I love dearly.

"She really loves you, Tucker. You know that, right?" my mother says.

I smile and give a slight nod but can't form words. I need to get upstairs to her. I need to see her. I just want to be with my girl.

"Do you mind if I see you at the rehearsal dinner later?" I ask her.

"Of course. Your brother is coming this way." She moves her head slightly and waves behind me.

I look and Eric is coming up to greet us. I say my good-byes and leave them sitting at the bar as I make my way to my room.

I'm anxious to get to Baylee. Her parents are set to arrive in about an hour from the airport for tomorrow's festivities.

The elevator ride feels like it's taking hours to move up to our floor and I'm tapping my foot in anticipation. Once the doors open, I'm running out to get to our room.

Once inside, I realize the room is quiet, except for the shower running. Baylee must still be getting ready. This can't wait so I make my way into the bathroom.

I move through the suite and open the bathroom door. The steam from the warm shower is fogging the bathroom. She's got the music from her phone flooding the small space and she's humming along.

"Baylee, baby," I call her attention.

"Hey, Tucker," she says, her eyes closed as she rinses the shampoo out of her hair. Her long dark hair is cascading down her back, and my dick is instantly hard behind the fabric of my sweats.

I toss my baseball cap off, along with my shoes and socks.

I discard my clothes as I move toward the shower, anxiously wanting to get closer to my girl. I walk right in and take in the beauty in front of me; I'm ravenous for her. I watch as the water cascades down her beautiful naked body. Her dark eyes watch me, stunned as I stand before her.

"I love you," I tell her.

"What?" She smiles, confirming she heard what I said.

"You heard me. I love you and now I'm going to show you just how much." I walk toward her, pulling her wet body against mine. I grab her wet hair with my left hand so that her gaze is completely on me. With my opposite hand, I cover her collar bone and feel her pulse quicken in anticipation. I crash my lips over hers. My kiss is passionate and frantic as the water beats down over us from above. I'm desperate for her.

Pulling away, I turn her around so that her hands are against the shower tiles, and I spread her legs wide. I take a step back and admire the perfect specimen she is. I take in the firefly tattoo she has on her shoulder, seeing it on full display. Knowing she got a permanent reminder of the nickname I gave her on her body drives me wild every single time I look at it. Starting there, I plant open-mouthed kisses down her back and spine.

Falling to my knees, I bite her ass and then proceed to spread her cheeks to find her folds are wet and ready for me. I slip my tongue through and blow on her swollen lips. The moan she gives as she drops her head against the tile reverberates off the bathroom walls.

"I've missed you all day, baby." I squeeze her ass.

"Tucker, please," she's panting as she answers me.

"What do you want, Firefly?" I want her begging for me.

I continue to goad her by kissing and licking her inner thighs but avoiding the one place she wants my lips. She's writhing and moaning, wanting my face between her legs to put her out of her misery, but I'm loving this game a little too much. Every little sound I'm pulling from Baylee is making my dick harder.

Finally, she's had enough and slides one of her hands through my hair, gripping my red strands. I would say it hurts, but something about this only turns me on even more.

"Tucker, if you don't feast on my pussy right now, I'll kick you out of here and torture you by making you watch me get myself off, and not let you have a taste for the rest of the weekend."

The fire in her eyes pulls a smirk from me. I love seeing her confidence shine through. She lets go and holds her stare for a moment longer until she sees me grab onto her and dive in to feast on her.

The minute my tongue connects on her, she lets out a loud moan and I do the same. Fuck, she's heaven. I flick my tongue, pulling sounds from her that are only heightened by the small space of this bathroom. I add a finger, then a second, and start pumping in a steady rhythm.

I continue to eat her out like she's my last meal, loving the way she pushes herself back against me. The water continues to hit us both, adding to the sensuality of this entire situation. Her tits are bouncing as she's reacting to my mouth on her.

With my fingers coated in her arousal, I use the opportunity to pull them out and she immediately whines at their absence. But it's then I start I move one of my fingers to her puckered hole. At first, I think she's going to stop her movements, but she surprises me, my confident Firefly.

She moans and moves her ass further into my touch, welcoming me more. I slowly push my finger in, while I continue lapping her juices with my tongue. Once I know she can handle it, I add a second finger and coax another moan from her.

"Fuck, I'm coming, Tucker. Oh, my God, yes, right there." Her body starts convulsing harder than ever before. It's intense for her and I hold onto her harder, nibbling on her clit to intensify her climax further, while I continue my movement with my finger.

"Yes, yes, fuck!" she screams in the shower, and I swear whoever shares a wall with us will hear her. It's hotter than hell.

"Oh, shit." She looks back, trying to push her wet strands off her face.

"Baby, it's okay." I look up, her juices coating my beard even with the water falling all over us.

"I squirted on you." She looks down and laughs. "That's never happened to me."

"I'm not mad about it. It's fucking hot." I smile up at her. "I swear it was the hottest thing I've ever seen."

"I can't believe that just happened. Tucker, that was intense," she says, trying to stand on shaky legs.

I grab her by the chin from behind and kiss her lips, still hungry for this woman.

She turns and wraps her arms and legs around me. I can't help but push her against the shower tile. Our kiss turns hungry, and my cock is at her entrance.

"Baby, fuck, I don't have a condom." I lean my forehead against hers.

"I'm on the pill," she pleads. She gyrates her pussy over the sensitive head of my dick and I nearly come from the contact.

"Jesus, Bay, you can't do that, or this party will end before it starts," I tell her.

"Please, just this once. I'm clean," she pants.

"I promise I am too. Are you sure?" I look into her eyes.

"Yes, please. I want this," she pleads. "I love you. I've always loved you, Tucker." She softly kisses me.

"You're it for me, Baylee." I kiss her lips.

I shift slightly and I'm already starting to ease into her. I've never gone bare with anyone and it's a whole other level. The minute my cock is buried deep inside her, I'm seeing stars. I breathe in and out through my nose, trying to compose myself. She's warm and tight, and if I don't focus, I'll be coming in the next sixty seconds.

"Shit, Baylee, this is incredible."

"Tucker, you feel so fucking good. Kiss me."

I do as she asks, I swallow the moan she lets out. She squeezes me tighter with her legs around my middle, and I start to pump into her while pushing her against the shower wall.

I can't even pay attention to the burn in my legs in this position as I continue to fuck her like this, because the way she feels as she tightens around my cock is bliss. I pull away from her lips and bring one of her nipples into my mouth, sucking hard. I can feel the walls of her pussy constricting around me and she's already coming again.

"Right there, Tucker. It's so good," she says as she's arching her back against the wall.

I pop off her breast. "I know, baby, I'm going to come right after you," I tell her.

I feel her tighten around me and the minute she falls off that cliff, I feel my balls contract. That warmth glides down my spine and my thrusts start to become more erratic. I bury my face into her neck, moaning her name and telling her how much I love her, until I feel myself spill ropes of cum into her. It feels endless, until my thrusts slow, and I finally slow my breathing enough to pull away, my eyes sated. I rest my forehead on the cool tile, while she puts her head on my shoulder. She's limp in my arms, after multiple orgasms in a short amount of time.

I pull away and luckily see I didn't leave a mark that will last longer than a few minutes.

"Fuck, that was fantastic." I laugh.

Her hair is wet and stuck to all parts of her face. Her eyes are closed, but her smile is nearly from ear to ear. She simply nods in agreement.

"Baby," I kiss her jaw, "you okay?"

"More than okay," she answers.

"Let's finish showering." I move her directly under the water.

"So you love me, huh?" She giggles.

"Yes, more than anything," I tell her, kissing her shoulder.

She drops little nibbles on my neck and slowly makes her way up to my face until she locks onto my lips. "I love you so much it hurts," she confesses.

Once she pulls away, I look into her eyes, pushing the wet strands of hair off her face and admiring this beauty in front of me—wondering what I did in my lifetime to deserve her as mine.

The way the energy shifts in the shower again, I can't help but tell her, "Baylee, we don't have time for another round."

"But you just told me you love me. That warrants at least two rounds." She waggles her brows.

"Well, we'll have to postpone round two for after dinner." I grab her chin with my thumb and forefinger and give her a chaste kiss.

"Hmm, maybe I'll just have to take care of you real quick, because your monster cock can't go around like that all throughout dinner. I mean, he needs some attention." She looks down and moves her small hand up and down my shaft, causing me to involuntarily shift my hips. Apparently, my dick is already half hard again.

"Baylee..."

But she's already getting on her knees. "I love you, Tucker. Now it's my turn to show you just how much." She opens for me and pulls me all the way down her throat. I've forgotten what my point was as she cups my balls and I'm lost in this woman I love.

CHAPTER 22

Baylee

LOOKING out the window of the plane, I'm lost in the bliss of sitting next to Tucker as we fly home. The wedding was beautiful. His brother and Brittany looked breathtaking as they exchanged vows and their reception was a blast.

We danced the night away and Tucker has some moves I didn't expect. I felt like I was on cloud nine with him. It felt like my heart was being carried away by the only man that has ever known me. I'm fortunate to be able to show him all the pieces of me now that we're together.

"I love you. Have I told you that today?" Tucker kisses my shoulder, pulling me from my thoughts.

I smile, still looking out the oval window of the plane. "Only ten times since we left the hotel room," I tell him as I pull my gaze toward him.

"Oh, well then count that as number eleven." He nuzzles his face into my neck where he proceeds to bite me, eliciting a laugh from me.

"Who knew you were such a sap?" I tease him.

"I know, right? I thought Clay would take the cake on that one. We'll keep this between us, because I have to keep my street cred." He straightens.

"Right. You're really intimidating," I mock.

"Agreed." He pulls his headphones out from his pocket.

"I mean, every strong, powerful man reads smutty books." I jut my chin at the audiobook cued up on his phone.

"I didn't hear you complaining when we tried that thing I read about last night, where I asked you to sit on my face," he whispers in my ear.

My cheeks flame at the thought of last night after we ran back to our room from the reception.

I bite my lip and smile, and he smirks in my direction, then puts his earbuds in his ears, satisfied he made his point.

About ten minutes pass before I feel a tap on my shoulder. I look over to find Tucker pulling an earbud out.

"I've been meaning to ask you something, but the craziness of the wedding distracted me. Why didn't you tell me you were seeing my mom all these months? She told me about your visits."

"Oh, I didn't think it was a big deal. I mean, I like hanging out with your mom." I shrug.

"Yeah, but why not tell me?" he asks, curiosity lacing his tone.

"When I first heard about her diagnosis, I was devastated. I started stopping by right around that time. But you and I weren't speaking and then we reconnected, and I didn't think anything of telling you. I never stopped." I shrug.

"But I was horrible to you, I never responded to your texts"—he runs his hand through his beard, something I notice he does when he's contemplating something—"and you still cared enough to see her. Thank you."

He grabs my hand and brings it to his lips to plant a kiss to it. I can see something deeper is plaguing him.

"What's bothering you, Tucker?" I ask him.

"This weekend things have just felt more real with her," he confesses.

"How so?" I ask.

He keeps my hand in his, playing with my rings. "Like I won't get to have her there when the time comes for my own big milestones in life. When I get married, or have kids in the future, she may not be there. I never put too much weight on that before, but the minute I got to Ohio and started to go through the motions with Eric, it all became so real. Her cancer has no cure. She might get years, but there's no guarantee of decades ahead. That scares me."

Right then I realize how defeated he is by what lies ahead and I'm gutted for him. I unbuckle my seatbelt and shift to sit facing him. I turn his face toward mine, caressing his cheek.

"Tucker, I can't take away your pain. Nothing I say will make this better. But one guarantee I can make is that you aren't in this alone. You have me and I'm not going anywhere. I love you and I'll love you through the pain, no matter when it comes."

His eyes are on me, and he nods slightly, bringing his lips over mine for a light kiss. This weekend brought us closer than I imagined, but it also made me realize this experience with his mom is really breaking his heart, bit by bit. I hope he realizes he's got me and so many more people that will hold him up during this time. His mom is doing well right now and he's got time to build more memories with her.

———

I can't help the nerves as I sit in Sydney and Jada's kitchen, waiting to tell them about Myles. Dr. Nuys told me it was time to get this off my chest with my new friends. Since the attack, I haven't had to tell anyone what happened. Everyone around me knows my story and my new friends only know this version of me, the one who transferred from Connecticut and doesn't talk about her past.

Part of facing what happened is letting people that mean something to me know this side of me. With the pre-trial conference coming up, Dr. Nuys thought this was a good time to explain everything going on before I have to go to Connecticut for a few days.

I don't know the outcome of that conference, but I do know that whatever the outcome, what happened isn't my fault. And I know my new friends won't judge me, still I don't want them to look at me differently; I think that's why I've been hesitant. They've only seen me like so many used to before Myles got his claws into me—confident and free. He took so much of that with him that night and in the months he dated me; I don't want to lose that all over again.

"Baylee, you're scaring us—are you okay?" Jacob asks.

"Um, yeah." I fiddle with the ring on my thumb, biting my bottom lip.

"Oh no, you're pregnant, aren't you?" Jada says, bringing her hand to her mouth. "It's okay, we'll help you. My sister went through this, and she still got through school. She's a nurse now." She nods her head reassuringly.

"No, I'm not pregnant." I look at her. "It's not that."

"Oh, okay. Well, if you were, just know you're not alone."

"Thanks?" It comes out more as a question. "No, I wanted to talk you three about something from my past. I transferred here because I was accepted to the kinesiology program late, like I told you, but the timing was sort of perfect in a multitude of ways. My life in Connecticut crumbled shortly after I found out I got accepted. Actually, it was slowly crumbling for a long time without me realizing it. I never told you all what went on there before I moved back to Boston." I cast my eyes down and my heart is hammering in my chest.

Sydney puts her hands on mine and I look up.

"Baylee, whatever it is, you can tell us." Her comforting gaze feels like a balm on my thundering heart.

I take a breath and let it out calmly. "Before I moved out here, I was dating someone. At first, he was really great. He seemed like someone I could envision being with forever and it soothed my aching heart when I couldn't be with Tucker." I give a sad smile. They know I had a massive crush on Tucker since I was a teen, I confessed that shortly after we started dating.

"But as the months passed, he started to throw hurtful comments my way. His snide comments stung. He'd say things that were demeaning and hurtful in ways that caused me to change the way I dressed, acted, spoke. Pieces of me started to chip away. I hid the real me so that I could appease him."

You could hear a pin drop, the room has gone silent as my friends just listen. So I continue to tell them the way Myles dug his claws into my skin.

"My roommates noticed the changes with time. And when I got the call from Orange University here, I felt like something snapped in me. I knew a change was needed. I called my mentor at the internship and she told me I'd be a fool if I didn't take the opportunity. My roommates agreed and I took the reins of my life again. Well, Myles didn't agree. And instead of telling me how he felt, he showed me with his fist."

Jada and Sydney gasp at my revelation while Jacob whispers "Fuck" under his breath.

I feel the moisture of my tears fall down my cheek as I recount Myles's attack. "Tucker was my first call that night and from there, it's all a blur. Myles was arrested, but his mom is a hotshot attorney in Connecticut. He was out on bail not long after. My pre-trial conference is coming up. I haven't told you, and I'm sorry about that—" I hang my head in shame.

"You don't have anything to apologize for," Sydney says.

"I do, because I feel like you've welcomed me in so willingly and I've closed myself off with this big thing," I tell them. "It's just that I sort of wanted to start over, but I realize now, with the help of my therapist, that I can't. It's a part of me. As much as I don't want it to be." I already feel lighter having told them.

"First, I can't imagine it's been easy, Baylee. Having to uproot your life and adapting to a whole fresh one, with a new school, so late in your academic career, after such a traumatic event. But to carry all that for all these months, I'm so sorry. Just know you don't have to apologize and I guarantee you, we support you. You're our friend and that asshole is a piece of shit for ever making you feel less than perfect. You deserve so much better. I imagine Tucker was beyond livid that night, and continues to be pissed knowing he ever laid a hand on you," Jada says.

"You have no idea." I give a small smile as I pick at a piece of string off my sweater.

"Well, that burly man does seem to care quite a bit for you," Sydney says while wagging her brows at me and fanning herself with her hand.

"Your boyfriend is sitting right next to you," Jacob says to her.

"Yes, yes, I'm well aware." She blows a kiss in his direction and winks.

Sydney and Jacob made it official last week and it's pretty cute to see them transition to romantically dating. The way he melts for her when she walks into the room is pretty epic. I love watching him just fawn over her.

Jada and I laugh as they bicker back and forth, and there's a refreshing lightness in the room after the heaviness I just dropped.

I once again realize I've been blessed by so many incredible people around me. I just wish the one thorn in my side, my brother, would come around. He's the one person I still haven't spoken to and have avoided since I started dating Tucker. I don't want to talk to him because I want to focus on putting everything with Myles behind me first.

It feels like that should be my focus and not Danny's selfishness. I'm the priority and what my brother is doing seems utterly childish. He should be checking on me and making sure I'm managing okay. But instead, he's been standoffish and putting his feelings and needs first.

———

It's November, and I'm packing for my pre-trial conference in Connecticut. I can't keep the nerves from multiplying as I get things in order, knowing I'll have to face Myles in the next forty-eight hours. It's the first time I'll be seeing him since the night he attacked me.

I'm going through my room, grabbing things for my meeting with the prosecutor tomorrow, along with items to wear for the conference. I'll be spending the night with my old roommates, sort of like a girls' night to distract me before my inevitable run-in with my monster ex. Tucker isn't loving the idea of me going without him, but it's what I want to do, and I need to face this part of my life on my own.

Before Myles, I stood on my own two feet without needing a man to conquer things for me. I'd like to tackle this on my own as well. Since the incident, I've been walking on eggshells in many ways. I finally told my new friends about the attack, and now I'll face Myles and put this chapter of my life even more behind me. Dr. Nuys and I have discussed that as much as this door of my life will never fully close, there are pieces of it that I can choose to hold on to as lessons versus fears. I won't allow this attack to hinder me and hold me back from my life. Myles has done enough damage, and I won't let him take my future happiness away too.

We discussed my decision to return to Connecticut on my own at my last therapy session. Dr. Nuys agreed that as long as I had a safe plan to stay with my friends and I felt comfortable doing this, it was a good decision. I have a restraining order against Myles, I don't think he'd be stupid enough to try anything heading into the pre-trial. Tucker put up a fight a few times, however, it's ultimately my decision.

My first stop will be the prosecutor's office, which I've never been to as we have only met via virtual meetings since my attack. Mrs. Lupchick, the prosecutor taking my case, was kind enough to interview me virtually, due to my desire to remain safely in Boston ever since Myles came after me that night.

Now that the pre-trial is upon us, I have to meet with my attorney tomorrow. She's kept me apprised on the case and has gathered evidence and done her interviews throughout the last couple months leading up to this week. I've felt so comfortable with her, and I'm grateful she's never made me feel like because of Myles's mother being a hotshot attorney, I wouldn't be heard. She feels confident we have a solid case and has been diligent about gathering as much evidence as possible. She's really glad I went to the hospital and called the police right away, as that really helps.

"Hey, Bay!" Tucker calls from the living room.

"Yeah, I'm in my room!" I yell as I fold a few more things into my bag. As much as this is *technically* my room, I only use it to keep my clothes in the closet until we can get around to organizing the closet in the main room.

I hear his footsteps down the hall. Once he's at my door, he stops and leans against the doorframe. "Any chance you've changed your mind and want company?"

I look over at him as I continue folding my clothes. "Tucker, we've talked about this. I want to do this on my own. It's important to me."

He walks into the room. Grabbing the items in my hand and tossing them onto my carry-on, he seizes my cheeks, looking into my eyes. "I'm just scared. He almost took you from me. He could've easily taken my world that night. So don't fault me for wanting to hold you closer. I know you want to do this on your own. But while you're trying to stand tall, I'm here wanting to hold you closer because I just figured out what loving you like this feels like."

He catches a tear as it falls down my cheek with his lips and I bring my hands to his wrists.

"I love you. I know you'd be there if I needed you to be. I appreciate it. And I promise you I'll let you know how things are going, step by step. This is just something I have to do on my own. Not because I don't want to do it with you, but because you've shown me I'm strong enough again. He didn't ruin who I am. I'm whole thanks to you, Tucker."

"I love you, Baylee. I know you can do this on your own, you are strong." He kisses me. "And if you feel like he's trying to pull you away from remembering that, you dig deep and hear me saying that from here, alright?"

I nod, the lump in my throat too big to allow words to come through.

"You're taking my truck tomorrow so that he doesn't recognize your car," Tucker tells me.

I've had my car at my parents' house this entire time, in fear Myles would cross state lines and follow me throughout Boston, looking for me once he got out on bail. When I heard the judge didn't put him on house arrest because it was his first offense, I knew keeping my car far from this apartment was the best decision.

"Are you sure?" I ask him.

"Baylee, this is non-negotiable," he tells me. "Now, take a break from packing and come eat. I got us take-out from that Thai place you love down the street."

"Oh, did you get those Pad Thai noodles with the extra spicy sauce on the side?" I clap, jumping up and down.

"Of course, baby. Let's go." He grabs my hand. "Oh, and my friend Hunter is coming over."

"Who?" I look confused.

"Hunter. He's the probie at the station. He doesn't know many people in town and I thought he could come over. He might be a good distraction. Is that okay?" He looks over his shoulder.

"Sure." I shrug.

As if on cue, there's a knock on the door as we walk into the living room.

Tucker opens the door as I start opening the lids of the food containers. My back is to the door, completely lost in the aroma of the food. I'm salivating at the thought of everything in front of me. This is the best distraction before the next forty-eight-hour nightmare of seeing Myles.

"Thanks so much for the invite, man." I assume that's Hunter.

"No problem," Tucker greets his friend. "Come in, the food's here. I want to introduce you to my girlfriend, Baylee."

I hear footsteps approach behind me.

I turn around and I drop the lid to one of the Thai containers.

OH. MY. FUCKING. GOD.

"You're the probie? I FUCKING LOVE YOU!"

"Jesus." Tucker throws his head back. "Are you fucking serious?"

Hunter, better yet—@huntsamillion as I know him, is absolutely gorgeous and he's standing right in front of me. His megawatt smile is even prettier when it's directed at me, and his dimples are so damn cute in person. I'm blushing, I can feel it.

"Baylee!" Tucker throws his arms out.

"I'm sorry, did I say that out loud?" I cover my mouth, even though I'm smiling behind my hands.

Hunter throws his head back and laughs. Oh my gosh, even his laugh is hot. Then he extends his hand out toward me. "Hi, I'm Tyler Hunter. It's nice to meet you. Thank you for having me over."

"Don't thank her, man! I invited you! Fucking traitors," Tucker protests.

"You are *so* welcome for the invite." I push his hand away and go in for a hug, savoring his toned body and I even breathe him in. I, Baylee Rios, am hugging Tyler Hunter. My friends are going to fucking freak.

"Baylee, baby, may I remind you that your boyfriend is standing right here." Tucker towers over us.

I pull away from Hunter. "Yes, baby, I haven't forgotten. But it's *Tyler Hunter*." I gesture. "He's famous!"

"Uh huh." Tucker crosses his arms over his chest looking less than amused. "I'm regretting this decision more and more by the second."

"It's fine, Tucky," I tell him with a wink.

"Bay, what have I said about that nickname?" he says with clenched teeth. "Now it will get back to Riv and you know that one won't let up."

"I won't say a word. I promise." Hunter gestures his hands as if he's zipping his lips and throwing away the key.

"See, he's not going to say a word." I point at Hunter. "You're the sweetest, by the way." I look over at Hunter.

"Should I give you two a moment?" Tucker says, annoyed.

"Do you mind? That would be great," I tease.

"I guess it's not as funny when it's your girlfriend doing the fawning, is it man?" Hunter taunts and I can see Tucker is rethinking this whole plan of having him over tonight.

When Tucker nearly growls, I move toward him and reach my hand up until he brings his face down so I can capture his lips. Then I whisper, "I only have eyes for you, Tucker. Always. That will never change. Even if you only have a hundred followers." I joke and smack his ass.

That pulls a laugh from Hunter and we move on to grab plates then proceed to eat our dinner. The lightness of the night helps alleviate the nerves I was focused on before, and I fall in love with Tucker even more for helping me forget all the heaviness I was carrying.

CHAPTER 23

Baylee

I MADE it to Connecticut earlier today and nervously had my meeting with my prosecutor a few hours ago. Going through the case, especially walking through the details of everything, felt nauseating. I'm glad she went through it though, because tomorrow won't be any easier. Seeing those photos of me immediately following the attack was brutal, but I think it was better to see them ahead of tomorrow.

It's amazing what our brain will do to preserve itself to help us cope from tragedy. In order to survive a hard time, I have felt like I remember the severity of that night in such a different way. Now that I see how much damage he caused me physically, I see just how significant this is and how devastating this will be if I don't ensure Myles serves time for what he did.

It makes me sick to think he could do this again. The moment I left Mrs. Lupchick's office—or should I say Fiona because she kept insisting I call her by her first name—I'm more determined to see Myles learn his lesson. No aggressor should walk away unscathed from something like this. He deserves to serve time. And Baylee Rios is no doormat.

I called Tucker right after my meeting with Fiona to tell

him how it went, and he was proud of me for that first step. I couldn't help the tears I shed. But I took a deep breath and told him I won't let that deter me tomorrow. I'm determined to see this through. I'll look Myles in the eyes in the morning and show him he didn't tear me down.

Now, I'm sitting in my old apartment with my girlfriends having a girls' night. This moment feels bittersweet because so much of this feels like my old life, like I've never left. Pieces of this are so comfortable to me, but I also don't want to go backward because I've gained so much from the life I'm living in Boston. I know the three of them will always be in my life in some way.

"Alright, so we got the update from the prosecutor, but what's the fun update you had for us?"

They already know everything between Tucker and I, but I told them I had something fun to tell them. However, I kept my text vague as to what it was.

"Well, last night, I met someone you might be interested in hearing about," I pull out my phone and open my Photos app.

"Oh my gosh," Brianna squeals. "Is it someone on the baseball team. Aren't you friends with the Gael's CEO or something?"

"Um, yeah, sort of. We're not that close yet, but she's really awesome. Maybe I can swing a baseball player meet and greet your way. But no, that's not the surprise," I say as I pull up the photo I want to show them.

I swing my phone to face them and all three gape at the picture in question. It's one of Hunter and I from last night, smiling from ear to ear, mostly at Tucker who is hidden on the other side of the screen scowling at us. My friends do a double take, their eyes nearly bug out of their heads.

"No. Fucking. Way!" Mandy yells. "When? Where? How?"

Alexis takes my phone from me and pinches the photo to

inspect it, probably wondering if it's photoshopped. "Tell me how this happened right this very minute!"

"Turns out he moved to Boston and…" I take a dramatic pause, "he joined Tucker's firehouse."

The three of them scream.

"That's fucking bananas!" Brianna gasps.

"What are the chances?" Alexis yells.

"That's it! I'm moving!" Mandy declares.

I'm laughing as the three of them lose their shit.

The rest of the night continues with the four of us going back and forth laughing, exchanging stories and simply soaking up time together. They never found a replacement roommate, so I sleep in my old room, and it feels like old times, but something is missing. I don't feel like the same Baylee that used to sleep here.

I've been chasing the old Baylee, hoping she'll return, but I think that version of myself will never quite come back to me. As much as I've been looking for her to re-emerge, a new version has erupted from the darkness. This Baylee is stronger and more equipped for what's ahead.

As I try to fall asleep, I close my eyes, picturing the ugly monster that lies ahead in the morning. But his clear blue eyes don't bring on the same terrors they once did. I'm no longer absorbing his words and believing I'm weak inside. Tomorrow, I get the opportunity to show him exactly who he tried to knock down and how I rose up despite his efforts.

***

"Remember what we discussed yesterday," Fiona whispers my way.

I nod as I sit next to her. I look up at the clock and realize we still have thirty minutes before everything begins. I'm antsy and need to move around.

"Do you think I can run to the restroom?" I look at her.

"Of course. You doing okay?" She looks at me, concerned.

"Yes. I just downed a ton of water this morning," I tell her.

I was so nervous I drank way too much water in fear I would be dehydrated. I may have overdone it. I internally roll my eyes. Myles's team still hasn't arrived, so I know I have some time.

I move through the courtroom and walk into the hall. Luckily the restroom is close by, and I push through to the door to the women's bathroom.

Once inside, I find an open stall. The courthouse is quiet and there's not much foot traffic throughout.

I'm washing my hands when I hear the door open. I'm not looking up, nor paying much attention to anything around me, when I feel a presence behind me. It isn't until I realize the body is much too close to my personal space that my hackles rise, and I look in the mirror to see those cold blue eyes staring back at me.

I say nothing as I hold his gaze, and it's in that moment I take note how different we are, as if we're complete opposites. His lightness in contrast with my darker features. His ice blue eyes to my almost black ones, along with his lighter hair to my raven locks. But inside, he holds all the darkness, while I hold all my light around me.

"Move," I demand.

He stands firm where he is. He wouldn't dare do anything mere feet away from the courtroom where he's being tried for assaulting me, would he? But his entitled ass might actually be living in an absolute fantasy, I guess.

"Should I say it louder?" I say with clenched teeth.

He steps away, his nostrils flaring.

I keep my eyes on him as I grab a paper towel. I won't fucking dare give him my back because he's fucking hostile.

When I make my way to the door he has the audacity to move closer to me, but not close enough to touch me. I feel my heart pounding in my ears, but I tame my breathing enough so he doesn't sense my fear.

"You fucking ruined my life," he spits in my direction. "I should've known a whore like you would fuck everything up. I was left here while you were away living your best life, and I now have to pay for your little sad story that you told the police."

"The only person who ruined your life is you, Myles. And—wait, how do you know anything about my life?" I ask him, realization dawning on me that he knows more about me than I'd like.

I look over at him, realizing that day when I felt like I was being watched was more than a feeling. Was he there?

"Oh, you connecting the dots? Yeah, I watched you, sweetheart." He sneers. *God, he's vile.* "You're a fucking temptress. I saw you walking on campus and guys just watched you pass by in your tight clothes, because you just ask to be looked at. You're a disgusting slut."

I tamp down the bile that threatens to come up. How did I ever find this person attractive? I let him put his hands on me. I let him touch me in the name of love... or what I thought was love.

"Look over there." I jut my chin toward the mirror. "You see that person right there?" I move a step back so it's only his reflection he sees. "He's no man. That right there is a person that's a sad excuse for a man. I'm sorry I ever let your fingers touch my skin because I was always too good for you. But today I'm not just standing up for myself against you; I'm standing up for all the people you could ever raise your hand to in the future. You need help, Myles."

He pulls his gaze away from the mirror and moves toward me, and I get the feeling he's going to do something physical to me. I stand there and continue, "Ah ah, I wouldn't think of doing anything. Mommy can't dig you out of an even deeper hole. Better keep your hands to yourself."

With that, I walk out of the restroom, a satisfied smile gracing my lips. Serves him right for thinking he can continue to try to intimidate me right before this pre-trial. But he knows the evidence we have will push this case even further. He knows his fate and he just needed to knock me down a few pegs to help his ego before *I* knock him down.

Once I reach Fiona, I sit down and she sees me smiling.

"Everything okay?" she asks, confusion in her tone.

"Yep. Myles followed me into the restroom and used a few toxic words to intimidate me. I didn't fall for it," I tell her, smoothing out my skirt.

She looks behind me and sees Myles walking into the courtroom, his complexion a few shades lighter than he was when he first walked into the ladies' room.

"Serves him right," I continue.

"I bet it does." She smiles.

———

I feel lighter walking into the apartment tonight. Today was draining, yet absolutely freeing in so many ways. Facing that courtroom was something I needed to do on my own, but getting home to Tucker is also a need of mine and I'm itching to feel his warmth underneath my fingertips.

The moment I open the door, I expect to see him waiting for me on the other side, but instead I'm met by not only Tucker, but my parents, my brother, my sisters, and Carolyn.

I can't hold back the surprise on my face. I think Tucker senses it when I look over at him.

I'm immediately pulled into a hug by my mom, followed by my dad and each of my siblings. It's a weeknight, so I assume my nieces and nephews stayed back as they had sports and after-school activities. My brothers-in-law must have taken them to those commitments. Danny remains cold toward me and Tucker, but I appreciate him coming despite what's transpired between us. I look over to find him standing further back than the rest of the family.

Once Tucker reaches me he whispers, "I couldn't help it, they just showed up. I texted but I assume you didn't see it as you were on 'Do Not Disturb.' Sorry, baby."

He moves to kiss my cheek and I bring my fingers to lace with his. I can't help but notice my brother's eyes swing to our connection then quickly look away. I see his jaw clench. It's hard to suppress my eye roll.

Carolyn comes toward me and pulls me into an embrace. "I'm so glad today went as well as it did. You deserve justice for what he did to you, Baylee."

Justice was indeed served. Myles received the maximum sentence for what he did, at least for a first-time offender. Obviously, I wish he could stay in a jail cell forever, but I think anyone that went through any type of violent act would want the same. In Myles's case, he'll serve a year in jail. Turns out, the case against him was my word against his for a while, until Fiona started gathering evidence a few months back. She came across my neighbor's doorbell camera, which caught a few images of Myles from the open doorway into my apartment that night.

The sound is choppy and, at first, I was worried his lawyers were going to argue it could've been anyone yelling at me. The video shows the assailant hitting me and the image of me getting knocked out. Had Myles decided to walk in the other direction, the evidence wouldn't have been as solid. But as luck would have it, Myles parked his car in the direction where he had to walk directly past the camera. His outfit matches that of the person attacking me and the evidence was damning for him.

He plead guilty. To add to this, Fiona jumped on the fact that Myles followed me into the bathroom right before the pre-trial conference, since there are cameras all over the courthouse. The judge would've probably been more lenient on his sentence, but she decided to hold firm on her decision. His attorneys, along with his mother chiming in, didn't want this to go on further to a long trial. So, he took the deal, and he's now going to be behind bars.

He will also be required to seek counseling and I do hope he can recognize his behavior is not something he can continue. Either way, I stood up for myself and hopefully put a stop to him hurting someone else in the future.

"Thanks, everyone, for being here. It's been a long day, but I'm really glad he's being punished for what he did," I say.

"We just wanted to see you and tell you how proud we are of you," my oldest sister, Ariana, tells me.

"Listen, I wasn't going to stay long, I have some plans, but wanted to say I'm glad that bastard is where he should be," my brother announces.

Before anyone can protest, he's already saying his good-byes. He's out the door without much more than a simple nod my way. I guess he's going to hold a grudge, and I honestly don't feel like figuring all that out right now. He needs to work his shit out. I'm not going to let that bring me down today.

My dad shakes his head and I can see the disappointment across his face. I give him a smile and a simple shake of the head to let him know it's not worth it right now.

"Should we order a pizza or something?" I ask the rest of our family.

"Actually, we aren't here to take up much of your time. We just wanted to swing by and give our congratulations," my mom says. "Your dad, Carolyn, and I have a night out to the movies planned!" She claps her hands.

"Yes, I'm dreaming of a big tub of popcorn." Carolyn looks excited.

Tucker smiles at his mom. "That sounds fun. Anything good out right now?"

"*Dirty Dancing*," my dad groans.

"Isn't that old?" I ask, confused.

"My point exactly!" My dad throws his arms out. "Thank you, Baylee! She gets it!"

Both Carolyn and my mom look at me like I'm a traitor.

My mom chimes in, "Baylee, for your information, *Dirty Dancing* is a classic and they're doing a special tonight where they're releasing it in theaters for forty-eight hours. So, Carolyn and I are going to see it. Your dad heard about it and wanted to join. So don't act like you didn't want to go, Thomas!" She points at my dad.

"You know Mr. Rios has a bad case of FOMO," Tucker whispers.

"Excuse me, I do not have whatever you just said. I'm healthy. I just had a physical," my dad retorts.

"FOMO is 'Fear of Missing Out,' Dad." I roll my eyes.

"Oh, yes, I do have that. But I just want the candy. I love Hot Tamales," he states matter-of-factly.

"You can't have those. The doctor just said your blood sugar was a little high," my mom throws to him.

"Then why am I going?" he pokes back.

"Oh my gosh, this is exhausting," Hannah, the third Rios sister says, pulling at Ariana's arm. "Drive me home. My own children don't bicker this much."

"I think it's comical." Sierra, my middle sister, snickers, as if this is the most entertaining thing.

"Alright. We're off," Ariana says as the three of them start hugging me goodbye. "Mom, Dad, see you later. Have fun and good luck, Carolyn. Tucker, it's good to see you and love seeing you with my sister." Ariana waggles her eyebrows at me. *Gross.* In front of our dad, nonetheless.

Tucker laughs and my cheeks flame. Awesome, this is how gatherings will be from now on.

Carolyn looks down at her watch and claps her hands. "Okay, we have to go. I need to prep with my pre-movie snacks. Let's go!"

"Thomas, no whining or you're getting a ride home from our girls and not hanging out with us. We're going to this movie with or without you," my mom declares.

"Fine, I'll go," he says as they begin to say their goodbyes and head out the door.

Once everyone has left, it's just the two of us and Tucker leans against the front door, his eyes bulging.

"What just happened?" he asks.

"They're all nuts and we're the normal ones," I declare.

"Agreed," he says.

"Can we start this over and I walk in and you maul me?" I smile sweetly.

"I like that plan better." He pushes off the door and grabs my face with his hands and kisses me hard.

We end up skipping dinner and going straight to dessert. And by dessert, I mean he gives me three orgasms—two in bed and one in the shower.

CHAPTER 24

Tucker

THE RELIEF I feel now that Baylee can start to live a life without that monster walking the streets is freeing. I was livid when she told me he watched her on campus at least once. Add that to the fact he followed her into the bathroom at the courthouse, I can feel my blood boiling.

It's been a few days since she returned from Connecticut and we're having our gathering at Clay and Abby's tonight for the season finale of *Love and Lost*. Unfortunately, I lost the battle of hosting. To no one's surprise, I'm fully invested as everyone predicted; I could do without Baylee's smug smile as we walk into Clay's apartment.

"What's the rush, Malloy?" Clay says as he moves out of my way so I can get inside.

"It's going to start," I say, making my way to the kitchen to set down the bags of chips and dip we brought.

"If I have to hear about how slow my legs are one more time, I'm going to lose it," Baylee says behind me.

"Bay, I told you, it's tradition—we have to be in our seats and ready by the time the show starts. We talk shit from the first scene to the last." I walk over to her and kiss her cheek.

"What's the appeal of this show?" she asks.

"It's addictive. What more could you need?" Kennedy answers for me as she picks her spot on the couch and throws a blanket over her legs.

"I'm excited, even though I've barely watched this season," Samara says. "I will say it looks like a hot mess. I did watch that episode they brought the drama by bringing ex-girlfriends into the mix and things got ugly."

"Sam, that's the whole point," Kennedy points out.

"What do you want from me? My life is chaotic enough as is. I have twins. I live in a state of constant drama." She gives her best friend a pointed stare.

Samara is a close friend of Kennedy and Abby's, but I've gotten to know her more throughout the last year. She's married to Ashton. They are parents to nearly-one-year-old boy-girl twins. Her husband stayed home so she could have a night off and she's loving life right now with the break here.

Abby comes out of the hallway with Ella in her arms; the baby is babbling and flapping her arms. She looks bigger than the last time I saw her, and she's got the cutest little dimples.

"Who's the prettiest baby?" I say as I bring my arms out to take her from Abby.

She lets me take her and I pull her close as she snuggles her sweet face into my chest. I know how much she loves when I put her up high and pretend she's an airplane. She giggles and smiles as I glide her through the air.

Once I bring her back to my chest, I blow raspberries to her cheek and she squeals in delight, probably from the tickle of my beard against her skin.

"Malloy, it's starting!" Abs grabs my attention and I move over to the couch with Ella in my arms.

Once we're on the couch, I make sure the baby is comfortable with me. I start explaining who everyone is on the screen and she's just as captivated as I am.

"Oh, Ella, you see, Trina has to be the one that gets picked or we're going to be so upset," I say as I pop a popcorn kernel into my mouth. She's more enthralled by the food than the people on the screen. She keeps trying to grab the bucket of snacks, but Abby is pushing toys in hopes they're more exciting. Sadly, it's not working.

"Here, baby girl, try this toy." Abby hands her a teether that finally does the trick.

"Oh, I think this is the one he's going to pick," Kennedy announces, pointing at the TV screen.

"You think Lonni's going to get picked over Trina? No way!" I declare.

"Remind me what's happening with this guy to the right?" Samara asks. She's completely lost.

"Bullshit, Malloy," Kennedy fires back.

"Twenty bucks, I'm right." I pull my wallet out and throw cash on the table.

"You're on." Kennedy does the same.

"I still don't get this show," Clay says from the kitchen.

"None of this makes sense. It's dumb," Baylee finally says.

"Shhh," the four of us say from the couch.

"Your negativity isn't welcome here," Abby says over her shoulder.

"Such a touchy group." Clay laughs, and Baylee joins as they continue their little party of two in the kitchen.

I smile because it's comical how serious we are about our reality television. I love it even more that Baylee has blended into my friend group so seamlessly.

We're missing Marissa and River tonight, who I consider to be the crazier ones in our unit. River is running errands with his mom and Marissa has to work on a case. She's a hotshot attorney in Los Angeles and this new case is taking up a ton of her time.

The night continues on and the finale is sort of lackluster if I'm being honest.

I get up and stretch. "I hate to admit it, but that was beyond lame," I announce to the group.

"I know! This finale was missing something," Kennedy says. "I can't believe he chose Trina." She's just pouting because I won the bet.

"Don't be a sore loser," I tell her.

"Don't be a dick," she shoots back.

Clay's phone chimes. "Hey, Malloy, you think you could run over to my mom's with me? River needs help moving some furniture. It's late but she's expecting that new couch early tomorrow and she needs help beforehand."

I look over at Baylee.

"Yeah, go ahead. I can catch a ride home," she says.

"You can hang out with us a bit," Abby says, pointing at Kennedy and Samara. "These two are staying here until River's done and we were going to open a bottle of wine and hang out. This one"—she holds out a sleeping Ella in her arms—"will be going in her crib."

"You sure?" Baylee asks.

"Of course. You're one of us now." Kennedy winks.

"You sure you don't mind if I head over there and come back over when I'm done?" I ask her, bending down to whisper into her ear.

"Yes, I think I can survive apart from you for a little while," she says.

I pull back and look into her eyes. "I promise to make it up to you," I say quietly as I push the stray hair away from her face. I lean in again and whisper into her ear so only she can hear me, "Maybe between your legs." I bite her earlobe for extra effect and hear her intake of breath.

I chuckle as I pull away.

"Oh my gosh, go already," Abby says, rolling her eyes. "I can only imagine what you're whispering to her."

"Don't be jealous that you and Clay aren't in the early stages anymore." I stick my tongue out at her.

"She isn't jealous, asshole." Clay moves toward his fiancée

and kisses her. "Love you, baby," he says as we head out the door.

Once we leave the apartment, we head to the car and Clay is giving me a look that makes me uncomfortable. Finally, I can't take it anymore and break the silence.

"What, man?" I say as we descend in the elevator.

"You really love her, don't you?" he asks me.

"Yes," I say as I pull my phone out.

"I mean, you see forever with her," he says as a statement and not a question.

"Yeah, I would say so," I say confidently.

"Wow, that's big. I mean, she's young," he says as the doors open and we walk out.

"She is," I admit.

"What does she think?" he asks me, looking over at me.

"We haven't had a conversation about the future really."

"Don't you think you should?" he asks me, surprise etching his features.

"Well, it's not like I'm asking her to have my babies."

"Okay, sure, but don't you want to know where she stands? Isn't she like a decade younger than you?" he asks as he opens his driver door.

Once we're both in the car and buckled, he starts driving and continues the conversation.

"Yeah, she's twenty-two... almost twenty-three, actually. I'm thirty-two. But age is just a number at this point, no?"

"Hey, I'm not judging. I promise. I'm just talking this through with you."

"I know, man. I just don't know what to say. I mean, I can't help who I fall in love with. It's not like I've looked at her since she was younger and saw this happening. It just happened in the last year, I can't stop it now," I admit.

"I know, but I think it warrants a discussion. She's the age she is and has a career to build. You're at a different point in life. So, what if she wants to wait ten years to get married, then what? You wait until you're in your forties to get married? Then you're in your mid-forties to have kids? I'm just asking the questions."

I sit back and allow his words to sink in. They're valid and it's not like I haven't considered these things, but I've simply allowed her love be enough for me. Whatever comes with that, I'll accept. I just want Baylee. Whatever I get in return, I'll take.

"Honestly, man, I love her. She's the reward, and the gifts I get with her love are just extra little bonuses that I'll take along the way," I say, a small smile taking over my features.

"I like that. Little bonuses. I might have to steal that, man." He chuckles.

"No, don't. I sort of like it. I'll have to use it on a card, or something." I laugh.

He smiles and turns on the radio. I meant everything I said, because I feel peace with Baylee in my life. She brings me all the best parts of life I never thought I needed to make me whole. So, whatever she wants to bring me to add color to the already vibrant life I see with her, I'll accept.

———

Baylee

"So, we're dying to know… how are things with Malloy?" Abby asks.

I sip my wine and smile. "They're really good. Tucker is perfect." I can't help the flutter in my chest over how much joy I feel that he's really mine in this way.

"What she really means is how's the sex? Let's be real, he looks like a beast," Kennedy says, and I nearly spit my wine out.

"Kennedy!" Abby looks over at her friend. Then she swings her gaze to me. "That's not what I meant at all!"

"Don't mind, Kennedy. She has no filter," Samara says, "she's just like that."

"I won't apologize for asking the question no one else will," Kennedy says.

"Actually, I would totally ask that question," Marissa says through the phone.

I look down, having completely forgotten she called in shortly after the guys left. She was bummed to have missed the show.

"Hi, Baylee, I know you don't know me well, but I have no problem asking that question," Marissa clarifies.

"It's true. She's super invasive," Abby confirms.

I look over at Samara. "Don't look at me. I barely know you, I wouldn't ask you. I couldn't even confront my aunt about a dick purse at my wedding."

"Huh?" I look at Kennedy. Now I'm really lost.

"It's a long story. We don't have time for that right now. Let's stay focused." She grabs my hands. "Baylee, I adore my fiancé, alright? But let's be real. Your boyfriend—he's gigantic. Like he should be living in a forest with an ax or something. He must be proportional, no?"

My cheeks flame.

Kennedy stands from her seat and points at me. "She's blushing, Marissa," Kennedy squeals.

"I fucking knew it!" Marissa screams through the line.

"You two are so bad. Leave her alone," Abby says. "You don't need to tell them anything." Then leans in. "Even though you are super red." She winks and that only intensifies the heat I'm feeling on my face.

If only they knew it's not just the size I'm reacting to, but the damn piercing. I bet they have no idea he's hiding that damn jewelry on his anaconda. I mean, no one flaunts that kind of shit on their dick. It's so hot though.

Did someone turn on the heat in here?

"Okay, fine, don't answer the question about how well-endowed he is," Kennedy says, "because River wouldn't appreciate that. But how's the sex?"

"I'm so glad I missed the show and called for this part of the night," Marissa says.

"You know I'm right here, right?" we hear Marissa's girlfriend yell in the background.

"Yes, Josie, I love you!" she says. "Malloy is a big teddy bear. I just need to know if he cries after sex or something weird."

I laugh, because I honestly can't wait to meet Marissa in person.

"No, he doesn't cry after sex. Gross!" I scrunch my nose. "I could never. Have you had sex with someone who cried after sex?" I look at everyone at the table.

"Well, no, but I had one guy scream 'touchdown!' and it was not a touchdown for me, if you catch my drift," Kennedy says as she takes a big gulp of wine.

"That's sad." Abby pats her friend's hand.

"I mean, it was a long while ago, but I had sex with a guy in high school and he was like a jackrabbit, but that might be normal in high school," Samara shrugs.

"I mean, I'm not attracted to guys, but I don't think you should ever think that's normal, babe," she says through the phone.

"I second that sentiment," Josie yells from afar.

We all laugh and nod our agreement.

"Oh, then I guess that's my horror story." Samara laughs.

"Um, I appreciate you bringing me in even though I'm so much younger." I look around.

"Hey, none of that." Abby winks.

"Hold on, how young is young?" Marissa asks.

"I'll be twenty-three pretty soon," I tell her.

"Oh, please," she laughs, "I live in LA, Baylee. That's nothing. Josie is twenty-five."

"I'm twenty-six!" Josie declares.

"Fuck, I'm an asshole," Marissa whispers.

"You're the worst," Abby tells her.

"She loves me," Marissa tells us, "just like you do, Abby."

"Surprisingly, I do," Abby says sarcastically.

"Honestly though, I do appreciate having you all to hang out with. My friend group is small after everything with Myles," I admit.

"You mean that asshole in Connecticut? May he rot in Hell," Marissa says.

Everyone here knows what happened. I know Tucker needed his friends to lean on and I'm glad he had so many important people around him to help navigate his feelings as he struggled. I know he had a hard time seeing me hurt, even if I thought he wasn't suffering.

"Yeah, well, I appreciate all of you here with me. I'm readjusting to living in Boston, and I like being back." I smile at those sitting at the table with me, even though Marissa can't see me through the phone.

"Sometimes it's in the time of darkness that we find our clarity. I'm sorry yours was full of pain as well. But it led you to us and we're grateful you're here now." Abby grabs my hands and the rest of them put their hands on hers.

I try hard and fail to hold back the tears that form in my eyes. When I look up, I see them looking at me with the same tears in their eyes. I'm lucky for the crew I'm slowly building in my time here. I have my girls back in Connecticut, but here in Boston, I'm building a new group and it's beginning to stitch my heart back together.

CHAPTER 25

Baylee

"I **LEFT** instructions on how to thaw the breastmilk here." Abby shows Tucker and I the written-up instructions on the counter. "I also have a list of phone numbers on the fridge if you have an emergency, aside from our own numbers, of course. Clay and River's mom is out of town visiting her friend in New York this weekend."

We move around the apartment while Abby shows us some of Ella's favorite things. We're watching the baby and Lola while she, Clay, River and Kennedy go out on a double date tonight. We're excited we could step in and give them a night out.

"Abby, you're hogging their attention. I need to give them explicit Lola instructions," River whines.

"Riv, you can't be serious." Clay looks over at his twin while bouncing Ella on his knee.

"Dude, Lola has a very specific bedtime routine when she's with new people," River explains, while Kennedy rolls her eyes from the couch. Meanwhile, Lola is glued to Tucker's side.

"Why the hell is my dog obsessed with you right now, Malloy?" River looks disgusted by this.

"Beats me." He scratches behind the golden retriever's ear, and she leans into his leg even more. "But I don't mind the love."

"Well, I fucking do." River comes over and puts his face right in front of his dog. "Lola baby, Daddy will be back so soon and bring you back home, okay?" Then he proceeds to kiss her and hug her.

I don't know River very well, but he's definitely obsessed with his dog.

"Malloy, Baylee, she should be good after her next bottle in about an hour or so. Once she has that, just read a book. I left one out. It has the animals with the textures on the page. She loves touching those as you read. She had her bath already and the white-noise machine is on. Just make sure you put on a fresh diaper before bed and the jammies that I laid out. You know how to turn on the baby monitor?" She looks at us.

"Yes, Abs, I can turn on a baby monitor," Tucker answers her.

"Great." She nods at us, then turns to River. "Okay, the floor is yours."

"Finally!" He rolls his eyes as he stands and turns his attention to us. I assume he's going to explain something, but I should've known it would be over-the-top for River.

He reaches behind him and pulls out a typed-up paper. I should amend that statement. It's front *and back*, typed.

"Alright, my Lola—" he starts when he's interrupted by Kennedy clearing her throat. "So sorry, *our* Lola is precious and has needs that must be met."

"You're kidding me with this, right Riv?" Tucker says as he grabs the paper and starts scanning it.

"I'm not kidding. She's very precious," he says.

Tucker looks over at Abby. "You're going to dinner, not leaving the country, right?"

"River, what did you do?" Kennedy makes her way over.

"He typed a fucking thesis." Tucker holds the paper above River's head.

Kennedy laughs. "I thought you were kidding."

"Absolutely not." He looks shocked she would suggest such a thing.

"We aren't doing any of this. Now go, before Baylee and I decide we're going on a date and you guys are shit out of luck," Tucker says.

"At least look it over, man," River says.

"Sure, whatever you say." Tucker starts folding it and putting it in his pocket.

Clay laughs as he kisses his daughter, and Abby says her goodbyes as well. Then he hands me Ella.

Soon they're waving and closing the front door and we're alone with a baby and a dog, and I look over at Tucker. "You really going to look over that list?"

"You kidding me? Absolutely not." He scoffs. "He's so fucking crazy."

"Why is Lola obsessed with you tonight? She *is* following you everywhere," I comment as I notice she hasn't left his side since we arrived.

"Oh, I stuck a bag of bacon in my pocket to screw with River." He laughs.

That makes me start laughing and then Ella joins in and she grabs my cheeks with her chubby hands. She looks at me with those cute dimples popping out and her beautiful blue eyes. She's absolutely stunning and it's hard not to imagine what my babies will one day look like. That day being far down the line, when I have my life in order, but one day nonetheless.

"What should we do, pretty girl? Should we sit on the play mat?" I ask her as I bounce in place. She giggles and I take her over to her little play area in the living room.

Tucker joins us and we lay down as she starts playing

with the objects in front of her, kicking her feet and babbling with joy.

"I love hearing her sounds," Tucker confesses.

"I know. There really isn't anything better," I say.

"I don't know if I've ever heard her cry. She's one of the happiest babies."

"Remember when my sister's baby cried for, like, three hours straight for her first Thanksgiving?" I cringe.

He drops his head into his hands. "Oh, gosh. Don't remind me. I think I lost my hearing for two days straight. I remember walking my mom home and asking if all babies came like that."

"I think I used that memory to keep from having sex with my first boyfriend because I was scared." I laugh.

"Dude, she had some lungs on her." His eyes go wide. "Now she's all shy. So weird."

"I know. Nothing makes sense." I shake my head. My niece is quiet all the time now and my sister says of her kids, she's the quietest one.

We soak in all of the little coos and giggles Ella lets out as she plays. She soon starts to rub at her eyes, and we realize it might be time to start to wind down. I get her bottle ready and as I head back, I see Tucker has taken her back to her room.

While in her room, he's gotten her changed into her pajamas and has started reading her a book. She's focused on touching the pages and babbling along with him. He smiles when she tries to read along and I swear my ovaries explode yet again as I watch them interact. He's the whole package and I fall in love with him more each second I watch him in all these different parts of life.

Once he finishes going through the book, he looks up and I move into the room. I hand him the bottle and instead of getting up, he decides to feed it to her, as if he's done it a million times before. She's eager to take it and starts drinking quickly. He moves slowly in the rocking chair, his gaze fixed on her, and she moves her hand up. She tries to touch his face, but is only able to graze her fingers on the bottom of his beard.

I let them finish up the routine and walk out with the monitor. I see him place her in the crib. I can see she's out cold; it's good to see her parents being gone tonight didn't affect her too much in her routine.

I feel Tucker's arms wrap around me as I wash a few dishes in the sink, his beard nuzzling into the crook of my neck.

"Do I get to have a little time with you now on the couch?" he asks.

"That sounds nice." I turn my head to capture his lips with mine. I feel him slide his tongue along my lips and I open for him. "We cannot let this go any further, sir. There's a baby in the other room."

"That's too bad," he says as he breathes me in.

I dry my hands and we move to the couch. Lola has been sleeping on the couch for the last forty-five minutes, but once we sit down, she repositions herself so that she's resting her head on Tucker's leg.

We turn on the television and find a movie. I settle my head on his shoulder, but then he pauses it, causing me to sit up and look at him. Tucker has a serious expression. "You think you'd want to have kids?"

"Now?" I ask in a panic.

"No, Baylee, not now." He chuckles.

I smile. "Yeah, eventually. Probably down the road, if financially it makes sense. I would like to be married for a few years first. But when the time to have kids happens, I'd most likely still be in school, so my partner would have to be able to support us. After undergrad, I'll still have to earn my Doctor of Physical Therapy degree, which takes three more years." I bite my lip because I'm not making assumptions that he'd be the one by my side, even though that's what I want. I've got a long road ahead of me as a student.

"Your partner? Who's the one putting a baby in you if it's not me?" Alpha Tucker is always fun when he comes out. He grabs me and pulls me to straddle him. Lola moves to lay on the ground.

"Well, I want it to be you, but I didn't want to assume." I shrug my shoulders.

"Baylee, what makes you think I don't want that?" He brings his hands to my hips and the vulnerability in his eyes feels like I can see into his soul.

"I'm young and I don't know if you want to wait for me. I don't know if I'm what you want, Tucker," I confess, moving my fingers through his hair.

"Shit, I forgot you're young. This is over." He goes to move me off his lap and starts laughing. "I obviously know our difference in age. That's why I asked. Listen, I love you, Baylee. I want to respect your career, and I want to see you realize your dreams. I also want us to move forward. If you see yourself having kids and having a future with me, I want that with you." He brings my lips to his.

I deepen the kiss and continue to move my hands through his hair. I feel him grow beneath me and I grind against him. I swallow his moan, and I can't help but think we're not passing this babysitting task here, although Ella's safely sleeping in her room.

"I honestly can't wait to get you home, Bay," he whispers against my lips.

I bite his lower lip in response.

"And just so you know, I'm not trying to rush you, I only asked because when the timing is right, I do want that with you. I want to have everything with you," he says as he rests his forehead against mine, our breathing labored. I let his confession seep into my heart, and I let my own heart take off with it, because I think everything I dreamed of is coming true with this man.

———

The minute we get home, the pent-up energy from the evening has hit an all-time high and we're ripping off each other's clothes, throwing them along the floor of our apartment. We don't even make it to the bedroom.

Once we reach the kitchen table, we're down to our underwear and I get down on my knees. I pull on his boxers until his cock springs free. I'm salivating at the thought of having him in my mouth. I lick my lips and gaze up at him. He's towering over me, his eyes hooded as he stares at me.

"I love you," I tell him as I open my mouth and swallow his cock. I take him deep, until the head hits the back of my throat. Tucker gathers my hair into a ponytail and starts urging me on.

"Fuck, you suck me off so good, Bay," he moans, his eyes on me the entire time.

I look up at him, my head bobbing on his dick. His encouragement only spurs me on. I'm so wet knowing how much power I hold, even though I'm the one on my knees right now.

He's pumping his hips as I feel the velvety skin of his dick. I feel the piercing as I scrape my teeth slightly on his length, something I've learned sets him off and he rewards me with a guttural moan.

"Yeah, Firefly, right there." I move a hand toward his balls and squeeze.

He pulls me off him and I can't help the confusion that probably takes over my expression.

"I want to come in that pussy tonight," he says as he pulls me upright and picks me up. The way he easily lifts me, you'd think I weigh nothing, and to him, that could easily be the case.

He places me on the table and opens my legs wide. He looks at my body as if he's mesmerized. "You're so fucking wet for me, baby. Did sucking me off make you hot?" He stares at me, stroking himself.

I'm squirming, anticipating the feel of him. Since he went bare inside me, we've gone without a condom a few more times and I crave him that way more often than not.

"Look at the way you're staring at my dick, like you're starving for me." He glides himself through my folds and I arch my back, pinching my nipples.

"Please, Tucker. I need you. Fuck me," I beg.

Without warning, he thrusts inside me and I'm so full, it's perfection and bliss all in one.

"This is my pussy," he says and he begins a punishing pace that's addicting. I wrap my legs around his middle and lock them. The slapping of skin and our moans get louder as we chase our high. I swear this kitchen table is moving across the floor as his thrusts get stronger and I don't even care.

"Fuck, Baylee, you better get there, baby," he says.

All of a sudden, he's grabbing me and moving me toward the wall. He's fucking me up against it and it's so fucking hot knowing he's got this kind of strength. I can feel all of him perfectly.

He's moving his lips down my neck, nipping as he goes along my jaw to my collarbone, then bringing his hand to my breast and pinching my nipple. I scream out as that jolt causes me to feel it down to my pussy.

This angle hits perfectly as his cock is rubbing on my G-spot and soon I'm seeing stars and screaming as I climax. His thrusts start to quicken and he's soon pumping harder, falling off his own cliff. I feel the warmth of his cum shooting into me and I pull his lips into a punishing kiss. I have no idea how each time feels better than the last.

Once we come down from our high, he puts me down and I stand against the wall, breathing heavily and trying to find the strength to stand on solid ground.

"Fuck, Baylee, watching my cum running down your thighs is fucking addicting," he says, as he catches his breath while trailing kisses down my jaw.

I'm still panting, feeling like my limbs are Jello at this point. Without another word, he carries me to the shower, where we wash each other off and I fall asleep within minutes of my head hitting the pillow.

Hours go by, but I'm woken up by the sound of Tucker's voice on the phone.

"Yes, this is he."

It's a one-sided conversation. *What's going on?*

"Where is she?"

Is it still dark out? I reach to grab my phone from my side of the bed and see it's only one-thirteen in the morning.

"Yeah, I'll be right there. In the ER?"

He's getting out of bed and putting on his clothes.

I rub my eyes and sit up. "What happened?"

"My mom's in the hospital. I have to get to her."

CHAPTER 26

Baylee

"RIGHT NOW, WE WAIT, MR. MALLOY," the doctor says as I stand in the hall holding Tucker's hand. "The next twenty-four hours are critical. I need you to understand that."

We just got here and Tucker can't sit still. We're getting our first update from the doctor as the nurses tend to his mother in the emergency room. We came outside to give Carolyn some privacy as they change her into a gown.

She looks so frail, and it's hard to see her like that. She'll be admitted to the intensive care unit soon; we're just waiting on a room to become available. How did she spiral like this?

As if reading my thoughts, Tucker speaks up, "I don't understand what happened. She seemed fine the other day."

"Her last round of chemotherapy was too much on her. This can happen. I understand it seems like it's out of left field, but her treatment is strong due to how aggressive this type of cancer is," the oncologist, Dr. Arroyo, explains. "Mr. Malloy, I want you to understand, it's important we focus on making sure we stabilize her and keep her comfortable."

Carolyn wasn't feeling well earlier and had called the neighbor. She didn't want to inconvenience Tucker, so she opted to stay home rather than go to the hospital. Luckily, the neighbor stayed with her late into the night. When Carolyn got up for some water she collapsed and the neighbor called an ambulance. We are grateful someone was there to call for help.

"She'll be okay, right? I mean, she'll come out of this?" he asks and his voice cracks. I swear my heart breaks right along with it.

The doctor looks at him and I see the turmoil in his gaze. "Mr. Malloy, right now, it's a waiting game. Unfortunately, her body suffered a great deal. She's in the right place and now we wait for her body to stabilize and get stronger. The longer she can get that rest and recovery, the better, alright?" He puts his hand on Tucker's shoulder and Tuck nods at him.

With that, the doctor leaves us and enters Carolyn's room. I hear the doctor speaking to the nurses, asking for an update on the room upstairs.

"Tucker"—I move myself in front of him so he looks at me —"tell me what I can do."

He puts his arms around my waist, nuzzles his face into the crook of my neck and tightens his grip around me. He breathes me in and whispers, "It's too soon. I can't lose her, I'm not ready. It's not her time yet, Bay."

I run my hands through his hair. "I know, baby. She's strong and she's surrounded by the best to care for her," I say, hoping I sound reassuring. I'm saying it for him just as much as I'm saying it for myself.

Carolyn has been such a force of nature in all our lives and she hasn't had enough chance to fight this. For so long she hasn't even looked sick. Only recently she started to lose her hair from the chemotherapy, and her body began to show the changes. The cancer is starting to eat away at her in ways that remind us of the evil it really is.

Tucker pulls his face away as if a reality hits him. "Fuck, I told Eric and haven't really checked in about his flight."

"I did. I hope that's okay," I confess. "He knew you were

busy getting information on her so I texted him. His flight took off about twenty minutes ago; he should be here in about ninety minutes. He'll grab a ride from the airport and meet us here. Brittany is with him."

"Thank you." He blows out a breath and runs his fingers through his hair. "I'm glad he'll be here. I can't imagine this is easy for him being far away."

"Yeah, I know it must eat at him being a plane ride way instead of a car ride," I say.

"It's not easy. Either way, one of them has to give something up with someone leaving family behind," he says, looking down.

Right then, there's commotion in the room and soon they're pushing Carolyn's bed through. One of the nurses spots us, along with the oncologist.

Dr. Arroyo motions for us to follow them as they make their way out of the emergency room.

"Your mother's room is ready in the I.C.U. All her belongings are in the bag. Did you have anything in the room you have to grab?" he asks.

"No, we didn't drop anything off," I tell him. "Did your mom have anything else other than the stuff they placed in the bag?"

"No, I have her wallet on me," Tucker says.

"Okay, great. She's still groggy from the medication we gave her. She's breathing on her own, which is a good sign. We'll continue to monitor her once she's settled in her new room. Her labs came back and they were as I suspected; the chemo is what caused this reaction," he explains. "They're a little strict upstairs, so I'm not too sure they'll let you spend the night tonight, but due to the hours, they might let you stay now that we're getting close to morning."

"No problem. Just let us know. My brother is headed into town as well. We can take shifts if needed," Tucker explains.

Once we arrive at the elevators, Carolyn and her team take

one and we wait for the other. The minute our doors close, Tucker looks at me.

"She is so quiet and frail, Baylee. I can't look at her without thinking that I might not hear her voice again. What if the last time I talked to her was it?" He looks completely shaken.

"She needs you to look at her and think of her walking and talking again, Tucker. Right now, she needs you to have a positive outlook. She's fighting for her life. It's our job to fight right along with her, got it?"

I get where he's coming from. I'm having the same concerns as him. But I'm having to fight the urge to fall off that cliff of fear and thinking of the last time I spoke to her. So I'm focusing on the fact that she would want me to think about her walking out of this place with us and forming new memories. That's what we all need right now.

"But if you're going to break, you grab my hand, pull me out of the room, and have that moment with me. Then when you walk back in that room, you pull yourself back together. Got it?" I tell him. "She needs us whole, because she deserves all of us standing with her. Not pieces of us."

He nods with tears in his eyes. I know his heart is breaking. My sweet teddy bear of a man is so soft inside and all I want is to take away his pain.

I walk up to him and to bring my palm to his cheek. "I love you, Tucker. You aren't alone in this."

"I know. I love you," he says just above a whisper, his voice hoarse.

"No matter what, you will get through this."

He nods and leans into my hand. Eventually he moves his face and kisses the inside of my palm. The elevator doors open and he grabs my hand and pulls me out. I follow behind him, forcing myself to compose my emotions.

Carolyn needs our strength right now. That is the new mantra I keep repeating in my mind until I believe it myself.

It's been over twelve hours and no change in Carolyn's condition. My parents have been texting all day, asking how she's doing. They've offered to bring food to the hospital, but we've told them we'd let them know if something changes. There's so many rules in the I.C.U. regarding visitors that we've told them to stay home until we know more.

Right now we're in the cafeteria as they're going through shift-change and they don't allow family members in the room during that time.

"Okay, explain that again," Tucker's laughing for the first time since he got that call in the middle of the night. "You ingested something thinking it was clams and it was snails? How do you confuse the two?"

"Dude, I had no idea." Eric's holding back a laugh himself and Brittany is wiping tears from her eyes. "I ordered, the food came and I just started eating."

"I left you alone at the table for two minutes and you couldn't even handle a simple meal on your own," she teases.

"What can I say? I'm lost without you." He blinks in her direction, and she pushes his shoulder in a playful manner.

I really do love them together. Eric was the biggest player in high school. He was the star lacrosse player, and had a new girlfriend practically every week. I never thought he'd settle down and he took his time, but Brittany seems like a great fit for him. They compliment each other pretty well.

"The best part was seeing he consumed the entire appetizer plate of them by the time I returned." She laughs.

"I was starving." He throws his arms up.

"Eric, I was gone for half a second. Really, stop being dramatic."

"We'd been busy that day." He emphasizes with his eyes doubling in size. With the way her cheeks redden, I can fill in the blanks.

"Okay you two, we can stop there with the story time from the honeymoon, thank you. Younger brother ears here." Tucker covers his ears.

"Yes, your innocent ears are so delicate and all." Eric rolls his eyes.

"Exactly. He is oh so innocent and all," I say as I scoff.

"I really am. Baylee is such a bad influence," Tucker says, popping a tater tot into his mouth.

"I'm sure." Eric narrows his eyes.

"So, Baylee, how's the new school?" Brittany changes the subject before the conversation gets awkward and I'm the one with the reddened cheeks.

"It's good. I really love the program. I'm hoping to get a job soon though," I add. Now that Myles is no longer a threat, I feel comfortable getting a job again.

"Oh yeah? That sounds great. Somewhere specific?" Eric asks me.

"I mean, ideally a paid internship would be nice at a physical therapist's office or something. That would be a dream." I smile. "But I think starting with a coffee shop or something along those lines would be a good for now, then this summer going back to interning in my line of work would be ideal."

"How exciting," Brittany says.

I look over at Tucker and he simply smiles at me. Brittany and Eric start chatting about something together and he leans over to whisper to me.

"You know you don't have to work if you don't want to right now. You can focus on school if you need to," he tells me.

"I appreciate that, but I think it might be good for me. I'm used to working a few hours a week. I always save up a little for myself too." I reach over and kiss his cheek.

"Just know the offer stands if you change your mind, Firefly." He winks.

"Sorry to break things up, but maybe we should head

back up to the floor. They said after eight would be a good time for us to return," Eric says, looking at his phone.

We gather our trash, and grab the extra snacks we got to take to the room.

Taking this time downstairs gave us the energy we were longing for after hours of sitting in Carolyn's room, watching her lying there in the same state with no change. It's been draining seeing her so weak all day. My heart hurts for her, in addition to seeing the pain in the eyes of both Tucker and Eric throughout the day. I was hopeful as the hours passed, but when I saw she made no change, it felt as if a piece of me kept breaking seeing that she wouldn't improve. It's encouraging that she hasn't gotten worse though.

The intensive care unit is situated in its own dedicated wing. We arrive on the floor from the elevators, move through the double doors, where security scans our guest passes and the nurses' station is straight ahead. The minute we walk in, we can tell something is immensely wrong.

It's as if things are moving in slow-motion. I look over and see the doctors, respiratory therapists and nurses rushing into Carolyn's room. I stand there, motionless, unable to understand what's happening.

I have no clue how much time passes before someone comes to speak to us, but it feels like all the air is pulled from my lungs before I finally take a full breath. I brace myself, prepared to hear she's gone. My eyes are full of tears, and I reach for Tucker's hand, not even pretending that my own hands aren't shaking.

"Are you Carolyn Malloy's sons?" the charge nurse comes up to us to speak to us.

"Yes, we are." Both Eric and Tucker stand up straighter. I still see commotion in the room, what looks to be a doctor is still inside with nurses and other medical personnel, so I have to assume she's still alive, right?

"Your mother's heart stopped and we called a 'code blue'

right before you entered the unit," she begins, "that's why you saw all of us running around. We were able to stabilize her, but she's currently intubated."

Tucker squeezes my hand and I audibly gasp. It's hard to see Carolyn from here because her room is still full of people moving around. I blink and I feel the moisture from the tears I was holding back.

"Once we have some more answers, we'll update you. We'll know more once tests start coming back." She goes back in the room, and we walk up to the glass and stand in shock at how quickly things changed from when we went downstairs.

None of us say anything and the numbness feels all-consuming as we simply stand there, feeling as if so much of our world is crumbling right before our eyes.

It feels like hours pass before someone from the healthcare team comes out and allows us to go inside. We try to keep our composure, the lightness we carried up here from downstairs long forgotten.

I watch the cyclical way her chest rises and falls with the intubation machine. This isn't fair. All I want to do is scream. She deserves more. Tucker and Eric deserve more.

Tucker stands at the end of the bed and he's frozen. The shock is palpable from him. I look at him and reach my hand out, he puts his hand on the blanket and touches her feet. I smile softly. He used to do that for her when she worked long hours as a nurse at school. She used to complain her feet hurt from running around all day. Even all these years later, he remembers.

I leave him there and walk up to her side and grab her hand. "Hey, Carolyn, it's Baylee. Tucker, Eric, and Brittany are here. We're all here. If you wanted all the attention, you've got it. But now it's time to stop all this and wake up, alright?" I move my fingers along her palm, hoping she'll react, but I get no response.

Eric grabs her other hand and starts talking to her. Brittany moves to her shoulder and starts talking to her about all the shows she has to tell her about, so she needs to wake up because she needs her crime show buddy. We give her all these little moments she has to look forward to. The only person that hasn't spoken to her is Tucker, who has only stayed at the foot of the bed, moving his hands along her feet, silence plaguing him.

I look back and see him looking down, most likely lost in thought.

I move over to him and touch his shoulder. "Tucker, talk to her," I whisper.

He looks from me to her, tears streaming down his face, silent sobs wracking him. He takes a breath to compose himself.

"Ma, I still need you for some of my firsts," he finally admits. "I need you to sit in the crowd and watch me marry my girl." A sob breaks free and he quickly tries to hide it.

I hug his side, trying to comfort him and kiss his arm, hoping he can feel my love by his side.

"I'll be right back, okay?" I look up at him.

He simply nods and I turn away.

I pull out my phone from my back pocket as I walk out.

When I'm in front of the elevators, I make a call.

He answers on the first ring and it's a balm to my aching heart.

"Dad, I need a favor."

CHAPTER 27

Tucker

"HUNTER, the minute I think I know you, you surprise me with something else," I tell him as I walk into his house.

Hunter looks back at me. "Well, don't be too impressed. I don't own it. It's a rental."

"How did you find this place?" Clay asks as he takes it in.

"The parents of one of my buddies owns it. I was stationed with their son in the Army. He was killed in action and he was one of my best friends. When I was honorably discharged from the Army, his parents offered it to me to rent. I was sort of bouncing around at the time and I decided to take them up on it."

"It's pretty cool," River says. "I love the paneling and the kitchen counter is awesome." He's running his hand along the entire island.

"Yeah, my buddy's dad is a contractor so he put his heart and soul into this place. I guess they decided to travel the world after Georgie died. They couldn't be here anymore. Everything reminded them of their son. He was an only child and their hearts were broken. They couldn't sell the place, which I get, but they also couldn't stay here all the time."

"I understand that," both Ashton and Clay say.

Hunter invited us over for a guys' day to BBQ. Ashton tagged along today; Samara's husband isn't one to hang out with us often. He isn't a firefighter, but he's River and Clay's friend from childhood. He needed to get out of the house and he's a pretty cool guy. I don't mind the extra friend today.

It's been a week since my mother's health scare. She's finally out of the woods and I'm shocked to say she made it out of that dark time. I honestly thought we were going to lose her.

My brother just returned to Ohio today. I thought I was going to have to shove him onto the plane. He was incredibly hesitant to get in the damn car I called for him. I do understand the hesitation though. After she coded and was intubated, it was touch-and-go for a while there. As if a miracle came over her, about twenty-four-hours later, she pulled at the tubing and was awake.

The relief we all felt was something I can't even describe. Baylee's parents were there by that point and it felt like we all threw a small party once we saw my mom's green eyes open and look over at all of us. I think I smiled for two days straight. I was simply on cloud nine for multiple reasons.

Baylee is with her now that she's situated back at the house, along with a home health nurse my brother and I hired to be with her. Luckily my mom didn't argue with us on this. She agreed it was necessary and Elliott is a kind woman that came highly recommended by the nursing staff at the hospital; she seems knowledgeable about the type of cancer my mother has been diagnosed with. She has also been very optimistic with my mom's ability to bounce back after what she just went through. I'm feeling more hopeful about her being able to continue treatment after we get her feeling better.

"Okay, so let me get this straight," River starts, "you're a veteran, you workout, you have a nice place, you're now a firefighter, you have that smile, and tattoos. Add to the that a motorcycle, second income with this damn social media platform, and you cook? Why aren't you married?"

Hunter just stands there with a sly smile and shrugs.

"You're hiding more, aren't you?" River asks.

"You guys, you're here to BBQ, not to braid each other's hair, am I right?" Hunter says.

"Oh, now you've intrigued him. He's like a dog with a bone," I say.

"Well, that's what you're missing. You need a dog," River says.

"I hear yours is cool. Maybe I should just take her," Hunter says.

"The fuck you will. My Lola is exactly that—mine. Who the fuck does this guy think he is?" River says to the group.

"The whole package apparently," Clay says back. "I bet Lola loves him more than you."

Oh, not the right thing to say, Clay. *Yeesh*. I start grabbing a few items to take outside to help Hunter start grilling.

"What did you say to me, brother? Take it back. That was below the belt." He points at his twin.

"I said what I said." He laughs as he grabs a chip.

"Ella calling me dada is completely happening now. Before it was a cute little joke, now it's really happening, Clay. Fuck. You." He flips his brother off.

"Sure, Riv." He rolls his eyes.

"You just wait," he tells him.

"Okay, Riv. I'm shaking over here." Clay smiles.

"Just you wait. You'll be crying soon," he taunts. "And I'll laugh in your face when she is says 'dada' this and 'dada' that. And she'll refer to you as CLAY." He throws his head back and belts out an evil laugh.

"Okay, you guys. Can we start making the burgers? I'm starving," I yell over my shoulder in hopes I can stop them from arguing.

"You're exhausting, you know that, Riv?" Clay says back. "I have no idea how Kennedy handles you half the time."

I close the door behind me and start putting the items down next to Hunter outside.

"Those two are a lot," he says looking out at his backyard.

"Believe me, I know. But they're loyal. I'm still getting to know Ashton, but he's known them since they were kids so he must be a saint." I laugh.

"Probably true." Hunter laughs as he grabs items and gets things started for lunch. "Glad to hear your mom is doing better."

"Thanks, man. Same. Baylee was my rock during the whole thing," I tell him. Beyond that, if I'm being honest.

She kept me grounded and I don't know how I would have gotten through it all.

"Listen, I didn't get a chance to tell everyone, but—" I get interrupted.

"If I have to hear those two bicker a second longer, I might lose it," Ashton says as he makes his way outside on the patio.

"They're still fighting over Ella calling River dad first?" I ask.

"Yes. It's exhausting. Seriously, why does Clay even fall for it?" Ashton shakes his head. "I came over here for a break, but I think my twins are easier than they are."

"I think you might be right," Hunter says.

"So Hunter, how's it going at the firehouse? These guys making your life hell as a probie?" Ashton asks him.

"It's not too bad, I expected worse." He flashes his relaxed smile Ashton's way. "After the Army, I think I can handle just about anything."

"True. Have you been back to civilian life long?" Ash asks him.

"I got back about three years ago. I traveled during that time around the States before I settled on Boston. Jerry and

Scarlet had reached out when I was traveling and told me about wanting to rent their home out, so I jumped on the opportunity." He throws the first few burger patties onto the grill while River and Clay join us outside, unfazed by the heated discussion we left them with in the kitchen.

"You two finally figure everything out?" Ashton asks them.

"Of course." River smiles.

"You made a bet, didn't you?" I roll my eyes.

"Always," Clay answers, clinking his glass with mine.

"You two are so annoying with your bets," Ash chimes in. "And yet we'll all take a side and throw money in by the end of it. My money is on Clay winning this as he is the actual father and she lives with him."

"I'm very persuasive, you know." River looks way too confident.

"You're ridiculous, Riv," I tell him.

"Malloy, you really don't know me, do you?" He laughs. "Back in the sixth grade, Clay's girlfriend couldn't even tell us apart."

"You really are a dick. This asshole went half a lunch period sitting next to her acting like me until I showed up. You know how embarrassed she was when she realized it wasn't me she was sitting next to? She broke up with me the next day." Clay shakes his head as he takes a drink of his beer.

"Well, you found out she wasn't for you thanks to your loyal brother," River retorts.

"It's not like I was going to marry her, man," Clay answers back.

"Do you have a speaker or something so we can play some music to drown them out?" I look at Hunter. "This is just going to keep going on and on."

Hunter makes a face before walking off, hopefully in search of a speaker. As much as the Nichols brothers might bicker, it's the exact distraction I needed after the stressful week I had with my mom being in the hospital. The only thing I'm missing is my girl by my side.

I pull out my phone and open up my texts to find the latest photo she sent me of her with my mom sitting on the couch smiling into the camera. My whole heart is staring back at me in that selfie and there isn't anything I wouldn't do for those two. It's a reminder that Baylee proved to me that we're a team and I owe her for loving me with her entire soul.

I got a ride from River this morning, leaving my truck with Baylee in case something came up with my mom. This is my first shift back since my mom got sick. Yesterday was the BBQ and I spent the evening over at my mom's house, while Baylee had to study with a group at the library.

My mom looks much better than she had been prior to her incident. She seems to be getting her appetite back, however, she has taken a break from the chemo since that was what prompted the heart attack. We have an appointment coming up to evaluate how we'll move forward. From the tests performed at the hospital, it seems there wasn't any damage to her heart wall with the cardiac arrest, which is a relief.

The one-eighty our lives have taken in such a short time has really put everything into perspective. I'm just grateful she's still here and I look at everything around me and feel like I'm looking at my life with a whole appreciation I didn't have before. I'm not taking any second with those I love for granted and I think the amount I've told Baylee I love her is starting to make her crazy.

I woke her up this morning to tell her and she nearly threw a pillow at my face. Granted, she was out studying until an ungodly hour, so she had every reason to be pissed, but I couldn't be gone on a twenty-four hour shift without telling her how much I'd miss her. She had to know and, of course, I had to kiss her all over before I walked out that door.

She forgave me after a few orgasms, obviously. The smirk on my face gets River's attention.

"You're thinking something dirty, aren't you?" He parks his truck.

"None of your damn business." I look over at him.

"Oh, it's really dirty then." He laughs.

"Fuck off," I tell him. "Also, thanks for the ride."

"No problem," he says as he hops out. "Glad I could help."

We start walking in and Clay catches up to us as he yawns. "Morning. Ella was up all night teething. I might need an I.V. of coffee," he says on another yawn.

"Maybe our captain could make his famous coffee today for ya," Riv tells him.

"I'll need it on rotation," Clay says. "It's brutal. I never knew it could be this bad."

"Sorry, man." I clap him on the shoulder.

"It's fine. Abby has a huge deadline today for a design. Hopefully Ella gives her a few hours this morning because we're both dragging."

We make our way in, greeting some of the guys from the last shift.

Once we put our things inside, we make our way back to get updates from the last shift. It was busy for the guys so we go about getting our supplies checked. I start going through the checklists and moving along the truck. River and Clay, along with the others, are doing the same. The banter is the same as always, the familiarity of it all feels like exactly what I need, as I recognize that my family here is truly formed with these guys. They're the brothers I gained without even realizing.

It's only then I notice we're a man short. I look over my shoulder, taking note that I don't see Rios anywhere. I walk around the truck and count the number of guys and see we are truly missing him in rotation. I walk into the station and don't see him anywhere.

"Hey, Cap, did Rios report in today? Or did he call out for today's shift?" I ask.

At first he looks at me confused. He grabs his clipboard and checks, shaking his head. "No, he should be here. You sure he's not out there?"

"I didn't see him. Maybe I missed him. I'll go check again," I tell him.

"I'll try his phone just in case," my captain says.

I make my way out, concern coursing through me. As much as Rios and I aren't on speaking terms, we still have a history. He's been my best friend more than not for most my life. And now, if anything, he's my family, so I can't help but worry that he hasn't called to check in. That's unlike him.

I do another check of the station without any sign of him anywhere. I ask the guys and now I have a few others looking for him. His car isn't in the lot, nor have any of them heard from him. I'm in the kitchen, while some others are looking for him in the locker room. I'm standing talking to River and Clay. Hunter is looking down at his phone, wondering what we should do, when we hear some commotion from the front of the station.

"Where is he?!"

I know immediately it's Rios; at least I know he's alright. The guys look around in confusion at Rios's tone.

I pocket my phone and prepare myself for what's coming. The moment the door swings open, I see the fury on his face.

"You fucking married my sister?!"

CHAPTER 28

Tucker

OKAY, so maybe we didn't think this through entirely.

Let me rephrase. I do not, in any way shape or form, regret my decision to marry Baylee. But what we didn't think about was the ripple effect of Rios and how he might react. Because in the moment everything happened, we were thinking about ourselves and the people around us. That was our main objective, that was our purpose.

The night my mom suffered her cardiac arrest, my heart shattered. Baylee saw the ground beneath me was crumbling. When my mom was in that bed, intubated and everyone was talking to her, telling her to get better, the only thing I could think about saying to her was how much I wanted her to come out of it to watch my life move forward. I had finally found my forever and my mom wouldn't get to see that start for me. The threat of her loss was crippling.

So Baylee offered me a gift. And it wasn't a small one. She called her parents to the hospital. Then she pulled me aside and asked if I wanted to marry her with my mother present, because she wanted that too. It wasn't about the romance and flowers like they do in the movies. Baylee and I knew we wanted to be together; that we wanted forever. She gave me a gift with my mom present. Was it legal? No. But it was a chance to do it in front of my brother, and most importantly, have my mother by my side. It wasn't picture perfect, of course. It wasn't the traditional wedding I'd always imagined, but life doesn't make plans within our control.

We called the chaplain the hospital had, and we did just that. It was about giving our hearts a little bit of love while they were also breaking. There were tears, while also tenderness. In that moment, I threw up a wish to whomever was above that if my mom came out of this, I would ask Baylee to marry me properly, with a ring, and have whatever wedding she wanted.

Since then, Baylee has called me her husband, knowing full well what we did isn't considered legal in the state of Massachusetts. But to her, she says her dreams became a reality—being tied to me in that way. She said her heart is mine, and mine hers. Going and getting that paper, with my mom awake and present in a different way—she'd do it for that purpose. But in her eyes we're married, the paper would just be a formality.

That night, I fell more in love with that woman, if that's even possible. I owe her for showing me how selfless she can be to ensure I'm cared for. She knew I would feel immeasurable pain had my mom not made it that night.

Her parents didn't ask any questions. They showed up and it was as if they understood what it meant to us to go through with our nuptials.

It wasn't until later that her mother confessed she always knew the love her daughter felt for me. She always knew Baylee would live her life at her own speed and she's a force to be reckoned with. Stopping her would never work and she knows I would never try to keep her from fulfilling her dreams.

I think after that night with Myles, they saw I would never do anything to put Baylee in harm's way. I would walk through fire to keep her safe. Her father simply hugged me and told me to keep her safe and shed a few tears when he pulled away.

The rest of the night, we sat vigil at my mother's bedside, hopeful she'd come out of it. Once my mother was conscious and breathing on her own, Baylee's parents promised not to discuss what had gone on in the hospital room, giving us a chance to announce to the family however we chose.

We weren't sure if we would move forward with a small service at the courthouse, or if we'd do an engagement and a full wedding with a proper ceremony and reception. We've been so tired and adjusting to getting my mom back to her normal routines that we haven't made any major decisions at this point. I just know I'd like to make it official in whatever way makes Baylee happy.

Now that Rios is here at the firehouse, it's obvious someone let it slip and I need to figure out who. I didn't get a text from Baylee, so I'm assuming she's unaware he knows at this point.

You could hear a pin drop in the kitchen right about now. The shock across everyone's faces would be priceless if it wasn't at my expense. Rios makes his way toward me and he's about to advance on me, but River and Clay stop him.

"Hey man, not here," River says.

"This fucker thinks he can marry my sister and get away with it!" Rios points at me while yelling in my direction.

"There's an explanation." I put my arms up in surrender.

"Malloy, you're a piece of shit!" he yells.

"Watch it," Clay says in his ear. "Why don't we take a walk before the captain hears you?"

"Too late. Malloy, Rios, let's go. Now!" our captain says from the doorway.

I look up and stand straighter. I then direct my gaze at Rios and stare at my old best friend until I see him compose himself. River and Clay hold on to him until he finally stands up and pulls himself from their grasp. "I'm fine. It's fine, I'll go." He fights himself free and walks off.

I nod at the guys without a word. I know they all want answers, especially because I've been around them since my mom was discharged and I haven't mentioned anything about me and Baylee. I hated keeping it to myself, but I was still figuring it all out. Especially without talking to the rest of Baylee's family, we wanted to wait until we had spoken to them first.

Once we sit down in a makeshift space the captain uses as an office from time to time, Rios scoots the chair further from me, the immature asshole. I have to hold off the eye roll.

"Care to explain the spectacle out there, Rios?" Cap begins.

He thumbs over at me. "Malloy married my sister behind my back."

I look down because that's literally what I did. I know better than trying to interject unless spoken to.

Our captain looks over at me. "That's ballsy. Is this true?"

"Yes sir, it is." I nod. "It's not so plain and simple, but yes, I did marry her. It's not legal though, sir."

"Fuck legal, Malloy. You know that's not the point," Rios interjects.

"Rios, quiet," Cap says. "Malloy, what do you mean it's not legal?"

"It was done in the hospital without a marriage license. It was sort of spur of the moment when my mom was intubated."

"Alright, Rios, then what's the problem?" Cap looks at Rios, already over this conversation.

"Cap, Malloy is really playing this down. He went behind my back with my little sister, who is ten years younger by the way," he emphasizes.

"Is she underage or something?" Cap asks.

We both answer, "No!"

He brings his thumb and pointer finger in-between his eyes. "Again, what's the problem here?"

"Cap, if I can be completely transparent here?" Rios asks and our captain nods. Rios continues, "I asked Malloy not to date my sister. He did it anyway. And now he married her? It's bullshit." He huffs and crosses his arms.

I look over and it's hard not to see how immature he looks beside me. I wish he could hear himself.

"Okay, here's what's going to happen. First, this family drama stays out of my firehouse, understood?" He looks at Rios.

He's met with silence from Rios, whereas I respond with, "Yes, sir."

"Rios, did you understand what I just said or do you need a note to the doctor to check those ears?" Cap asks.

"Yes, sir, I understand," Rios says.

"Great. Next, for your little tantrum, you'll both be taking on cleaning responsibilities during shift. Meaning, you'll mop, clean dishes, keep this firehouse tidy, etcetera. Give Hunter the night off. He cooks, you two clean, got it?" He smiles.

"Yes, sir," we both say, lacking enthusiasm.

"Wonderful." He claps and moves to leave the room. "Oh, I almost forgot"—he turns to look back at us before leaving the room—"if I see this type of behavior again, I'll transfer your asses. Got it?"

"Understood," I say.

Rios says, "Yes, sir."

We are left in silence and shortly Rios leaves the room shortly after without even glancing my way. I lean forward, resting my elbows on my thighs and rub my temples.

Letting out a silent curse and realizing it's only the beginning of this fucking shift, I pull out my phone and text Baylee:

Cat's out of the bag

BAYLEE

WHAT?

Rios showed up on shift out for blood

BAYLEE

Why is he so annoying? Let me find out who
opened their mouth

I love you

BAYLEE

Love you more, husband 💋

I can't wait to see those lips somewhere on
me later, wife

BAYLEE

Calm down… your shift just started. Let's not
get all hot and bothered so early

Right then a call comes in and I stand up and make my way through to meet the guys in the apparatus bay.

We're getting a call. Love you

BAYLEE

Love you. Stay safe 💚

"Sounds like congratulations are in order," River says with a sly smile across his face. "I guess Hunter isn't the only one keeping secrets."

"Hey, why am I being labeled as the secret keeper?" Hunter says as he rushes to get suited up.

"I know you've got stuff you're not telling us. I'll figure it out. You're a guy full of mystery. I just know it," River says, pointing at him.

"Let's talk about it later." I jut my chin as Rios makes his way past us.

I honestly want to talk about everything with the guys,

but I also don't want to cause more friction. Tensions are high as it is when we go on a call, I don't need to add more to it with the news of Baylee and I getting "married."

"Don't think I'll forget," River scolds.

"Believe me, I know," I say. "You're my ride, remember?"

River rubs his hands together, remembering he'll get my undivided attention, and I regret getting that ride with him. Between the two brothers, I'm wishing I'd asked Clay instead. I look over at the other Nichols brother and I can tell he knows exactly what I'm thinking. The laugh he lets out confirms it too.

———

The moment I walk into the apartment, Baylee sits up on the couch, yawning. From the blanket hanging off the opposite end, it looks like she slept in the living room.

"Bay, why are you out here?" I drop my bag at the door after locking up behind me.

She stretches her arms above her head, rubbing the sleep from her eyes. Even as she's waking up, with her hair haphazardly pointing in all directions, she's still the most beautiful woman I've ever laid eyes on.

"I just got up and fell asleep again. I wanted to wait out here for you," she says. "My class got canceled today." She rests her head on her hands as she waits for me to walk over to her. I lean over and kiss her lips.

I look over at the coffee table and see some crafting supplies laid out.

"What's all that?" I gesture.

"Oh, your mom taught me how to cross-stitch last time I went over there. Dr. Nuys told me picking up a hobby outside of school might be good to get my mind off everything with Myles, and your mom said embroidery is fun. She wasn't wrong. Turns out I'm not bad at it." She shrugs.

"So that's the design you went with while sitting across from my mom?" I look at her.

"Well, obviously not. This is what I'm doing while I'm here. The 'Fuck Cancer' design is the one I do while I'm around your mom. She likes that one." She smiles brightly.

"That's a relief. I was hoping an embroidered dick wasn't something you were doing while hanging out with my sweet mother." I laugh, although I wouldn't put it past Baylee to do something like that.

"It's not just any dick, Tucker; it's yours, obviously. Don't you see how I put a shimmery thread right there and embroidered your piercing to show it's your dick?" She gives me a *duh* expression.

"How could I have missed that?" I deadpan.

"How was your night?" She changes the subject, even though I know she's holding back a laugh at how ridiculous this entire conversation has been so far.

"Long. I felt like the minute we got back to the station and got comfortable, there'd be another call. It was one thing after another, but all the calls were successful. No losses, so that's always positive," I tell her as I move toward the kitchen.

"That's always a good thing," she says. "Your mom was doing well when I left the house." She stretches again and yawns.

"Why don't you go to bed and try to catch a few more hours of sleep if you don't have class?" I say as I grab a mug.

"Because I missed you and now that I don't have class, I want to spend it staring at you and maybe touching you all over," she says.

I look over my shoulder and catch her looking at my ass. "Excuse me, were you checking me out?"

She bites her lower lip and finally looks up to meet my eyes. "Maybe. Can't I ogle my husband?" The smirk she gives me tells me she only has one thing on the agenda this morning.

I can't help the way my dick reacts to the smoldering way her gaze keeps taking me in. "Well, if you crave something, why don't you come show me what you'd like."

She throws the blanket off her and makes her way over. The way she confidently strides over to me shows the Baylee I remember from before that monster got ahold of her. I don't see the vulnerable person she was the night I got that call from her anymore. That heavy shield that kept her down with fear and shame is no longer holding her back. She's standing tall and strong again. Seeing that beauty shine brightly from her is something that only makes me feel pride for this woman I love.

The moment she's within my reach, I bring my fingers through her hair and she leans into my touch.

"I hope you know that without you, I don't exist." I brush my lips against hers.

"You're a ray of light, Tucker." She runs her fingers through my beard.

"Now I know what life looks like with you in it. I can't exist without you by my side, Firefly." I grab her cheeks and kiss her, deepening the connection. I swallow her moan, intertwining our tongues. She grabs my forearms, and I feel her dig her nails into my skin and it only turns me on.

"I love you, wife," I say when I pull away slightly. I know our vows still need to be official, but that piece of paper doesn't prove to me that she's mine. This right here, holding her in my arms is the only proof I need. From the way she smiles before I once again bring my lips back to hers, I know she feels the same.

"I need to taste you," I tell her. "Now."

Instead of waiting for her to react, I pick her up and put her on the kitchen island. She yelps and giggles as I move her to sit down, moving her legs wide in front of me. I bring her lips to me again, moving my hands into her hair, tugging slightly, coercing another moan out of her. Her sounds are only making me harder behind my sweats. She moves her legs around my middle and pulls my body closer to her. I can feel her nipples hard against my chest.

I pull away from her slightly and move my hands down her front, squeezing her breasts from the outside of her shirt.

"Mmm," she moans and I love how reactive she is with her breasts.

I'm about to pull my hat off my head, when Baylee shakes her head.

"No, the hat stays on. Turn it backwards," she orders.

I do as she asks and the moment I do, she moans and bites her lower lip as she nods in agreement.

"How wet are you for me, baby?" I ask her.

"Why don't you put your mouth there and find out for yourself?" She grabs my face for a punishing kiss before pulling away. "I've missed you all night and my vibrator wasn't enough for me."

I groan as I begin alternating between kisses and nibbles down her body until I reach her navel. I grab the waistband of her sleep pants and begin to tug everything down in one fell swoop. I throw everything to the ground, exposing her to me and bite my knuckles. She's perfection.

I see her glistening pussy staring back at me, ready to be devoured. My dick is aching behind my sweats, but he's going to have to wait right now.

"Fuck, Tucker, you're killing me," she whines.

I love seeing her antsy. I simply chuckle and it just gets her more irritated.

"So impatient this morning, wife," I lean in and take a bite of her inner thigh and immediately run my tongue up her leg, which pulls a moan from her lips. I see the goosebumps forming along her skin.

"Tucker, please," she begs.

"What do you want, baby?" I ask, taunting her even more.

"You know what I want." She writhes even more, looking down.

I'm so close to her pussy, I blow air onto her folds and she moans even more.

"Tucker, please fuck me with that tongue of yours," she nearly yells.

"Like this?" I run my tongue through her center, which causes her to arch her back and she lets out a scream.

I hold her thighs open as I continue the strokes with my tongue, keeping my eyes on her. I add a finger, then another, pumping into her, curling it inside of her to rub against that sensitive spot. Watching her lose her mind as I move through her pussy only gets me more turned on. With all her sounds getting louder, I'm sure I'm going to blow my load before I get inside her.

Baylee brings her hand over my hat and holds on as she rides my face. Fuck, the sounds she's making are so hot. It only spurs me on to fuck her harder with my mouth.

"Yes, damn it, Tucker, right there," she's screaming, and soon, I can tell, she's climaxing. "Oh, yes... I'm... yes, fuck, yes."

Her legs start shaking and I stop holding them back. She constricts my head with her thighs as her orgasm takes over. She arches her back, and her body convulses as I taste her on my tongue.

I don't give her much time to recover before I'm standing and pushing my sweats down my legs until my cock springs free. I had plans to carry her to our bed, but I honestly can't wait another second.

The minute my dick is out, I bring Baylee closer to the edge. She's still panting and looking down, her smile sated.

"I need to be inside you," I tell her.

I run my cock through her folds, and she reacts because she's still sensitive. She spreads her legs apart, welcoming me.

That's all the invitation I need, and I line myself up and thrust to the hilt.

Her top is still on, and I take the chance to push her shirt up and grab her breasts as I thrust into her. I pinch each nipple and pull a moan from her, which spurs me on even more. I bend forward to pull a nipple into my mouth. I pop off one breast and move on to the other, giving each equal attention.

I can't help the punishing pace and we both chase our highs. It doesn't take long until I feel Baylee's walls constrict as her next orgasm crashes over her. Her climax lasts for some time and her screams ricochet off the walls. I see the sweat beading off her forehead and I continue to pound into her.

Once she's coming down, I slow my pace. I'm convinced I can get another out of her.

"One more, baby," I demand.

I change my angle slightly, bringing one of her legs up on my shoulder. Right then, she moans and I know my piercing is hitting differently than before. The minute she feels the change, she arches her back and I begin at a faster pace. I bring my thumb to her clit.

"Shit, Tucker, right there," she moans.

"You close?" I feel my own orgasm looming.

"Yes, keep going... right there," she demands.

I keep at it at the same pace and soon she's screaming my name. The minute she climaxes again, I feel my own orgasm hit me. My vision goes black, and my thrusts slow down as I empty into her.

"Fuck, that was..." I say as I drop kisses along her chest and neck, eventually kissing her lips. "That was intense."

"I would agree." She smiles against my lips.

"Maybe we should take a shower?" I ask her.

"Yes, maybe we should. Maybe we can get dirty again in there too." She winks.

My girl is insatiable.

CHAPTER 29

Baylee

I LAY on Tucker's chest, running my finger through his chest hair, admiring the ink along his left pec. I don't think it matters how many times I see his exposed torso, I'll never be over how toned and beautiful he is.

"Your body is incredible," I say just above a whisper. "I can't get enough of you." I bring my head up, rest my chin on his chest and look up at him, my smile soft and sated.

"Well, if that's your way of asking for another round, please give me at least thirty minutes. I think my dick will fall off if we have sex again. I can't keep up with your young ass." He squeezes my ass under the sheet.

I laugh and lay my head back down. "I'd never pass up another round, but no, that's not what I meant. I'm just saying, I'll never get sick of touching you, or looking at you and knowing you're mine."

I love this time together when we just lay here; moments where the silence isn't uncomfortable and we can just bask in what we're building together.

Running his fingers up and down my bare spine, he breaks the silence, "Do you want to make it official, Bay?"

I can't help the panic that washes over me like a bucket of

cold water. My head snaps up and I wish I could've controlled my reaction more.

"Why? Do you not want to?" Masking my disappointment is futile. He can read the hurt all over my face.

He brings his palm to my cheek and lean into him and close my eyes.

"Baylee, the thought of truly being your husband completes every fiber of my soul, do you understand me?" With his words, my eyes snap open and look straight into his. I feel like everything in me is firing on all cylinders.

"But you have to understand, I'm at a different part of my life. I'm a decade further into life than you—I've partied, I'm deep into my career, reaching my goals already. You're just at the starting line, and I don't want you to think I'm going to hold you back, or try to rush you," he tells me and I can see the turmoil on his face.

"Why do you think you'd hold me back? I want this with you," I tell him.

"Even if you don't see it right now, you might make little decisions on your path that will take you right versus left, up instead of down—because of me. I don't want to do that to you. I want you to become a physical therapist if that's what you want. I want you to do all the things you desire."

He seems really conflicted right now, and I pull myself up, revealing my breasts as I kiss him, then straddle him. There's nothing sexual in what I'm doing, but I never got dressed after we had sex last.

"Tucker, I understand we're ten years apart and at very different stages in life. That's never going to change. You know what's also never going to change?" I wait for him to answer.

He shakes his head, his gaze on my face as he glides his hands to my hips.

I move my hands through his ginger hair and he closes his eyes. I savor how much I love touching him beneath my fingertips. Then I bring my face inches away from his. "Tucker Malloy, I've loved you since the moment I understood the meaning of the word. And I'll love you as strongly on my last day on this Earth. Nothing will change that. There's nothing about loving you that would hold me back. If anything, you're helping me soar. So, yes, I want to make this official. I want to reach further with you by my side."

He beams a brilliant smile at me and it's hard not to smile back. Unexpectedly, he grabs my hips and flips me onto my back. "Baylee, you're everything I never knew I needed." He drops a kiss to my lips and it feels like home the moment I feel him against me.

He pulls away and whispers, "I love you more than I could've imagined, Firefly."

"I love you," I say back then capture his lips again. Everything I could've hoped for is finally coming true with this man I dreamed of—with this man I've loved for so long.

———

Boston has done us dirty right before Thanksgiving. Damn this cold front that's come in; the windchill alone can be felt down to the bone.

As soon as I open the door to the sandwich shop, I'm instantly assaulted by the warmth and relieved to be inside rather than outside with the rest of the pedestrians. I wore so many layers, and yet I swear it feels like I'm in a short-sleeve shirt. If this is just November, what will mid-January feel like?

"Bay, over here," my brother calls from the corner table he sits in. I look over and the smile he's sporting looks too casual for someone that should feel like shit for the way he treated his ex-best friend.

He gets up to greet me with a bear hug. He wraps his arms around me, but I don't return the gesture.

"It's so great to see you," he says, unfazed by my stiffness.

I take my seat, still defrosting from the cold outside, rubbing my hands together. I'm about to greet Danny half-heartedly when our server prances to the table.

"Hi. I'm Penzy. Is there anything I can get you to drink?" She smiles wide at me.

What a unique name. I look at her name tag to see if I misheard her. Nope. It's actually Penzy. Interesting.

"What a unique name." I smile up at her. "I'll take a hot tea please."

"You got it." She smiles wide.

"I thought it was a different name too," my brother says after she walks away. The moment he speaks, my smile drops. He notices the change in my mood and clears his throat.

"Thanks for accepting my invite to meet for lunch." He rearranges his utensils. He finally looks uncomfortable. Good. He's been an absolute ass and needs to figure his shit out.

"Well, I wouldn't have come. Tucker convinced me to," I say, looking at my nails like I have better places to be.

"Really? Why?" He sounds surprised.

Because he's a better person than either of us, you asshole, I think to myself.

"Danny, why am I here? I have studying to get to and Thanksgiving food to prep," I say with little emotion in my voice.

"Here." He passes me a gift.

"What's this?" I look at it, puzzled.

"A gift." He chuckles.

"No shit." I roll my eyes. "Why?"

"It's your birthday tomorrow, Bay," he reminds me, as if I don't know.

"I know it is. Why are you giving me something?" I'm stunned, my brother usually doesn't go out of his way to gift me anything. He's usually giving me something randomly when he sees me weeks after my birthday and it's never the size of a jewelry box. Last year he got me a sweatshirt two sizes too big for me and it wasn't even the style I'd ever wear. I'm convinced an ex-girlfriend left it behind.

"Well, I got you something special and I wanted to give it to you. Open it," he insists.

I roll my eyes once again because it's uncontrollable around siblings, and unwrap the ribbon. I pull off the lid and reveal a gold paperclip necklace with my initials dangling off it.

"I went to the store and she said it's all the rage right now. You can switch out the charms, but I thought you'd like the initials—you know, B and R." He looks so proud.

"Oh, so this isn't just to solidify the fact that I'm Baylee Rios, then?" I snap. I might be reading too far into this, but something about this gift feels more like a territorial thing. I have a feeling it's purposeful and I'm more pissed about it than anything.

"Would you rather have M for Malloy then? You're not really married, Baylee," he says and it stings.

"Well, we will be," I say, placing the gift back in the box and push it back toward my brother. "And you have some nerve acting like my feelings don't matter, Danny."

"You can't be serious about this marriage?" He laughs, but there's no humor.

I look up at my brother, and right then he seems unrecognizable. "Danny, for so long, I looked up to you. I thought you wanted what was best for me. I thought you cared for my well-being. But all you wanted was me away from Tucker. So much so, you were blind to all the bad in my life, as long as it kept me from your best friend. You didn't even see how miserable I was. You didn't see the abuse I was enduring at the hands of a monster. First with the emotional and verbal abuse, then I had to endure physical abuse. Luckily, I got out of it. I'm one of the fortunate ones who can say they got out. I'm now with someone that looks at me and sees beauty and possibility. But when you see us together, you see anger and resentment. How is that possible?"

I see his anger right then. He isn't even reflecting on his behavior. He's selfish even in this moment. Where did he go wrong?

"He was my best friend. And you're my favorite sister. How could you two do this?" he seethes.

"How could we do what? Love each other? See that's what I don't get. All we're doing is loving each other. And you could be a part of simply being embraced with more love. But instead you're choosing to fill your heart with hate. That's your choice, Danny. I'm not choosing that path. Go ahead and be angry, but I'm not. I'm choosing to be loved by this beautiful man at my side. And I'm choosing to be married to him too. Because I've loved him for far longer than I haven't." I stand up.

"It won't last," he says, staying seated.

"You're wrong," I say, looking down at my brother. "But you know what? One day you'll realize how wrong you've been. This moment right here you could've made better choices. Actually, there were many moments in the last year or so you could've reacted differently. But you'll one day regret those choices. And I'll be waiting for you to come back, because I'm your sister and I love you, no matter what. But you'll have a lot of groveling to do with many others. I hope they have the heart to forgive you, Danny," I tell him. "And I hope it's not too late; because time is precious."

With that I leave him sitting there, staring at me as I make my way through the restaurant.

I decide to head home, the cold a smack to the face the minute I take a step outside. Danny found out about the nuptials at the hospital after overhearing my parents, because he'd forgotten his bag for work at their house and had stopped by before that shift. When he walked inside unannounced, he overheard them talking about that night and what we had done.

They hadn't known Danny was in the house when he snuck out as quickly as he had shown up, he went straight to the firehouse, looking to confront Tucker. Everything blew up from there.

I end up ordering a ride and the moment I step inside the apartment, I realize it's still quiet. Tucker had some errands to run while I was out with Danny. I decide to grab some of my books and laptop and sit at the kitchen table to get ahead on my studying. Finals are coming up quickly after Thanksgiving.

I'm an hour into this chapter when Tucker gets home and my eyes are heavy. I stand and stretch my arms in the air.

"It is beyond cold out today." He shivers.

"I know, I was glad to get home," I say.

"I wasn't expecting you home before me," he says, a concerned look on his face.

"Yeah, it didn't go so well," I say, scrunching my face.

"I'm sorry, baby," he says, pulling me to his chest, then planting a soft kiss to my lips. "Maybe I can make it better?"

"Yeah? What did you have in mind?" I smile up at him.

"You go hide in the bedroom and I'll get things ready out here. I'll call when you can come out." He smacks my ass, and I yelp with a giggle.

I make my way to the room and decide to take a shower and get into pajamas. Sounds like a night in is the perfect way to spend the rest of the evening.

As soon as I get myself dressed in some warm PJs, there's a knock on the door.

"You ready?" I hear Tucker's muffled voice.

"Yes," I answer.

"Good. I'm all set out here," he says as he opens the bedroom door. I'm all moved into his master bedroom now and I make my way through our shared bedroom and into the living room.

When I walk out to the space, my jaw drops. "You did all this while I was in there?"

"Yep," he answers, all satisfied with himself.

"Tucker, in no way did you do this by yourself." I smack his shoulder.

"Ouch! Why don't you women understand that I bruise easily!" He rubs the spot.

I roll my eyes and make my way through. He put out snacks for a movie night in the living room, along with a makeshift cotton tent and twinkle lights. He also ordered my favorite pizza and has some LED candles out on the table. I look over at the television and see *Sixteen Candles* cued up, which is my favorite movie. It's a pretty old choice, but my mom loves it and I fell in love with it too.

"Happy early birthday, Bay." He motions for me to sit down.

"Wow, pulled out all the stops. I'm impressed." I sit down. "Admit it, though—you had help."

"A man never divulges all his secrets." He winks.

"Uh huh." I give him a side eye. "I know you had help and it was a woman's help. No way River or Clay did this. Nor Hunter," I say, looking around. "I say Abby. Or Kennedy."

"Wanna make it interesting and put some money on it?" he says, serving a slice of pizza on my plate.

"Obviously," I answer, "my final vote is Abby."

He gets this mischievous look on his face, but doesn't say anything else and presses play on the remote.

"Hey, who was it? Did I win?" I yell.

"Shhh, the movie is going to start," he says.

"You're infuriating," I say as I take a bite of my pizza.

"You love me," he says. "Happy birthday, baby."

"Thank you for this," I tell him.

Everything about the evening feels like a dream. After the disastrous encounter with my brother, I thought my night was ruined, but this makes up for it.

After we eat and I enjoy too many snacks, I snuggle into Tucker's side. But when the movie comes close to the end, I can't help but sit up and watch attentively.

"Oh, it's the best part," I declare.

"Why is this such a big deal each time you watch it?"

"Shush." I wave at him as I watch the screen as if I don't know what's about to happen.

I watch as Molly Ringwald comes out of the church to find Jake Ryan standing at the Porsche waiting for her. Oh, my heart.

"Oh, how romantic." I nearly melt into a puddle.

"Are you fucking kidding me?" Tucker shifts and complains behind me.

"Tucker, why don't you—" I look over to make him pay attention, but that's when I see him positioned down on one knee, holding an open box with a ring for me.

"Oh my fucking God," I whisper.

"Baylee Grace Rios," he begins, "I've known you most of my life and all of yours. And in each second of knowing you, you've held a piece of a memory, capturing a part of my heart and making it brighter. You've surprised me now by showing me that our love is ever-evolving. It's messy, captivating, honest, fun, difficult—but, most importantly, it's going to shift in ways we least expect. And I want to be the person you shift with in this life forever. Will you marry me?"

"Yes, always yes!" I jump into him, toppling him over and kissing him, tears flowing down my cheeks.

"I love you so much and I'm so happy right now. I was already happy, but now I'm even happier because of you and our forever," I tell him, peppering his face with kisses all over.

"I love you, Baylee-almost-Malloy, for real this time," he tells me.

"For real this time." I smile at him.

Tucker

EPILOGUE

I thought I'd feel nervous. Even one butterfly would be normal, right? But as I stand next to Baylee, it just feels right with her by my side. Yes, we jumped right into this, but at the same time, it doesn't feel sudden. It feels right. The minute we made the decision in that hospital room to get married, even though it wasn't with the necessary paperwork, it simply felt like it was meant to be.

Here we are on our official wedding day at City Hall in front of her parents and my mother. This time we've added her sisters, their significant others, and their children. My mother is better today, and my brother and his wife returned to celebrate us, which is a great surprise. Rios was invited, but isn't here and that's his choice. I can see it disappointed Baylee, even though she put on a brave face when she showed up to find he was the only one not in attendance today.

I gave Baylee the option to do a big wedding, but she opted out of it. She wanted to keep expenses down and to save for a big trip this summer when she's off for break. The holidays just ended and we're soaking up the last few weeks before she returns for the new semester.

This next term is supposed to be her final one before she's officially a college graduate, although, she may push a class or two into the next fall and take a little bit of the workload off her back. She doesn't see the point in rushing to finish all her courses this spring if she can spread a few of the classes out and finish in the fall. She'd still walk this spring with the rest of her class. She needs to decide soon though.

Kennedy offered her a summer internship at the Gaels facility with the physical therapy department, and I told her she should take it. Baylee doesn't want any handouts, but I told her Kennedy wouldn't offer if she didn't think Baylee deserved it. Working with a sports team is her dream, so this is exactly what she'd love to do.

I look over and catch the smile on my mom's face and my heart swells. Seeing her sitting there, looking better than she had months ago brings me so much joy. What a difference a few months makes. Baylee catches me looking at my mom and her smile doubles. She squeezes my hand, and I know she feels the same relief I do.

Before we know it, we're declared a married couple and I kiss my bride.

I whisper to her, "I can't believe it's official."

"Believe it. You're stuck with me now." She laughs.

"I can't wait," I tell her, dropping another kiss to her lips.

"Okay, lovebirds, let's go. They need us out of here." Eric slaps my shoulder.

We make our way through and head out into the hall. We're about to find a spot in the building where we can take a photo, when we encounter someone we least expect holding a bouquet of flowers tied with blue ribbon.

"Danny?" Baylee says.

"Hey," Rios says, "you look beautiful. Here, I brought you these. I thought I'd bring your something blue, even though I got here a bit late. That snowfall last night made me late. I'm sorry." He looks genuinely apologetic.

"It's okay, man. Thanks for coming," I say. I do appreciate the gesture, and I know Baylee appreciates him showing up for us.

She takes the flowers and gives him a small smile. Then she hands me the flowers and I nod. She turns to her brother and wraps her arms around his neck and hugs him; they embrace for a long while. I look over and see her mom wipe a tear from the corner of her eye. I can see the toll this has taken on their family. It was never our intention for that to happen.

Rios pulls something from his pocket, revealing a small gift box. Baylee looks hesitant at first but finally takes it from him and pulls at the bow to open it. When she opens it, I see the tears pooling in her dark brown eyes. I move closer, the protectiveness coming over me. Once I'm closer, I realize the small smile that's formed on her lips. I look down and notice the necklace with an initial hanging off it. She pulls it out and it's then I see the delicate M dangling off the gold chain.

She reaches for her brother right then and those tears she was holding back finally break free. I walk away, giving them the space they deserve. I look over my shoulder and see them pull apart. Rios whispers something to Baylee. Then she nods and a smile pulls on a corner of her lips. Maybe despite all that's happened, everything will be okay in the end. It'll take time, but I'm hoping we can start to rebuild what we lost recently.

"Shall we take that family picture?" My mom, the eternal optimist, says as she comes up by my side.

"Yes, let's do that," Ariana says.

We find a spot where someone can snap a photo and it feels like something finally clicks. That crack in our armor may have been mended today and I feel a little lighter as we walk out of City Hall.

———

"You didn't think you'd get away without celebrating, did you?" River says as I open my front door.

I rub my hand down my face, preparing myself for all the people walking through my house for this celebration I didn't ask for.

It's the weekend after my wedding to Baylee and we're celebrating our wedding with a friend gathering per the request of our little extended family we've built.

"Just so you know, they made me come and I feel like the seventh wheel," Hunter declares as he walks in.

"I'm here against my will, if it makes you feel better," I whisper.

"I heard that." Abby points at me, narrowing her eyes. "You owe me this, especially after I helped you with *Sixteen Candles* night!"

"I knew it!" Baylee yells. "You owe me money!" She points at me with the biggest smile like she won the lottery.

"My protégé is learning," River says from the kitchen. "Nice, Bay-Bay."

"I don't like that nickname." She scrunches her nose.

"Yeah, I heard it right when it came out and have to agree." He nods in agreement.

Ella squeals in agreement right then and I go to grab her from the carrier. "Come here, sweet girl."

When I pick her up, I give her kisses on the cheek, which causes her to giggle and I assume it's from the beard. She's in a new phase of pulling on my beard, so she attaches to me, pulling on the hairs as I try to slowly pry her little fingers off my face.

Once I succeed in removing her hands from my beard, I put her on my hip and start looking at all the treats everyone brought. They told us not to do a thing and they'd bring all the food. Kennedy was adamant that we not lift a finger. She said because we weren't doing an official wedding, we had to let them do something.

"Wow, you guys went all out," Baylee says. "This is a lot of food." She starts lifting lids and looking at all the containers.

I'm about to lift a lid to something that looks like a cake.

"Oh, that's a surprise." River slaps my hand.

"Geez, Riv!" I yell. "What is it with everyone hitting me all the time? I'm a delicate person."

"Poor baby," Clay says, batting his lashes.

"Do you need Baylee to read you a bedtime story and put you to bed now?" River asks, pouting.

I cover one of Ella's ears and mouth, "Fuck off."

River flips me off with both middle fingers. Then he steals his niece. "I'll take her. I don't want her to, you know, grab your hair or something and hurt your delicate scalp."

"Asshole." I roll my eyes.

Baylee comes up to me and pats my chest. "It's okay, baby. Not all of us are built big and strong. Some of us are just built big."

I look down at her and she laughs.

"You're evil. He's rubbing off on you, you know that?" I tell her.

"I know. I sort of like it." She has an evil gleam in her eyes.

"Okay, everyone, let's grab plates and go eat." Kennedy claps and starts ordering everyone around.

We make our way through, grabbing food, then sitting at our dining room table. We ended up adding some chairs so everyone can sit together.

It's a loud bunch. Samara and Ashton couldn't make it as the twins ended up getting a bad cold. But they called earlier to send their well-wishes. Marissa was going to call in, but she has a court appearance she has to prepare for. She ended up having to text and said how crazy we are and that was her way of saying congratulations. That's her style anyway.

Once we're stuffed to the brim with food, everyone begins

clearing our plates and we start laughing about little things here and there. I love the dynamic between all of us.

"Alright, now for dessert." River stands up and the way he's excited about this, I'm scared about what's coming.

"Why do I feel like I should duck or something?" I say to the table.

"Because River and Clay were literally in charge of it and no one knows what's coming," Kennedy says.

"Actually, just River. I had nothing to do with it," Clay says.

"What do you mean?" Kennedy asks.

"Yeah, he said he wanted to do the dessert," Clay explains.

"He said the two of you were in charge of dessert because you knew what Malloy would like. That's why I let him have that duty," Kennedy says with panic in her tone.

"Why am I getting more concerned?" Baylee says, her eyes bouncing between Kennedy and Clay.

"Because I know River and he's up to something," Clay says.

"Oh, fuck." Kennedy puts her head in her hands.

"What's the big deal?" I ask. "Did he make the dessert or something?"

"No, it's not that," Kennedy starts.

"What am I missing?" Abby finally asks. "Is someone allergic to something?" She's looking around the table and then something clicks. "Oh *no*." Her eyes go wide.

"What the fuck is going on?" I ask, throwing my arms up.

"He wouldn't," Clay says.

"You know he would," Kennedy deadpans.

"Now you guys are scaring me," Baylee says.

"It's nothing to be scared of. Just promise to continue to be friends with us after this if our assumptions are correct. Okay?" Abby says.

"Ookayy," Baylee says.

"No, seriously, you have to promise," Kennedy says.

"Do you want me to sign something?" Baylee asks.

"That's not a bad idea. Do we have time for a notary? Better yet, anyone here a notary?" Kennedy asks.

I look over at Hunter and he's got a smirk on his face because this is amusing for someone that has no idea what's going on. Not that I know what's going on either. We probably look like absolute clowns.

Finally, River makes his way over with the dessert. It's still covered with only the top exposed. But we're still unable to see it, because he's blocking it and we can't see anything yet.

"Alright. So, before I show you what I got done for you, I just want to say that we love you both very much. Well, I should say—Baylee, we love you. Malloy, we're just happy you found someone we love so much more than you." There are laughs and I just nod.

"We hope you find forgiveness on those days where you disagree and find light on the days when the dark is finding ways in. But most of all, always find ways to laugh. Find ways to let love in through all corners. And always remember you have great friends to share your memories with. We love you," he says.

What a true friend. That's such a kind thing to say. He's truly an amazing person and we're lucky to have him. I don't know what we did to find an amazing support system around us and he's become our ringleader. Our center that has his goofy moments, but has a heart of gold.

He puts the dessert in the middle of the table and for a second we're all smiling. Then the image sinks in.

The words written on the cake are perfectly fine: Congratulations Baylee and Malloy!

Kennedy has her face in her hands. Abby's holding back a laugh. Clay is looking at his brother, trying not to murder him with his eyes. Baylee looks over at me, her mouth agape. Of course, River's completely proud of himself.

Hunter looks at each of us and finally says, "I have no idea how I ended up with such a fucked up group of friends who watch reality dating shows and celebrate a wedding with a cake that's decorated with what looks like a dick purse in the center. But hey, who am I to judge? Congrats Baylee and Malloy."

The End

Hunter

Spring is finally here and I'm gliding through traffic on my motorcycle to the station. This past winter was brutal, which was to be expected. I knew it would be, but I missed my bike. It's been nice to have her out to ride lately, now that the weather's been more compliant.

I reach the station and park alongside some of the crew. Taking off my helmet, I'm met by Malloy walking in.

"Well, good morning, Mr. Baylee." I snicker.

"Good morning. You just love calling me that, huh?" He laughs.

"I do. You're smitten," I tell him.

The way he looks at his wife is truly awe-inspiring and I like seeing my friend so enamored.

"She does make me happy." He smiles.

"There's nothing wrong with that. How is the semester treating her?" I ask.

"Good. Glad she decided to push those two classes to next semester, delaying her finish to next December. I think this spring would've been too much on her if she had taken all those classes right now. Now she can focus on what she needs, and still walk in May, but finish the coursework with time in the fall."

"Good. I bet she's happier. And her job?" I ask.

"She likes it," he says, "it's flexible hours and walking distance from the apartment."

Baylee got a job at a cafe near their place and she seems to like it. They have early hours, but they don't stay open late, which Malloy says she prefers.

Right as we're going inside, Rios approaches and greets us both.

"Good morning," he says, then looks over at Malloy. "Good morning, Malloy."

"Morning," he says back.

Rios walks ahead and Malloy stands at the doorway.

"You okay?" I ask him.

"I guess that's progress. That's the first time he's greeted me in a personal way at work."

"Baby steps," I tell him.

"Yeah. It'll never be what it was before and that's okay. But hopefully the tension will start to lift for the sake of our families."

"I agree," I say as we make our way to the lockers to deposit our belongings before getting a report from the previous crew.

I'm still a probie, with a few more months left of my one-year probationary period. Time's flying and I'm really enjoying firefighting. I find the work satisfying, and I like the camaraderie. It's the brotherhood that I was seeking after leaving the military.

The life I had back in Nevada was miserable and I haven't been back since graduating high school. I have nothing left there. The family I was born into only shares blood with me. Aside from that, they gave me nothing and I haven't looked back.

Throughout the years, I've gotten to pick and choose who

will be in my life and I feel blessed with the people that surround me. These guys are part of that because they have truly become a part of my chosen family. As we prepare for our shift, checking our gear and washing the truck—the laughter and interactions between them—I feel so grateful I survived so much to come back to this life.

We get everything in order, and a few hours go by seamlessly. Right as we're about to go inside to get some food, the alarm goes off for a call. We make our way to the truck.

The sun is beating down now that the day is well underway. As we drive into the city, I realize the address is an elementary school. My heart accelerates, realizing this might be a child we're dealing with. Those calls always make me a little more anxious. When a call comes in, the most we know is it's a medical emergency from the nature of the call, not if the person is an adult or child.

We park the truck outside the school and personnel are waiting for us out front, directing us to where the emergency is. Our captain is getting information and we listen in as we walk through to where the injured person is needing our attention.

"Anaphylaxis in one of our kindergarteners. He was playing after lunch and got stung by a bee. He's allergic. Seems to have escalated quickly. They gave him a dose of Benadryl. Then they gave him a shot of the EpiPen, but he's still having a reaction. He's puffing up really bad. The swelling is everywhere on his face."

We are all listening in as we make our way through. I'm taking mental notes. Anaphylaxis is a serious issue and can indeed escalate quickly. All those interventions with no relief is worrisome. We pick up our pace as we continue to the nurse's office.

We see some commotion at a small office up ahead. Now that I take in my surroundings, this school looks like a private one, with state-of-the-art facilities. That being said, this nurse's office is tiny, yet so many people are congregated inside, I assume, around this child.

"Alright everyone, please step aside, and let us take a look," River announces. He can be serious and commanding when he needs to.

Everyone looks panicked, some adults and students are in the small space, and they clear a path.

"Like he said, please step aside. If you're a nurse, you can stay. But anyone else, please move outside. You can wait there, but we need you out of the way please. Thank you," Clay says.

I crouch down, my role is to take vitals. I put my equipment by the child's side and start to evaluate the allergic reaction. The boy is quite puffy. His eyes are almost completely shut and he has hives all over.

"Hey, buddy," I say. "My name's Tyler Hunter. But these guys call me Hunter. Can you talk or is your tongue swollen?"

"I can talk but it feels a little funny in the back of my throat," he explains.

"Alright. What's your name?" I ask.

"Noah," he says.

"Hi, Noah," I say. "Can you open your mouth for me so I can check for swelling?"

He does as I ask. "Good job. Your tongue doesn't look swollen, which is good. Your eyes are pretty swollen, which probably feels uncomfortable, huh?"

He nods. "I'm just going to keep looking around your arms, neck, and head. I have to see where the hives are. Is that okay with you?"

He nods again. "If you start feeling anything else, just let me know."

"Okay," he answers.

"And my buddy, Clay, will be helping me out here."

Clay introduces himself.

We start assessing him and taking note where the hives are. The nurse is giving her report to our captain, and I overhear that the sting was on a spot that may have been near an artery. From my experience, it could have simply hit the blood stream and I wonder if that accounts for why it spread so quickly. She got the stinger out quickly. But even so, if his allergy is severe, that could be why he had such a significant reaction.

"Were his parents called?" I ask.

"His mother was called," the nurse tells me. "She works nearby. She should be here shortly."

Even though Noah most likely can't see me due to the swelling around his eyes, I still crouch down directly in front of him as if he could see me. "Noah, your mom's been called, but you'll have to take a trip to the hospital in our cool ambulance. Okay, bud?"

"I'm scared," he says with such a small voice.

"I know, but you know what?" I say.

"What?" he asks.

"You get the cool lights on," I tell him.

"Promise?" he asks, only slightly amused, his fear still at the forefront of his thoughts.

"Promise," I tell him.

We start getting Noah onto the gurney and I talk to him the entire time so he's not scared throughout the process. I'm about to walk away when he calls for me.

"Hunter, don't go. I want my mommy." His little hand reaches for me.

"It's okay, buddy." I grab his hand. "You're in good hands."

"Will you stay with me until she gets here?" he pleads.

"Oh, um." Shoot. I look over for some help, but the guys are packing stuff up. His gurney isn't moving just yet as they're trying to facilitate moving the equipment onto the bottom of the gurney.

"Sure, I'll walk with you. Let me just put my things under the gurney, okay?" I tell him.

"Okay."

I bend over and start packing up some of my supplies when I hear a woman's voice yell out.

"I'm here. Noah, Mommy's here. Baby, I'm so sorry!" She sounds desperate.

But that's not what has me shooting upright. She sounds familiar; it's a voice I haven't heard in years.

It's a voice that I'd recognize anywhere.

It's a voice that has pulled me from my hardest moments when I felt like I was never going to make it home.

It's the voice that brought me home.

It's *her* voice.

I feel her presence at the gurney, and I turn around. I'm standing next to the woman from my past. She's focused on Noah, doting over her son, who sounds relieved to know his mother is by his side. She hasn't noticed me yet. But I'm stunned in place. I'm paralyzed by her presence. It's like all my air has vanished from my lungs. She's taken my air because it's always been hers, since that night.

I continue to stand there. She must sense me and she turns to look over. It's then I see the shock overtake her features when she realizes it's me.

"Ty?"

"Indy…"

River walks up to us. "Do you two know each other?"

She stammers, "Um, yeah, we, uh—"

"Yeah. She's my wife," I finally say.

Find out how the Boston Embers series concludes with the love story between Hunter and Indiana in *Embers in Our Souls* coming in fall 2025. Preorder NOW.

Afterword

Malloy's character was never one I envisioned from the beginning of this series. At first, I thought I would redeem Rios, hoping his character would have a more bubbly personality. But as the series progressed, and I got to know Rios, it was clear his path was to be increasingly selfish.

Tucker Malloy's personality grew on me and I fell in love with the big teddy bear he revealed himself to be in my mind. By the time I saw him play out in my head, I fell in love with the idea of the age gap I saw for him. Baylee's character and her story past broke my heart, but it also fit their dynamic. This story is a hard one to read, but I love how well they come together in the end. Malloy is so lovable in book two, and he continues to carry that big heart throughout his story in Embers in the Dark.

I had a lot of change happening going into the third installment of the Boston Embers series. I decided to start fresh creatively with many things. I brought on a new editor with Ashley Matthews. Thanks to my incredible PA, I was introduced to Ashley in the fall of last year and we instantly clicked. And by clicked, I mean we have poked fun at each other whenever we find the opportunity. I value Ashley's ability to make a story stronger, pointing out ways to truly enrich the storyline. I value your insight so very much.

Speaking of my PA—Meghan, thank you for bringing joy and laughter to my life. I am grateful for our connection and your ability to help me brainstorm ways to keep me going in this busy author life. You help me stay creative, especially with social media. You are beyond helpful with graphics and helping me stay focused and connected with readers. Plus, you're always letting me know when Christmas is right around the corner. Thank you for being you and for not only being an amazing PA, but a wonderful friend.

Christiana from Concepts by Canea, I must start with thank you, first and foremost. You are so talented with your ability to take my descriptions and bring them to life with your craft. Your covers are beautiful and one-of-a-kind.

You came on to redesign the series covers with a positive attitude, and it has been a wonderful ride since. Not only did I have this request mid-series, but you blew me away with an extraordinary new cover design. I'm in love with how you brought Baylee and Malloy's cover to life. We aren't supposed to have favorites, but this one holds a special place in my heart. Having this one next to the rest of the series on the shelf will brighten my day. I love working with you and look forward to what book four will bring very soon.

I know my readers have been waiting on Malloy for some time and I hope he has lived up to the hype. I appreciate everyone that took part in my alpha, beta, ARC and Street team—you've all contributed to making this story stronger. Thank you so much for your notes and feedback. It's because of you that I can improve my work and continue to do this moving forward.

I have to give a special shoutout to April—you know why! I had you researching things for me on this book and I so appreciate you for that. You're a good friend. We had some good laughs on this.

To Joanna—you don't have to answer my calls to help me brainstorm and edit my book to find little errors, yet you are always willing to walk me through. Thank you for finding time in your busy schedule to guide me while my brain won't settle. I love you so much for being my person and helping me through so much in this crazy life of ours. You laugh through the busy nature life brings and I appreciate it all. Thanks for being who you are.

Thank you to my family for always supporting me as I'm constantly writing. I know it feels like I've always got a deadline or a computer in front of me. I love you all so much!

To all my readers—thank you for all of the support you have given me throughout the years. I still have to pinch myself that I get to do this. I am blessed to call myself an author. From having an idea to writing it into a book, I'm still surprising myself I get to do this. Thank you for taking the time to read my stories.

I am eternally grateful.

Stefanie xo

About the Author

Stefanie Castro is a Registered Nurse, certified doula and yoga instructor. She specializes in the field of obstetrics and loves everything about her career. She is a first-generation Brazilian American and is fluent in English, Portuguese and Spanish. Stefanie is a wife of 19 years and mother to her son and daughter, along with her very rambunctious Cavalier King Charles Spaniel, named Rusty.

She has grown in her love of reading throughout the years and now it's hard to find her without her Kindle by her side. Her favorite foods are popcorn and sushi. She is also very excited about Christmas and begins plotting next year's decor on December 26th. Stefanie has started two book clubs and is avidly reading whenever she has a free moment in her day. She loves to cuddle on the couch with her dog, along with a great book and a cup of tea.